Mint Frosting and Murder

Holly Holmes Cozy Culinary Mystery - book 9

K.E. O'Connor

K.E. O'Connor Books

MINT FROSTING AND MURDER

ISBN: 978-1-9163573-8-9

Written by K.E. O'Connor

Chapter 1

"I only managed two verses of *Silent Night* before a string broke on my harp. The carol ended up sounding more like *Blue Christmas* once I'd mangled my way through it. I should have stopped, but I was so looking forward to playing at the church service." Princess Alice Audley leaned on the kitchen counter as I stored leftover cakes in the Audley Castle industrial refrigerators.

And we had a surprising number of sweet treats left over. There was nothing wrong with the festive frosted donuts, cinnamon crisp apple tarts, or iced yule log, but the freezing weather meant visitors weren't brave enough to leave their homes, even for a slice of delicious cake and a wander around the festively decorated castle.

"You said learning to play the harp wasn't your thing. See the broken string as a sign," I said.

"A sign I'm useless at learning anything." Alice poked her bottom lip out.

"You're excellent at plenty of things."

She arched a pale blonde eyebrow. "Name them. I don't expect the list will be long."

I placed the final tray of gingerbread iced cookies in the chiller cabinet. "You're kind, generous, you always make me laugh, you're thoughtful, and—"

"That's my character. What about the things I'm good at? You're an excellent baker and great at historical

1

research. What do I excel in? Making a harp sound like I've trodden on a cat's tail?"

"You could be good at anything you put your mind to." I adored my best friend, and sister-in-law, but her wonderfully blonde ditzy head got turned too easily when she found the latest thing to learn. It meant she didn't stick at much for long. Although we stuck to each other, and that was good enough for me.

Alice flipped her hair over one shoulder. "When I spoke to Paris on the phone today, she reminded me one of our tutors said I only had half a brain, and if it weren't for my family legacy, I'd be a nothing."

"That tutor should have been fired." I turned to face Alice. "I hope your friends stuck up for you."

"Not really. If anyone spoke out in that class, they got picked on next. Everyone says going to a posh school provides you with the best education, but I wonder. I'd have been better going to a poor school like you. You didn't turn into too much of a delinquent."

"Princess Alice Audley! Don't be a snob. Maybe my school didn't have antique wooden desks, feather quills, and tutors wandering around in long robes, but I got a decent education."

She giggled. "You're describing Hogwarts."

I grinned at her. "I always get an image of that place when you talk about the colleges your parents sent you to."

"Hmmm... I don't know. I don't feel like I learned much. Certainly nothing useful. What's the point of Latin these days? Or knowing how low to curtsy when meeting someone with a particular noble title? You got everything you needed to have a successful career."

"I'm not sure being complained at by Chef Heston every day is everyone's perfect career path." Even though my boss could be a red-faced, shouting pain in my behind, I wouldn't change a thing about my job in the Audley Castle kitchen. It was stressful, the customers were demanding, but I adored baking. Almost as much as I adored my perfect little dog, Meatball.

"It's not every day, now." Alice smoothed a hand down her red gown. She'd been wearing festive colors since the beginning of December. Sometimes, she added tinsel around her neck. "Not since you've gone down to working part time. You're practically a lady of leisure since you married my brother."

I swatted Alice's hand away from the mint frosted cupcakes we'd been perfecting. "I still work four days a week. But now I'm with Rupert, it's nice to spend more time together." I smiled to myself. I'd been married to Lord Rupert Audley for almost eighteen months. After plenty of road bumps and diversions, we'd plucked up the courage to admit our feelings for each other.

And Rupert was exactly the kind of husband I knew he would be. Loyal, loving, funny, still with his nose permanently in a book, wonderfully clumsy, and always there when I needed him.

Alice's sigh swerved toward the dramatic. "I hate seeing you two together."

"Why?"

"Because you remind me of everything I don't have with Campbell."

"Alice, you and Campbell are great together. Although I never thought I'd see it happen. The man keeps his emotions so tightly buttoned up, I wondered if he was an android before he declared his feelings to you."

Alice and Campbell Milligan, the head of Audley Castle security, had dated for as long as Rupert and I were married. Alice had always had a huge crush on the surly, uptight, occasionally clever man, and he'd always been hopelessly in love with her. He'd just never admitted it.

She giggled again. "It does take work to get him to admit how he's feeling. His default answer when I ask him is always 'fine.' But he's been so grumpy since his accident. He's even trying my patience, and I've been in love with him for years."

"Last time I spoke to him, he reminded me of a hungry grizzly bear." Campbell had broken his foot and was covered in bruises after his brakes failed and he flipped a car into a ditch. Fortunately, he'd been the only one in the vehicle, but everyone had been worried about him. Alice had fainted when she'd heard he'd been in an accident, and when she'd come to, had been convinced he wouldn't pull through.

Unsurprisingly, Campbell made an awful patient. He hated being sick and told me he didn't have time to be unwell. But he had no choice but to submit to bedrest, since a broken foot took weeks to heal, and he wasn't allowed to put any weight on it. Doctor's orders.

"I'll take some cakes up to him after we've finished," Alice said. "Even though he never likes to admit it, your baking cheers him up."

"I've noticed him indulge a time or two in the past. Although I've also heard him complain you're feeding him too much and he'll get fat."

"Impossible! That man is all muscle." Alice sighed. "As much as I'd love to drool over his delicious muscles—"

"Please, don't."

She tutted. "We must focus on these cakes. I must ensure whatever we bake is spectacular, so I can impress my friends when they get here. I will perfect my chocolate cake."

I glanced out of the high windows. Snow had steadily fallen for two days. It hadn't let up once, and fifteen inches lay on the ground, making the castle frostily stunning in the lead up to Christmas. But being in the countryside in the beautiful village of Audley St. Mary meant the way in to the castle was tricky to navigate by car or foot.

"Are you sure they'll make it? Lots of people have already cancelled."

"They wouldn't dare miss Christmas at Audley Castle. We've been talking about it for months. Those ladies will find a way. And when they get here, everything has to be perfect."

I was already pulling out ingredients to make a fresh batch of mint chocolate frosted cupcakes with gingerbread men topping. "Your friends will love your baking, even if you don't think it's perfect. After all, you went to the effort of making it for them. They'll appreciate that."

She waggled a finger in my face. "Uh-uh. You've never met these particular friends, have you?"

"No, but I've heard plenty about them. They're your friends from boarding school, right?"

"Yes, we were in the same house. I wouldn't say we were natural friends, but when you get thrown together in a strange environment full of terrifying rules, bond quickly to survive."

"You make your boarding school sound like a prisoner of war camp."

"Sometimes, that's what it felt like. The tutors were mean. But I survived, and in part, it was thanks to my boarding school sisters. Because of that, we have an unbreakable bond." Alice wrinkled her adorable button nose. "They can be beastly when they want to, though. Which is why I'll show them my life is idyllic. And I'll prove that being voted most likely to say something stupid on a first date, and spend all my money on something dumb, was unfounded."

I paused from measuring out the cinnamon. It was a smell that reminded me of Christmas. "Did they really do that?"

"It was a joke. But I didn't find it funny." Alice grabbed my arm, causing me to fling flour in the air from the pack I held. "Make sure you don't mention I bought one hundred glittering wind chimes and put them around the castle. Those things drove Granny crazy."

"I suppose you don't want me to mention the money you invested in the doggy day spa, either?"

"That sounded like a sensible business investment. How was I to know dogs don't like saunas and hot tubs?"

"You could have asked Meatball." My delightful tan and white corgi cross was snoozing at home, no doubt in front of a roaring open fire after being spoiled by Rupert.

"Perhaps it wasn't the wisest investment." She grabbed a chocolate cupcake off the tray we'd already made. "Keep that just between us."

I grinned at her. Alice could have her head in the clouds, but she was smart and determined when she really wanted something. "We'll prove them wrong."

"I know we will. Because you're an amazing friend, and an even better sister-in-law." She wrapped me in a huge hug. "I couldn't have wished for a better one. Even though my daft brother took long enough to put a ring on your finger. I was worried he'd lose you to someone else."

Fortunately for me and Rupert, I'd had a crush on him since starting work at Audley Castle. I'd never thought it would come to anything, though. After all, he was a lord, and I was a commoner who worked in the castle kitchens. But true love shone through, and nothing could stop us from finding our way to each other. Even though the road was one of the windiest and most confusing I'd ever walked.

Chef Heston marched into the kitchen, still wearing his chef's whites. He slowed and stared down his long, thin nose at us. "Princess Alice. I thought you'd be finished by now. Do you need more time in the kitchen?"

Alice beamed at him. "We're just getting started. I tried to make some Christmas cookie crumble with the sweet mincemeat Holly made." She pointed at a burned offering on the counter. "It's all my fault. Holly said to watch the timer, but I got distracted when making icing for the cupcakes. Before I knew it, smoke billowed out of the oven."

I held back a smile as Chef Heston gritted his teeth.

"These things happen." His gaze shifted along the counter. "May I ask what that is?"

A sunken fruitcake sat next to the burned sweet mincemeat cookie crumble.

"That was my third attempt at a traditional Christmas cake. We put brandy and whiskey in this one. And when Holly's back was turned, I added a couple of extra measures of alcohol. I wanted it to be extra delicious. Then it wouldn't firm up. The edges got overdone, but the middle stayed soggy." Alice's mouth twisted. "Maybe you need a new oven."

"If I may, Princess, the oven is fine. Perhaps you put too much liquid in the cake." Chef Heston glowered at me. "You must use exact measurements. A decent instructor would tell you that."

"Holly did! I thought I was making things better. Still, third time is a charm. We're making mint frosted chocolate cupcakes next. Well, again. They'll work this time. We just need to sprinkle them with Christmas magic."

"A word, Holly." Chef Heston caught hold of my elbow and escorted me out of the kitchen and into the corridor. "Please, make her stop."

"Baking? But Alice is having fun."

"I'm begging you. She's wasting supplies. Don't think I missed the two ruined trays of food outside. The bottoms of the cookies were black!"

"Um... that was supposed to be a gingerbread wreath and sugar cookies with Christmas frosting. Alice got—"

"Distracted. Yes, she does that. But the snow has closed most of the roads leading to the castle. Half the Christmas food I've ordered has yet to arrive, and I can't see it getting here in time. The Christmas Day feast will be a disaster."

"Maybe some deliveries won't make it, but there's enough food in the store to last us a month."

"Only basic supplies. The festive ham and the gold crown turkey haven't been delivered. And I arranged for an imported European figgy pudding for the Duke. He adores his figgy pudding."

"You make an amazing figgy pudding. All you need are eggs, sugar, breadcrumbs, spices, dried fruits, suet, and brandy. What you'll make will be better than the one you spent all that money on."

"Of course it will, but it won't be the same. The Duke will know. And he expects things to be done a certain way." Chef Heston wrung his hands together. "Christmas is such a special event at the castle, but this weather will ruin everything. Most of the party guests have canceled."

I'd never seen Chef Heston this stressed, and his stress level usually simmered at a red-faced eight on a good day. "It can still be special. This year, the snow may make things a little different."

"Not just the snow. Last Christmas, you were my kitchen assistant, not a member of the family. You won't get a moment's peace, you know. You'll be expected to attend one event after another, go to all the local gatherings, and be a voice for the castle. Everyone will want to talk to you."

I bit my bottom lip. I didn't mind the occasional social event, but I wasn't a woman who enjoyed back-to-back parties. I needed down time with my dog, a plate of cookies, and my feet up. "That does sound exhausting."

He grunted. "That's what you get for marrying into the Audleys. People expect things from you. You're a part of the village. An important part."

"I like to think I was always special, not just because I married Rupert."

I got another grunt for that comment. But I understood what Chef Heston meant, and I'd experienced my share of social events and expectations since getting married. It was another reason I'd reduced my working hours. The family were active village patrons, and involved with many charities. We were always getting invitations to opening events, ceremonies, and galas. I found it intimidating, but I loved being involved in a community that had warmly welcomed me when I'd moved to Audley St. Mary.

"We can handle this. We know our way around the kitchen, so we'll make Christmas perfect for everyone," I said.

Chef Heston did a mock curtsy. "Whatever you say, Lady Holly."

"Oh, no. When I'm in the kitchen, I'm plain old Holly to you."

"If that's true, then get back in there and clear up the mess Princess Alice has made. Keep an eye on her and make sure she stays out of my precious supplies. She's a disaster. I don't know why I put up with her?" A rare smile crossed his face.

For all Chef Heston's bluntness and occasional rudeness, he had a good heart and a passion for making delicious food. He also had a soft spot for Princess Alice.

There was an enormous crash as metal hit the stone floor in the kitchen, making us both jump.

"Go! Now! Stop her before she burns the place down."

"I'm on it." I hurried away and poked my head around the door into the kitchen.

Alice was scooping up baking trays. She looked up at me and there were tears in her eyes.

I dashed into the kitchen. "What's the matter?"

She dumped the trays on the counter and sniffed. "I wanted to make sure Campbell had the perfect Christmas. He's been so down since the car accident. I wanted to give him something to smile about."

"He'll have a great Christmas with you. He's just in pain and hates taking his medication. He thinks it makes him look like less of an alpha male because he needs help."

"That would be impossible. My wonderful boyfriend is all alpha."

I resisted the urge to roll my eyes. I'd witnessed that alpha in action many times. He was as stubborn-headed as he was in love with Alice. "In a few weeks, the worst will be over. Campbell will be walking again, even if it is on crutches, then you can make plans for the New Year together."

"But I figured Christmas would be the perfect time to show him what a wonderful wife I could be."

My jaw dropped. "Wife! Is he thinking of proposing to you?"

"No. I'm planning on proposing to him."

Chapter 2

"I didn't know what to say after Alice dropped the marriage bombshell. Do you really think she'll go through with it?" I took a bite of the delicious pasta salad my husband had waiting for me when I got back from my kitchen escapades.

"It's the first I've heard about it, but Alice is always full of surprises." Rupert topped up my wineglass and picked up the napkin I'd dropped before settling in his seat at our cozy dining table. "And we know Campbell will say yes."

"Or his head will explode with shock. He's a traditional guy. Maybe he won't want Alice proposing to him. He could have his own plans." Although, if he did, he'd never share them with me.

"Campbell is smart. He'll say yes. And for all his roughness, he adores Alice."

I smiled and then sipped my wine. "He does."

"Almost as much as I adore you." Rupert caught hold of my hand and kissed the back of it. His blue eyes sparkled in the light of the candles he'd set on the table in our quaint cottage.

After we married, we'd wanted our own place, but needed to be close to Audley Castle and the family, so Rupert came up with the perfect solution. There were several cottages used by families that worked on the estate. One cute little place, sitting just beyond the shadow of the castle, had been empty for months.

We'd looked around and agreed it was perfect for us. Then, we'd spent a few months getting it renovated, before moving into our corner of paradise. There were dark wooden beams on the ceiling, the whitewashed walls were rough stone, and the furnishings were comfy.

I'd initially missed my staff apartment in the grounds, but it was lovely to have a space I shared with Rupert. And of course, Meatball.

"Did Alice tell you when she'd make this proposal?" Rupert said.

"Maybe Christmas Eve. But then she changed her mind and said Christmas Day evening. Or maybe New Year's Eve. She hasn't fixed on a date."

"Has she got him a ring?"

"Yes, but I didn't see it."

"I'm amazed my sister has kept this a secret for so long. She's usually a blabbermouth."

"Alice can keep important secrets when she needs to. Although this is the biggest secret she's ever had to keep. I'm excited for her. I hope Campbell doesn't get all gruff about it, though."

"Well, it's in his nature. Try not to hold it against him if things don't go according to plan."

"We'll be there for them, whatever the outcome."

The open fire in the dining room crackled as a log split. I looked over and smiled at Meatball, who slept in front of the flames, keeping his belly warm as he lay on his side. "Did he behave today?"

Rupert scratched a hand through his messy blond hair. "Yes, but he kept asking to go out, despite the snow. He misses you when you're not here. He dragged me to the castle and went inside to look for you."

"Meatball knows where I am. And it's too cold for him to stay in his kennel by the kitchen door. Even though it's heated, he'd be a frozen pup in no time."

Rupert pursed his lips as he studied Meatball. "He was acting strangely, though. He kept pawing at closed doors and whining. He was hunting for someone or something."

"Maybe he wanted a tussle with the Duchess's corgis. I heard she's got a new one." Duchess Isabella Audley was as dog mad as me and had an obsession with purebred corgis.

"She has. That makes eight. The castle will soon be overrun with those little monkeys." Rupert smiled as he shook his head. "Should I say something to Campbell about the proposal? Give him a heads up so it doesn't come as a shock?"

"Only if you want to risk your sister's rage."

His eyebrows flashed up. "You think Alice will be grumpy if I warn him?"

"There's nothing to warn him about. It's obvious they'll eventually get married, so it doesn't matter who asks who. Better for it to happen naturally. And Alice is right, it'll cheer up Campbell. The last time I saw him, he had a scowl on his face that even intimidated me." And having spent plenty of time with Campbell helping solve some of the castle's mysteries, I was used to his surly ways.

"It's just a shame our parents won't be here to witness the proposal," Rupert said.

I scooped more pasta onto my fork. "I thought they were arriving tomorrow morning."

"The bad weather has grounded them in Italy. They were only supposed to be there for three days before going to France and then coming here, but there were no flights going in or out. Everything has been canceled.

Even if they could drive back, they'd get stuck trying to get to us."

"I'm sorry they won't be here. It's good to have your family around you during the holidays."

He lifted one shoulder. "It won't be the first time they've missed Christmas. Of course, it's nice to have them here, but I see so little of them these days. Duty always comes first."

Although I was sad for Rupert and Alice that their parents wouldn't be staying with us over Christmas, a tiny part of me was relieved. It had taken them time to warm up to Rupert marrying a commoner. I'd had several tense conversations with his mother, reassuring her my intentions toward Rupert were honorable, and I had no designs on the Audley family fortune.

She'd remained suspicious for some time, but when she'd seen how happy we were together, she'd softened. Still, I often felt on edge around them. And they always put family duty and reputation first, sometimes to the detriment of their children.

Fortunately, Rupert and Alice had the wonderful Duke and Duchess living in the castle, and their grandmother, Lady Philippa Audley, also shared the space, so they were never alone, and always knew they were loved.

"We'll still have a wonderful Christmas. And we can call your parents on the day and share the good news," I said.

"Of course. But they're not the only ones who've canceled. I've been getting messages every hour from people who can no longer make it. All my cousins and aunts won't be here, nor my school friends. It'll be an intimate affair. Not like a few years ago, when we had to put people up in the games room on fold out beds. I think we had fifty staying that night."

I bit my lip. I remembered it well. We'd been run off our feet in the kitchen keeping up with the demands from the sometimes over-privileged guests, who'd expected luxury meals to be conjured with a snap of their fingers.

I sipped my wine and looked around the cottage. I was happy with small and intimate. I adored the Audley family, but it would be relaxing to have a low profile Christmas and spend time with those I loved the most.

"Will your granny Molly make it back for Christmas Day?" Rupert said.

I chuckled. "Since her husband introduced her to the wonderful world of pet friendly cruises, she's barely set foot on dry land. They're spending Christmas and the New Year in the Caribbean on an all-inclusive cruise. She's excited because there'll be a Barry Manilow impersonator on the ship. He's one of her favorites."

Rupert caught hold of my hand. "You're not disappointed, are you?"

I lowered my fork. "About what?"

"It just being a few of us here over the holiday. I don't want you getting bored with me."

My heart went out to this loveable, soft-centered man. "How could I get bored when everyone I love is right here?"

Rupert didn't look convinced. "It's good of you to say. I know this isn't what you planned."

"I'm saying it because I mean it. A quiet celebration over Christmas is what we need. It's been a whirlwind since I married you. You could have warned me you were so popular."

His gaze lowered. "Would you have said no if I did?"

"It would never have crossed my mind."

"You are happy? This is what you expected? I don't want you to want for anything."

I stood and kissed his cheek. "It's so sweet you worry about me being happy. I really am. And I want to enjoy the festivities without rushing around and missing half of them. Now, we'll have time to attend the tree lighting festival, go to carol services, and maybe go carol singing. And I've still got presents to wrap. There'll be plenty to keep me occupied. And I have a feeling Alice will want more baking lessons. She's determined to perfect her Christmas cupcakes."

Meatball lifted his head and barked.

A second later, Alice burst through the front door. "Help!"

"What's the matter?" I hurried over, easing the door closed to keep out the icy wind.

"It's Campbell. He's being so stubborn." She stamped across the wooden floorboards, leaving a trail of snow behind her.

"There's nothing new there," I said.

"No! You don't understand. This is an emergency. My boarding school friends have arrived." She gestured behind her.

"How did they manage that? I thought everyone canceled their travel plans because the roads are too dangerous," I said.

Alice shook snow off her pink wooly hat, then crouched to tickle Meatball's belly. "I told you they'd make it. Ten minutes ago, a huge SUV with snow chains on its tires pulled up. Paris, Verity, Tabitha, Delphine, and their assistant got out. And what do you think their first question was?"

"Where's the nearest fire so we can thaw out?"

Alice huffed out a breath. "Of course not!"

"Do we look insane for driving in such dangerous conditions?" Rupert said.

"You're not helping." Alice threw her soggy hat at him. "Where's Campbell?" She gulped in air. "I'm not ready. I

16

haven't perfected my cupcakes. Campbell is still wearing that grubby gray T-shirt and boxer shorts, and I hadn't even thought about dinner. It's all going wrong."

I walked over and squeezed her elbow. "It's nothing we can't fix."

"Who'd be irresponsible enough to drive them? The roads haven't been plowed, and with the drifting snow, there must be six feet of the white stuff on the minor lanes," Rupert said.

Alice groaned. "It was Crazy Dave. Delphine got her assistant, Emma, to drive them so far, but they ran into problems. They hired an all-weather vehicle, thinking it would get them through the snow. Emma did her best, but drove off the road in a blizzard. Crazy Dave was passing and heard their cries for help. After giving him a healthy tip for his services, they convinced him to drive them the rest of the way." Alice walked to the table and stole a breadstick off my plate, which she popped into her mouth.

"Where's Dave now?" Rupert said.

"Gone! He said he wanted to get home before the weather got bad. That man seriously has a screw loose. It's already terrible. But that's beside the point. As soon as my friends asked about Campbell, I raced upstairs and told him to put on his tuxedo."

"Why?" I held in a smile.

"That's what they expect. I told them Campbell is an international man of mystery, like James Bond. Just more delicious to look at and an even more amazing superspy."

"And they're expecting a smooth talking, tuxedo wearing, martini sipping charmer?" I said.

"And you've got a grumpy, broken-footed, boxer short wearing misery, who hasn't showered for days." Rupert chuckled.

"Exactly! I told him to get dressed and even got his tuxedo out, but he said no." Alice stamped her foot.

"So he should. Campbell's not a toy to dress up. And he's not feeling well." I patted her arm. "Does it have to be a tuxedo? Maybe a clean T-shirt and combing his hair would be enough."

"No! Well, it would be a start, since he looks gorgeous in anything. But he's being grumpy and rude. I can't let them see him like that."

I exchanged a glance with Rupert. Our quiet evening felt like a distant memory.

Alice grabbed my hand. "You'll get Campbell to see sense. He hasn't even brushed his teeth today!"

I glanced at Rupert again and gave an apologetic shrug. "What do you need us to do?"

She kissed my cheek, her cold nose pressing against my skin. "Come with me. I'll distract my friends while you and Rupert get Campbell dressed. Try for the tuxedo. It shows off his broad shoulders."

I wasn't so sure we would succeed, but I didn't want to stress Alice any more than she already was. When Campbell didn't want to do something, it didn't happen. "I'll ask him, but don't be surprised if he refuses."

"If he does, Rupert must order him to wear his tuxedo. He can't ignore a direct order."

Rupert shuffled his feet on the wooden floor. "The man is getting over a car crash, so I don't want to put him under pressure. Why does it matter what your friends think of him?"

Alice grabbed Rupert's coat from the closet and hurled it at him. "First impressions count, and my friends can be horribly judgmental. You know what they're like. They called you Stringbean for five years because you took ages to fill out."

"Campbell won't disappoint." I tugged on my snow boots, coat, and hat, and then tossed Alice her pink hat.

"Even if he disappoints them, he'll still love you. Give the guy a break. He's on a lot of medication. He also can't do his job, which is to protect you. I know he feels bad about that."

Alice groaned. "Less talking and more trudging through the snow. Follow me."

I tucked Meatball into his winter snow jacket, attached his leash, and we headed outside. The wind whipped snow into my eyes, and I grabbed Rupert's hand as we made our way toward the castle.

The lights were on in the grand entrance, and as we drew near, I spotted multiple footprints. Despite the bad weather, these ladies were still wearing their high heels.

Rupert pushed open the door and ushered us in first. The second I entered the hallway, I was confronted with an army of furs, glittering jewels, and clicking heels on stone tiles.

"Alice! What's going on? You dashed out so fast, I thought someone must have said something to upset you." A tall, slender woman in her early thirties with silky dark hair down to her waist strode over to Alice and kissed her cheek. Her skin was polished, and despite the late hour, her makeup was perfect.

"Sorry, Delphine. I wanted to bring Rupert and Holly to meet you as soon as possible," Alice said. "All of you remember my brother, don't you? And this is Holly, Rupert's wife, and my closest friend."

"Of course." There was a round of air kissing as everyone greeted Rupert and he accepted expensively fragranced hugs.

No one greeted me, although I got a few curious looks as I spent a moment getting familiar with names and faces. They were all beautiful and exuded wealth. Even Emma, the assistant, wore designer clothing and expensive looking heels.

"We're more interested in your gorgeous boyfriend, though," Delphine said. "Where is he? I insist on seeing him immediately."

"Anyone would think you were in love with the bodyguard, not our sweet little Alice." A stunning slip of a woman with jet black hair and huge dark eyes walked over. Under her fur coat, I glimpsed green silk. That was Paris. She was knockout beautiful. She must be a model.

"Maybe I am a little in love! Alice talks about the amazing Campbell Milligan so much, I need to be sure he's real," Delphine said.

"Of course he is! Why would I lie?" Alice said.

"You lied about dating Marcus Princeton." Verity shrugged a narrow shoulder and swept her blonde hair off her face.

"I never did! We went on one date. Well, half a date. He got food poisoning and had to leave early."

"That's what he told you." Delphine tittered, and the rest of the group joined in.

Tabitha shushed them, her blonde curls bobbing.

Alice stepped back to stand beside me. "Before we meet Campbell, I'd like you all to get to know Holly. She's special to me."

"Excellent. She can talk to Emma about our needs. And we require warming up after that awful journey. I want a hot chocolate and a brandy to go with it." Delphine held out her fur coat for me to take.

My cheeks flushed, but I kept my hands by my sides. It wasn't the first time someone had mistaken me for the help.

"No, you misunderstand," Alice said.

I caught her elbow and squeezed. "It's okay. We'll sort things out later. We can get to know each other better then."

Delphine shot me a sharp look, her arm still extended. "Where is Campbell? Let's look around, ladies." She tossed me her coat, then turned toward the stairs, followed by her gaggle of friends.

"Oh, no. Wait! He's not ready for guests. He was dressing when I left him." Alice dashed after them, flinging a desperate look my way.

"We want to see the wounded warrior. We'll be five minutes. And if he is only half-dressed, even better." Delphine strode up the stairs.

Alice was right behind her, which left me and Rupert no choice but to follow them after we'd tugged off our coats, hats, and boots, and I'd hung the nasty fur coat. The only fur I liked to see was on the back of a still living, free roaming, happy animal.

"Delphine is domineering," I whispered to Rupert as I unclipped Meatball's leash so he could run around and have a sniff. He zoomed off, looking like he had a mission to accomplish.

"She's always been like that," Rupert said. "And she's the leader of the pack. Be careful around her. Her tongue is as sharp as those nails of hers."

We'd made it up five steps, when the lights blinked out, there was a yell, and a loud thud in the darkness.

Chapter 3

A warm, firm hand clasped mine, and I held it tight, recognizing Rupert's reassuring grip.

"No need to panic. The snow must have taken down the power lines again," he whispered in my ear.

I nodded, even though he couldn't see me. "Is anybody hurt?" I called into the pitch black. "I heard a thump."

"That was me, walking into that silly stone urn on the landing." Alice's voice was so close to my ear, I jumped. "I've bruised my ankle."

"Is everyone else okay?" I said.

"We will be, so long as the ghost of Christmas past doesn't grab us." That sounded like Delphine a few steps ahead of me.

"I wouldn't mind him grabbing me if he's as gorgeous as Campbell is supposed to be." That sounded like Paris.

There was a gruesome amount of girly giggling.

"Verity, are you okay?" I said.

"No complaints here."

"Tabitha?"

"If you call being unable to see where I'm going, then yes, sweetie, I'm peachy."

"Emma?"

"All good. Thanks." She sounded further up the stairs.

I reached into my pocket to grab my phone. It wasn't there. In my haste to get out of the cottage, I'd left it behind. "Rupert, have you got your phone with you?"

"No. I left it charging in the bedroom. You?"

"Back at home. Alice?"

"This dress doesn't have pockets. Ladies, have any of you got your phones on you? We could do with some light."

"I go nowhere without mine. Hold on a second," Delphine said. "I'll get the torch function on."

"Hurry! I don't want to lose my footing and break my neck by falling down these stairs," Paris sniped.

"Then you should learn to walk properly in heels, darling," Verity said.

"I strut the Milan catwalk in heels twice this high. I assure you, I know what I'm doing with my designer footwear. Tabitha, you're a vegan."

"And your point?" Tabitha said.

"You eat carrots! They help you see in the dark."

"And visit the bathroom multiple times a day. All that fiber can't be good for you," Delphine said.

"It's amazing for me. And my BMI is under twenty."

"But your eyesight sucks," Paris muttered.

A light blazed at the foot of the stairs, and I turned to discover Saracen, Campbell's second in command, with a huge torch in his hand.

"Power's out," he said cheerfully.

"Ooooh! Is that the legendary Campbell?" Delphine said.

"No, this is Saracen. He works for us." Alice made her way carefully down the stairs to join him. "I'm glad you're here. Things were getting tense."

"Always happy to help, Princess Alice. Which way are you headed?"

"Downstairs," she said.

"No! We're visiting your boyfriend. You must want to check in on him and make sure he's okay. Perhaps he's afraid of the dark and needs a cuddle," Delphine said.

Alice pressed her lips together. "Campbell is afraid of nothing."

"He might be afraid of this lot when they get their claws into him," Rupert whispered to me. "I'm so glad I've got you. Otherwise, they'd be pawing over me. Delphine once suggested we date, even though she bullied me for years."

I squeezed his hand and smiled. "I'll protect you from the money grubbing socialites. Be back in a second."

He let go of my hand, not looking happy to be on his own with the ladies so close and giggly.

I caught hold of Alice's elbow and drew her near. "You go up first and check how Campbell's doing. Your friends aren't letting this go, so you'll have to make the introductions. Maybe if they get to see him, that'll be enough. You can present him in his tuxedo another day. A day when you have more time to prepare and get him in a better mood."

"You distract them, and I'll make a break for it. Ready?" Alice hitched up her floor-length gown and dashed up the stairs into the darkness.

I shrugged. I had no choice but to be ready.

Saracen grinned at me. "What's the plan, Lady Holly?"

His guess was as good as mine. "We should all stay where we are. It's not safe to wander in the darkness."

"Give me your torch," Delphine said to Saracen.

He glanced at me. "I'll lead you back down. You'll be safer staying in one room. The power should be back on shortly, and then you can look around."

"We're not common tourists. We don't want to poke around and stare at the dusty antiques. We're going upstairs to meet Campbell. Now, give me that torch." Delphine stuck out a hand and waggled her fingers.

Saracen looked at me again, and then Rupert. He gave a tiny shrug.

I stepped in front of Saracen. "None of you have seen Alice's renovation of the ladies' parlor. It's pretty. Let's go down, and—"

"Since when has the help been so involved with this family?" Delphine said.

I was glad it was so gloomy, so she couldn't see my cheeks flush.

"Holly isn't the help. I thought Alice explained our relationship." Rupert turned, so he faced Delphine and her friends, and had his back to me.

Delphine paid him no attention. "I'm going up, anyway, even if I have to do it alone and in the dark. I can't find my stupid phone in my purse."

"It's hidden under the cosmetics and anti-wrinkle cream," Paris muttered.

Delphine kept digging through the huge black leather purse hung over one arm. "You can talk. You brought three bags of luggage with you, and we're only staying two nights."

"My face is my fortune. I have to look after it." Paris smoothed a hand down her hair.

"This is ridiculous. I'm going. Emma, you're with me." Delphine turned and inched up the stairs, one hand gripping the bannister, which was covered in a green and red garland, the other hand outstretched to keep her balance.

Emma lingered on the stairs and pushed her dark-framed glasses up her petite nose. She looked at the rest of the group, but no one offered any useful suggestions.

"Wait! I'll go first and guide you." Saracen dashed up the stairs until he reached the front of the group. "Take your time, ladies. I don't want any accidents. It'll be impossible to get medical help here, with the snow being so bad."

"I'm sure a big, strapping man like you would take the best care of us if we needed looking after." Delphine caught hold of his arm and squeezed his biceps.

The torch wobbled in Saracen's hand. "I'm always happy to do my job."

Although I couldn't see in the gloom, I was certain Saracen was blushing.

Paris, Verity, and Tabitha pushed past Saracen and Delphine.

"Hey! I want to get the first look. That's not fair." Delphine dropped her hold on Saracen and hurried after them.

After a second of hesitation, Emma followed.

"I give up." Saracen shook his head and pointed the torchlight so they could see. He dropped back to join me and Rupert as we climbed the stairs. "I hope they know what they're letting themselves in for. Campbell's been snapping and snarling at me ever since his accident."

"He's embarrassed about what happened," I said. "After all, he's always bragging about what an incredible driver he is."

"Anyone would have done the same in those conditions. There was black ice all over the road, and it was hidden under the snow. It was the first day it really came down. And it looks like there'd been damage to the underside of the car. It's still being looked at," Saracen said. "Whoever drove it last must have hit a hole or ran over a branch. There was brake fluid leaking out. It's no surprise nothing worked when Campbell stamped his foot on the brakes."

I tried to ignore the giggling as Alice's friends headed closer to their target. "He'll be looking for someone to blame for that mistake."

"This is where it gets worse. Campbell checked the logs. He was the last person to drive that vehicle before he ran it off the road."

"Which will make him even grumpier," I said.

"No doubt. You should send him up some of those sugar-free gingerbread cookies you made me. They're delicious. Every time I eat one, it takes me back to the gingerbread cake my gran made every Christmas. I loved that cake. I loved her, too, but mainly because of the cake." He chuckled.

"I'm glad you like them. I've been experimenting to find the perfect recipe."

"If you want to put a tin of them in my Santa stocking, you won't hear any complaints from me."

I'd been providing sugar-free tasty treats to Saracen ever since he'd received a diabetes diagnosis. "I'll see what Santa can do."

"Thanks, Holly. It won't be so bad working over Christmas with all your treats around."

"You didn't volunteer to stay over the holidays?"

"Nope. Campbell twisted my arm and said he needed his right-hand man on site because he was stuck in bed. I don't mind being here over Christmas, though. Although it's kind of eerie with most of the staff already gone home for the holidays. The place is usually full of tourists and staff."

"We like to give everyone plenty of time off," Rupert said.

"Will somebody help me!" a male voice snarled from some distance away.

"Is that the ghost of Christmas past?" Delphine said from the top of the stairs.

"That was Campbell," I whispered. "What's he up to?"

"No clue. But he sounds as angry as a Christmas elf who got lumbered with the midnight delivery shift. I'll go see what's going on. Excuse me, ladies." Saracen brushed past Delphine and her group and disappeared into the darkness.

"Hey! Don't leave us," Delphine said. "Some bodyguard he is. Should we follow him?"

"We should follow the sound of that deliciously surly voice. That must be Campbell," Tabitha said. "Is that who we just heard?"

It was time for rapid diversionary tactics. The last thing Alice needed was for her friends to see Campbell in one of his epic, grumpy moods. They wouldn't approve, and she'd be heartbroken.

I squeezed Rupert's elbow. "We need to buy Alice time. Back me up if her friends question me."

"Always. Lead the way," he said.

"That wasn't Campbell. But I can take you to his room." I hurried up the stairs. "It's easy to get lost in all these corridors. And I don't want you winding up in the haunted wing."

"There's a haunted wing?" I could just make out Paris's alarmed face in the gloom as my eyes adjusted to the lack of torchlight.

"Oh, yes. Ghosts everywhere. That part of the castle always gives me the chills. And every visitor reports seeing an apparition. Some people even freeze to the spot in terror."

"There I was kidding about the ghost of Christmas past." Delphine looked over her shoulder. "Not that I believe in ghosts."

"I do," Paris said. "I once saw the ghost of a dead fashion designer. He'd come back to critique his range when it was showcased."

"Are you sure that wasn't an illusion because of the champagne?" Delphine said. "You barely eat for two weeks before a catwalk show. A few sips of bubbly, and you're away with the fairies."

"I know what I saw. Ghosts are real." Paris jabbed a finger at Delphine. "You should be more respectful, or they might visit you tonight and make you sorry."

"What rubbish. You! Take us to Campbell. Some assistant you are, not helping." Delphine pointed at me.

"We have already introduced Holly to you," Rupert said. "You know who she is."

Delphine smirked, turned, and continued up the stairs, Verity, Paris, Tabitha, and Emma trailing behind her.

"I'm so sorry about them," Rupert whispered. "Some people are snobs."

"Forget about it. I already have." It wasn't uncommon to encounter disdain from people in the Audley social circle. They didn't understand why Rupert hadn't married a princess or a lady. I'd given up explaining how true love conquers all, regardless of title or status. It was none of their business who Rupert loved and married. The most important thing was it worked for us. And it did.

I hurried up the stairs after the gaggle of socialites. "Turn left at the top, but be careful of the Venetian urns."

"We have been here before," Delphine said, a splash of acid in her tone. "We know where we're going."

"I don't have a clue," Verity said. "Don't leave me. I don't want to end up in the ghost wing."

"Ouch! Whatever I just walked into was hard," Paris said.

I gently nudged past them with Rupert to take the lead. "This way. Campbell's room is at the end of the corridor." They didn't know it yet, but I was leading them in the opposite direction to Campbell and Alice's room. It would only buy Alice a few minutes, but hopefully, that was all she needed.

"Are you sure it's this way?" Paris said.

"Yes. Not far," I said brightly.

"Alice must have moved her room since the last time I visited."

"It's easy to get turned around in the dark," I said. "We're almost there."

The end of the corridor was approaching, and the closed door that opened onto the turret staircase would be too suspicious to use. And there was no way I was taking them up there. For all the talk of a haunted wing, there were cold spots in the castle I didn't enjoy exploring.

I leaned in close to Rupert. "I need to check things are okay with Campbell and Alice before these ladies descend like sparkling vultures. Can you take over?"

"I'll do my best. But we're running out of options."

I kissed his cheek. "You'll think of something."

"Ladies, have you seen the woven tapestry we recently acquired? It came from the Lake Como area of Italy. This one is traditional scenes from the Villa d'Este gardens from the late eighteenth century." Rupert stopped by a tapestry that had been on the wall for years. "It's exquisite."

I stepped back on the pretense of looking, and while he had everyone's attention, tiptoed into the darkness. Once I was certain I hadn't been seen making my escape, I broke into a run, raced along the corridor, and straight to Campbell and Alice's bedroom.

I tapped on the door and pushed it open. Alice was on the floor, illuminated by torchlight. Next to her was a half-dressed Campbell with his tuxedo pants around his knees and a white shirt open to the waist.

I averted my eyes. "Sorry to interrupt, but they're almost here. Rupert is distracting them with the wall hangings, but they'll soon know we led them on a goose chase."

Alice sighed. "Oh, well, you did your best. But look! Campbell was putting his tuxedo on for me. Isn't he an angel?"

"I feel like a jerk," he grumbled.

"But you were attempting to surprise me. I feel so bad for scolding you earlier. I love you." Alice kissed him.

Campbell glared at me, daring me to smile or make a comment. I studied the flocked wallpaper in the gloom. Silence was the best option. It felt like one false step, and Campbell would explode.

He finally looked back at Alice. "Why do your friends have to see me now?"

"You know how determined they are." She fussed over his close-cropped hair.

"Can't you get them drunk and feed them? Then they'll forget about me."

"That'll come. There'll be demands for champagne any second." Alice tried to button his shirt. "My ladies love their bubbles."

He eased her hands away from his chest. "I can do it. You don't need to coddle me."

"I want to help."

"Alice! I've camped in deserts, scaled mountains, and toured dangerous jungles. I can take care of myself."

"Now, you don't have to. Not now you have me." Alice looked up at me. "Tell him, Holly."

I mimed zipping my mouth shut and tossing the key.

"Sensible move," he muttered as he buttoned his shirt.

"I knew that was the wrong way. Why did that idiot woman take us along that corridor?" Delphine was right outside the bedroom door.

"It's dark and easy to make a mistake. I thought we were going the right way, and I've lived here most of my life." Rupert sounded harassed.

"This is Alice's room! I remember now," Paris said.

31

Just as the door was shoved open, the lights came back on and revealed Campbell in his half-dressed glory.

Alice attempted to shield him, but she was half his size, and even though she spread her dress with her hands, most of what he had was still on display.

I backed away and joined Rupert in the corridor, powerless to stop Alice's friends pouring into the room for a good looky-loo.

"Sorry. I did my best to tempt them with the tapestries, but they soon figured out something was wrong when you vanished," he whispered.

"You did a great job," I said.

"Oh, my goodness! What a gorgeous man." Delphine shoved past Paris, a lecherous look on her face. "I see now why you like him so much."

"He is delicious." Verity licked her lips. "Well done, Alice. I didn't think you had it in you."

Alice was desperately trying to get Campbell back on his bed without hurting his foot. "Thank you. I mean, of course, I have it in me. I don't know what you mean."

Saracen hurried into the room. "Power's back on."

"Well observed," Campbell said. "Give me a hand, before Alice hurts her back lifting me."

"Of course, boss." Saracen placed down the torch, and between him and Alice, they got Campbell back on the bed and a blanket covering his modesty.

"Well, this wasn't how I expected these introductions to go." Alice clasped her hands together and pasted on a brave smile. "But here we all are. Campbell Milligan, I'd like you to meet my school friends. Delphine Augustus, Paris Gallo, Verity Kingston-Blythe, Tabitha Orleans, and... oh, where's Emma? We didn't lose her in the dark, did we?"

"Forget her. I sent her to sort the luggage. Emma's not here to socialize." Delphine held out a hand to be shaken. "It's a pleasure to meet you, Campbell."

He gave it a brief shake. "Alice has told me all about you."

"When she sent us pictures of you, I couldn't believe she'd bagged such a hottie."

Campbell shifted on the bed and winced as his foot moved. "I'm very happy with Prin... Alice."

I pressed my lips together, trying hard not to smile. It had taken Campbell months to stop calling Alice *Princess Alice* every time he said her name. Just like it had taken me a while to stop calling Rupert *Lord Rupert* after we'd started dating.

"Now, I have an important question. What do you see in Alice?" Delphine said.

Campbell's eyes widened before his expression hardened. "She's perfect. Kind, sweet, always helping those who need it. She doesn't judge people like a lot of others do. And Alice always looks for the best in people, even if they don't deserve it."

"We all do that." Delphine leaned close, Verity, Tabitha, and Paris hovering behind her. "Are you hoping to get a title out of this little arrangement?"

"Delphine, that's enough!" Alice's face flashed scarlet and then went pale. "Campbell's in love with me, and we're very happy together. Don't spoil things with your spiteful words."

"I'm not spiteful. I'm curious." There was a malevolent gleam in Delphine's eyes.

"Ignore Delphine. She's jealous of everything you've got," Verity said. "Always has been."

"How could I possibly be jealous? I've got the delicious Clay at my beck and call. He does anything for me. Just last week, he got me a stunning diamond bracelet. I asked where the matching necklace and earrings were. I'll get them next month." Delphine's smile appeared frozen on her face. "Not that there's anything wrong with you, Campbell, but I doubt you're buying Alice diamonds every month."

"I don't need anyone to buy me diamonds," Alice said. "If I want them, I'll buy them for myself. I'm not with Campbell because he gives me gifts."

"We can all see why you're with him," Paris drawled. "He's luscious. Let's have another look at those abs."

All the high-heeled ladies tittered. Alice and I stayed silent.

"Shall we go downstairs and open some champagne?" Rupert said. "We can have a pre-Christmas party to celebrate your arrival."

I was glad Rupert was attempting to take the heat out of this awkward situation. If it wasn't diffused soon, Alice may throw Delphine out a window.

"Perfect! You're an angel, Rupert. You. Go sort the champagne for us." Delphine waggled a finger at me. "Emma will help. She'll be in my room, wherever that is."

"Delphine!" Alice said. "Holly is my sister-in-law, not the help. I've told you several times she's married to Rupert."

"My mistake. It slipped my mind." Delphine gave me a saccharin smile that was as false as her shiny hair extensions.

Alice hurried into the corridor and leaned in close. "Ignore Delphine. She's being beastly. She can get like that, sometimes. She's probably hungry."

"It's fine. I'll find Emma and sort everything out." I was glad of an excuse to get away from this uncomfortable gathering.

She hugged me. "This Christmas will be perfect. Once Delphine settles in, she'll be nicer. You'll be best friends by the time she leaves. I promise we'll make the best of this situation."

I caught Campbell's gaze through the open bedroom door, and he winced at me. We both realized a quiet, relaxed Christmas was now a distant memory.

Chapter 4

Half an hour later, Alice's friends had left Campbell alone, freshened up in their rooms, and descended into the ladies' parlor. They were sipping on champagne and trying some of Chef Heston's Christmas lobster truffle canopies.

Despite Alice's assurances Delphine would behave, she was still being curt to me and abrasive to her put upon assistant, Emma.

Alice sidled over as I stood by the open fire, breathing in the warmth and rubbing my hands together, despite not being cold. "I've ruined everything. Campbell is barely speaking to me after my friends barged in on him."

I forced a smile. "You've ruined nothing. But I feel sorry for Campbell. He hates being vulnerable, and getting caught with his pants down and you helping him may have sullied his superspy image."

"I know! And he was being so sweet by trying to put his tuxedo on."

"All he wants to do is make you happy."

"He does. And he's a teddy bear under that grumpiness. I'll make sure my friends back off and leave him alone until he's feeling up to receiving visitors. Bursting in like that was rude. I should have been firmer with them."

I glanced over my shoulder to make sure Alice's friends weren't listening to our conversation. "From my limited experience with Delphine, it seems when she sets her mind on something, nothing prevents her from achieving it."

"That's her in a nutshell. She's always been the group's leader. Verity and Tabitha go along with whatever she tells them to do, but Paris sometimes stands against her. They've had some wicked cat fights over the years."

I put an arm around her shoulders. "You have interesting friends, Alice."

She shrugged. "They used to be nice. At least, sometimes."

"Alice, when are Rupert's friends getting here?" Verity called out. "I broke up with Arthur Sidmouth the Third last month, so I need a new catch of the day. A handsome one. He needs to be rich, and I don't want anyone with a weak chin."

"They're not coming." Alice turned away from me. "The bad weather has meant everyone canceled. I'm amazed you were able to make it."

Delphine set down her glass and crossed her arms over her pale pink silk blouse. "You promised us an enormous party, a banquet, and a masked ball. All I'm seeing so far are servants out of their place, warm champers, and attitude."

"I can't control the weather," Alice said. "We had everything planned, but everyone's been canceling all week, ever since the snow started. They either couldn't get a flight into the country or didn't want to risk driving."

"We made it. So should they," Delphine said.

"We'll still have fun." I tried to sound breezy, but my words came out high-pitched. "It'll just be a more relaxed Christmas."

Delphine paid me no attention.

I shrugged off her rudeness and turned back to the wreath-draped mantel. I had no interest in making friends with someone so shallow.

There was a tap on the door, and a second later, Chef Heston appeared. "Sorry to interrupt, but the Duke is looking for you, Lord Rupert. Something about a family portrait. He needs your help to figure things out."

I didn't miss Rupert's relieved sigh at being given a reprieve. "Thank you. Tell him I'll be right there."

I hurried over to him. "Don't leave me. If Delphine keeps jabbing at me, I might set Meatball on her." I looked around for my furry buddy, but he was nowhere to be seen. It wasn't like him to go missing for so long. Maybe he'd picked up the unfriendly vibes and was staying away.

"I'm sorry, but you know what the Duke gets like when he lands on an idea. He can't shake it loose until he finds the answer." He kissed my cheek. "I'll be as quick as I can."

I didn't blame Rupert for wanting to get out. If I had a valid reason for escaping, I'd do it, too. The giggling and shrieks from Alice's friends had caused a low-level headache.

I shot a longing look at the door as Rupert walked out. I took a step toward it. Maybe I could slip out unnoticed.

Alice's hand gripped my elbow. "Oh, no. Not you, too. I need support."

I arched an eyebrow, my patience prickling. "I only ate half my dinner before you dragged me here. Don't I deserve a time out?"

"Have a lobster truffle puff. They're delicious." She grabbed one off a silver tray and handed it to me.

I took a bite. It was excellent. You could always guarantee delicious nibbles from Chef Heston.

Alice pursed her lips as she studied the group. "Maybe it is time for a change. It'll be tricky to cut ties, though.

My parents are friends with their parents, and the connections go back generations. It won't be easy to remove them from my life."

"You don't have to cut them from your life completely. Delphine seems poisonous, though. Do you have a difficult history?"

"Not really. I mean, I shoved her in a duck pond once. She's never forgiven me for that."

"I'm sure she deserved it."

"She did. She called me a chubby idiot who had air for brains."

"I'd have done more than shove her in a pond if I'd overheard those insults." I tucked my hand through Alice's elbow. "Just because something has always been done a certain way, doesn't mean it has to continue. When you and Campbell have a family, do you want to inflict the next generation of Delphines on your children?"

Her pale eyebrows flashed up. "What a shocking thought. I'd never do that to them."

"But you're prepared to do it to yourself?"

Alice tutted. "You're too clever for your own good, sometimes."

I smiled at her. "I have my moments."

"When are you and Campbell getting married?" Delphine said from the other side of the room. "I hope you have the ceremony here and don't go back to his unimportant little hometown. I won't be your bridesmaid if you do that."

Alice narrowed her eyes at me and then turned with a false smile on her face and headed over to her friends.

I stayed back a few paces but remained close in case she needed support.

"We haven't made it official yet, but I'm sure it'll be soon," Alice said. "Wherever we marry, it'll be perfect. And I've yet to decide on my bridesmaids."

"You'll have us. We made the pact in school to be involved in each other's weddings," Delphine said. "I'll be chief bridesmaid."

"Why do you get that role?" Paris said. "I'll look better in any gown than you."

"You'd look like a stick insect. You fashion models are far too thin. Eat something before you vanish."

"It's why I get so much work. And I've just landed a huge campaign for a new perfume. My face will be everywhere."

Delphine rolled her eyes. "Get the work while you can. You're getting forehead wrinkles."

Paris gasped and dashed to the mirror above the fireplace, pulling her skin taunt as she twisted in the light.

Delphine smirked. "I don't know what the world is coming to. All you Audleys are marrying down." She glanced at me, and her stony gaze ran from my head to my toes and back up.

I grinned at her and stuffed a lobster truffle puff into my mouth.

Alice thumped down her champagne flute. "That's enough! Holly is one of the sweetest, smartest, kindest people I know. Not only that, but she's a genius in the kitchen."

"Oh, yes. I'd forgotten that was how she wormed her way into your lives. You know what they say about the way to a man's heart..."

"I did no worming," I said calmly. "I was fortunate enough to get a job in the kitchen, and Alice was kind enough to make friends with me. That was how I got to know Rupert."

"I made friends with you because you're an amazing person," Alice said. "I feel privileged to have you in my life and delighted you married my brother. You're too good for him."

"The kitchen assistant is too good for the lord?" Delphine shook her head. "Are you sure you're feeling well, Alice? You're not pregnant, are you? You've gained more weight."

I opened my mouth to insist Delphine apologize, but Alice got there first.

"No, I'm not. And I've never been better. Holly has opened my eyes to what true friendship means. She's always there when I need her. She makes me laugh when I'm sad, or just sits with me and feeds me cake if I don't want to cheer up. She gave me the courage to follow a path to true love, and she's helping to make me a better person. And so what if I'm a little curvier than usual? Campbell loves my figure."

There was a second of stunned silence. Tabitha, who stood just behind Delphine, did a silent clap and winked at Alice.

"We do that for you, too," Delphine said. "Isn't that right, ladies?"

Verity, Tabitha, and Paris mumbled their agreement, but seemed uncomfortable at the possibility of offering Alice genuine support.

I was at a loss for what to say, and as I glanced around the room looking for a distraction, I realized Meatball still hadn't returned from his castle exploration. Where had he snuck off to? He'd better not have his nose in the Christmas food.

"Has anyone seen Meatball?" I said, more to myself than the group.

"I don't eat meat," Tabitha said. "I'm vegan."

"It's not an entrée. Meatball is Holly's dog." Alice peeked behind a chair. "Didn't he race off somewhere when we arrived?"

"He did. But it's unlike him not to check in." I poked my head out the door. "Meatball!"

There was a bark some distance away, and then claws on the tiled flooring grew near. Meatball turned the corner, and he wasn't alone. There was a cute, fluffy corgi by his side, trotting along, her little tail up.

"Oh! You found a friend." I crouched and caught hold of him, giving his belly a tickle. "Who is this beautiful girl?"

Meatball ruffed out a joyful bark and sniffed his lady friend.

"There she is! I've been looking for her everywhere." Duchess Isabella Audley approached from the other end of the corridor, swathed in pale blue silk.

"This is your new pup?" I said.

"Yes. And she's so feisty. Much like Meatball. It's probably why they're friends. Every time I turn my back, she disappears to find him."

"Oh! It makes sense now. Meatball has been asking to visit the castle. He's been looking for his new playmate, too. What's her name?"

"Dottie. She doesn't get on well with the others, though, so I'm glad she's found a friend in Meatball." Duchess Isabella picked up Dottie and kissed her head. "Dottie, meet Holly."

"She's adorable." I let Dottie sniff my fingers, and after she seemed happy with my scent, gave her a gentle tickle.

Dottie's tail thumped back and forth, and she leaned into my touch.

"I believe I've introduced an alpha into my pack, and they're struggling to get used to the new reign of corgi rule," Duchess Isabella said.

"Meatball will be glad to have a friend. They're welcome to hang out together anytime you like."

Meatball was wagging his tail, clearly thrilled by this new arrival to the corgi contingent.

"Duchess Isabella. I thought I recognized your voice."
Delphine appeared in the door, all smiles and air kisses.

"It's nice to see you again. I'm surprised you made it
through the snow. Wouldn't it have been safer to stay at
home?"

"I wouldn't miss one of your incredible parties. We've
been looking forward to Christmas at Audley Castle all
year." Delphine placed her back to me.

I rolled my eyes and crouched to pet Meatball some
more. He was much better company than Miss Airs and
Graces.

"Well, I hope we don't disappoint. It'll be an intimate
affair, this year. But of course, make yourself at home.
You're always welcome. How are your parents?"

"They're taking their Christmas break in Aruba. We
have a home there."

"You didn't want to join them?"

"And miss coming here? Of course not. You
always host such elegant parties." Delphine continued
simpering around Duchess Isabella, whose answers,
although polite, became increasingly short.

I kept petting Meatball and ignored Delphine, since
that was what she was doing to me.

"If you'll excuse me, I need to get this little one to bed."
Duchess Isabella tickled Dottie under the chin.

Delphine went to pet Dottie, but her growl made her
step back and frown.

"Don't mind Dottie, she's never sure about new
people." Duchess Isabella glanced my way and flashed
her eyebrows up. "It takes a while for her to warm up to
anyone."

Meatball whined and lifted one paw off the ground.

"You can't go with her," I said. "You can see Dottie
tomorrow, though. Perhaps we can arrange a walk
together?"

"That sounds perfect. Dottie adores the snow, even when it's so deep she can't see over the top. She even chases snowballs." Duchess Isabella chuckled. "She's keeping us on our toes with her antics."

Dottie tried to get down to be with Meatball, but Duchess Isabella shook her head. "Time for bed. Play time tomorrow. Good night Holly. Delphine. Enjoy your evening." The glitter of amusement in her eyes suggested she knew what I felt about this evening's entertainment.

Delphine nodded and smiled until the Duchess and Dottie were out of sight. She turned to me, and the fake smile was gone.

"Get more champagne. And since Alice reckons you're so amazing in the kitchen, we need more food, too. Nothing greasy. Can you handle that? Proper food this time, not those fishy puffs."

I stared at the empty glass Delphine held out, and stepped closer, but kept my voice low. "Since you're on such good terms with the family, you know where everything is. Help yourself to anything you like." I turned before she protested and strode away, whistling for Meatball to follow.

My heart raced, but I had to stand up to Delphine, or she'd bully me the whole time she was here. And as much as I wanted to support Alice, I was done being trodden on by her entitled, snobbish school friends.

Meatball wagged his tail as he trotted along, and I let out a slow breath. Life as a dog was simple. If only I could get away with focusing on walks, food, belly rubs, and sleep. But I'd known what I was getting myself into when I married into the family. And for the minor problems it caused, I wouldn't change a thing about my life.

Just being away from that gaggle of giggling ladies and back with my dog relaxed me, and my headache faded.

I pulled on my thick gloves, grabbed my hat, and shoved my arms into my coat. I attached Meatball's leash, and we headed into a wintry wonderland. The freezing air was welcome as it stung my cheeks, and with every step we took away from the castle, I relaxed a little more.

"Which way should we go, Meatball? We need to stick to a path, or you'll get lost under the snow." I pushed a gloved finger through the snow and couldn't touch the ground.

His head shot up. He growled at the gloomy trees up ahead.

"It's just a squirrel or a deer. No need to worry." I kept him on his leash in case he chased the wildlife. Although I liked snow, I didn't want to traipse through it and get frozen toes hunting for Meatball while he went on an adventure.

Meatball barked, and he didn't stop.

I peered into the gloom. I still couldn't see what had alarmed him. "Let's go another way. Somewhere the night critters won't disturb you."

He pulled on his leash, his nose fixed on the shadows. His behavior made me uneasy. Was something out there?

I was gently tugging him along the path, eager to move on, when a bush rustled. And was that someone deep breathing? Fear skittered down my spine.

"Hello. Is anyone there?"

The rustling grew louder, and a second later, a man burst through the bushes.

He yelped as he toppled over and landed face first in the snow.

Chapter 5

Meatball tugged so hard on his leash, it slipped through my fingers. He raced through the snow, disappearing into a snowdrift in his attempt to reach the fallen stranger who wore a black tuxedo. Hardly the outfit of a burglar, but you could never be too careful.

I chased after Meatball. The snow soaked the bottom of my coat and froze my knees. "Meatball, get back here!"

Meatball kept barking and running. At least, he attempted to run, but his little legs were no match for the snow, and it stuck to his fur in big, round clumps, slowing him down. He pushed on regardless.

Whilst keeping a careful eye on Meatball to ensure the snow didn't swallow him, I kept shooting glances at the stranger. As he'd fallen, he'd dropped several wrapped packages covered in bright red Christmas paper and bows. Anyone intending to steal from Audley Castle, or sneak in to do something they shouldn't, wouldn't bring gifts.

I finally caught Meatball and scooped him up. He was heavy, thanks to the balls of snow stuck in his fur. He struggled for a second, then licked my cheek, relieved to be off the frozen ground and safe in my arms.

I stopped close to the stranger. "Are you okay? You gave me a scare by appearing out of the darkness."

The man wiped snow off his face and blinked several times. "Sorry to startle you. I'm trying to get somewhere. I'm not sure I'm in the right place, though."

"Where do you need to be?"

He scrambled to his feet and brushed snow off his long black coat. "Audley Castle. I see a castle, but is it the right one? Do you know? I've not been here before."

"Oh! You're in the right place."

He blew out a breath that fogged in the freezing air. "Thank goodness. I was losing the will to go on. I didn't realize how cold it was when I started. And three miles seems a lot farther in the dark and snow." He smiled at me. "I'm Clay Osbourne."

I arched my eyebrow. Was I supposed to know that name?

When I didn't answer, his mouth twisted to the side. "And you are?"

"Not certain you should be here."

"Ah! Well, I should. I mean, I don't have an invitation, but my fiancée is staying in that castle. At least, I hope she is. I've been trying to get her on the phone, but she's not picking up."

"Who's your fiancée?"

"Delphine Augustus. I wanted to surprise her, but it didn't go as planned. When I couldn't reach her, I drove here. But my car ran off the road a few miles back. Anyway, I braved it and carried on by foot. The trouble is, I didn't pack any snow boots, and I lost the feeling in my toes half an hour ago. But by then, it was too late to turn back." Clay sucked in a breath. "I am sorry I frightened you. When I heard a voice, I hurried to get to you before you vanished. You're my angel of mercy. Both of you." He grinned at Meatball.

The more we talked, the less concerned I was that Clay could be up to no good. "I didn't expect anyone to be out this late, especially not when it's so cold. I'm

Holly. I live here. And you'll be happy to know Delphine is here, too. She arrived with her friends earlier this evening."

"At last! Luck is on my side." Clay gathered the fallen gifts, stuffing the smaller ones into his coat pockets. "This was supposed to be a surprise. Delphine always loves grand gestures."

I got a good look at Clay as he drew nearer. He was around thirty, with shoulder-length blond hair and a strong jaw line. Even in a soggy tuxedo, he looked handsome. Maybe he was a model. I could imagine Delphine liked her men picture perfect for any photo opportunity.

"Holly, what are you doing out there? Is everything okay?"

I turned and saw Saracen in the doorway, holding up a torch. I waved him over. "We have an unexpected guest."

"I'm not in trouble, am I?" Clay said. "This was meant to be fun. I thought Delphine would be impressed by me making such an effort. She never seems happy with me these days. These gifts are all for her." He held out a bedraggled parcel, the paper soggy and the bow limp.

Saracen joined me and glared at Clay. "You're trespassing on private property, sir. I could arrest you for that."

Clay's eyes widened. "I'm here for a good reason. I was just explaining to Holly."

"I don't think Clay means any harm." I felt sorry for him, and he appeared more hopeless than harmful. "His car ran off the road a few miles away. You weren't hurt, were you? We've had a few accidents around here because of the bad weather."

Clay exhaled slowly, his gaze cautious as he studied Saracen. "No, I was going slowly. I could barely see beyond my headlights, and I don't know these roads."

"Only idiots go out in weather like this," Saracen grumbled. "You'd better come with me."

"You're not locking me up for trespassing, are you?"

"I'm thinking about it." Saracen jerked a thumb over his shoulder. "But I'd rather figure things out in the warm."

"Of course. You'll come, too?" Clay said to me.

"Well, I do live here. And it is cold. Let's get inside and warm you up. I'm sure Delphine will be happy to see you."

There was an ear-piercing shriek from the castle entrance. As I rubbed my ear and frowned, I spotted Delphine, Verity, Paris, Tabitha, and Alice standing by the open door.

"Clay! It is you! What are you doing out there?" Delphine went to step into the snow in her heels, then hesitated and remained where she was.

"I came to surprise you, darling." Clay strode ahead of us, all smiles and easy swagger. "I couldn't stand the thought of not seeing you over Christmas. It would have been a miserable holiday without your beautiful face in it."

Delphine gasped. "You came just to see me? Ladies, did you hear that?"

"I risked life and limb to get here. I almost died when my car spun off the road."

Saracen and I followed Clay back to the castle.

"How romantic. Clay risked his life to be with me." Delphine pressed a bejeweled hand to her forehead in a mock swoon.

"I've been calling you for hours. I got worried when you didn't pick up and thought something bad might have happened to you."

"Oh, my phone is somewhere in the bottom of my purse. I'm always losing it in there. And I've been having such fun with Alice that I forgot to check my messages." She held out a hand to Clay.

"It was an adventure getting here. But it was worth it." Clay kissed Delphine on the cheek and then nodded at her friends. "Nice to see you all."

"Let's go inside and celebrate my handsome hero." Delphine simpered around Clay, while her friends stood back, looking mildly green with envy. Only Alice looked unimpressed.

"Let's get inside," I said as I joined the cooing party. "Clay can tell you the story of how he survived the epic snowstorm of Audley St. Mary while we warm up."

Clay clapped his hands together and rubbed them briskly. "Great idea. Is there anything to eat? I'm starving."

"Holly will get you something. According to Alice, she's a genius in the kitchen, and is always happy to serve." Delphine caught hold of Clay's arm. "You come with us."

I bit my tongue. There was no point in telling Delphine I wasn't the hired help again. She had it in her head I was below her in social rank, and nothing I did would change her mind.

"You good?" Saracen said to me.

"Yes. Thanks for the help."

He lifted one shoulder. "That guy would never have gotten so close to the castle if Campbell was fit for duty. Maybe don't mention this to him? I don't want to get in trouble."

"Mention what?"

Saracen grinned. "Need a hand in the kitchen to fill the posh lady's order?"

"Sure. And there are gingerbread cookies with your name on them, if you're interested."

"Now we're talking."

Half an hour later, and after two platefuls of sandwiches and a mug of coffee, Clay was retelling the epic battle of how he survived the snowstorm to get to his beloved for the third time. Each time, it became more embellished and harder for me not to yawn and feign politeness.

Everybody else seemed enthralled by Clay and his heroic adventures, especially Delphine, who almost sat in his lap, one arm wrapped around his shoulders.

Alice poked me in the ribs with her elbow. "Campbell wouldn't walk through the snow for me."

"He would."

"He'd complain if he did."

"Alice! Campbell escaped from the castle with you when you were a murder suspect, and you went on the run together. He almost lost his life and career to protect you and ensure your name was cleared. Campbell would die for you in a heartbeat."

"Oh! Well, yes. That was decent of him."

"More than decent. A little snow would never stop Campbell from getting to you if you needed him."

"Maybe so." She sighed and flopped back in her seat. "But why won't he ask me to marry him? I've been dropping hints for months, but he can't hear me. I've yet to figure out if the man is stubborn or stupid."

"He's stubborn." I leaned closer. "And I have firsthand knowledge that marrying into the Audley family is challenging. Maybe it's one he's not ready to embrace."

Alice reared back. "I don't know what you mean. We're the perfect family."

"You're perfect. You and Rupert are a joy to be around. But I've had trouble with your mother, and I'm still not sure she trusts me. She worries I'll run off with the family silver the second I get the chance."

51

"She's frosty with everyone, including me." Alice gripped my hands. "You are happy being one of us, though, aren't you?"

"More than happy. But perhaps Campbell has his concerns about joining the family. As much as I love Rupert, I was nervous about stepping into this role. Lots of things have changed since I married him. I'm not complaining, but it takes some adjustment. I was fortunate Chef Heston was happy for me to keep working in the kitchen." Baking was a passion I'd never give up. "Maybe Campbell is concerned about what his role will be once you're married."

"It won't be any different. He'll remain as head of security for Audley Castle. He'll be my protector. Even more so when he's my husband."

"Isn't that a conflict of interest? He might put your safety before his own because his emotions cloud his judgment. Or he may abandon his post when he's supposed to protect somebody else because he's worried about you." I'd seen Campbell battle with this dilemma more than once, before finally confessing his feelings for Alice. "Campbell is his career."

Alice sighed and smoothed her dress over her knees. "I want Campbell to be happy. I'd never dream of taking away his career."

"Have you discussed that with him? Or have you only been dropping hints about tiaras, six-tier wedding cakes, and how many bridesmaids you want?"

She wrinkled her nose a few times. "Perhaps I have been more focused on the wedding rather than what it would mean for him. You commoners are so difficult."

"You posh people are so weird."

"I'm not posh."

"And I'm not common. Neither is Campbell."

Alice grinned at me. "It's our differences that make us the perfect best friends. I'll talk to Campbell and let him know if he wants to keep working at the castle, we'll figure things out. Do you really think that's the only reason he hasn't made a proposal?"

"Campbell doesn't talk to me about matters of the heart. Have you mentioned it to Saracen?"

"I cornered him a few weeks ago and demanded answers. He went bright red, lost the ability to talk in complete sentences, and pretended someone was calling him on the phone. I got nothing."

"I need to go to bed." Delphine stood, waving at Clay to remain in his seat. "I feel a migraine coming on. Emma, come with me. You'll need to sort my things."

Emma had discreetly tucked herself in one corner with a large plateful of food and a glass of champagne. She quickly set down her glass and hurried out of the room ahead of Delphine.

"Do you need anything?" Alice said. "I've got pain medication for your migraine if that would help."

"No. I've got everything I need in my room. I'll see you all in the morning. Then the celebrations can really begin." After a brief round of air kissing everyone but me, Delphine left the room.

"I wouldn't mind going to bed, too," Alice whispered, "but it looks like the girls are just getting started. As their host, it would be rude to sneak away."

Another champagne bottle was popped and the bubbles poured, and we were swiftly surrounded by more giggling and gossip.

"Would you object if I snuck off?" I said.

"Don't you dare! If I have to stay and endure this lot, so do you. As my sister-in-law, you're obliged to remain. We'll stick it out for another hour and then make our excuses. Delphine has already used the headache excuse, so we'll have to come up with something else."

"Have I ever told you using the sister-in-law card all the time will wear out? You only get so many chances to pull it out before I object." I checked my watch. It was heading toward midnight, and I wasn't a night owl. I was used to dawn starts so I could get the baking done before the café opened for visitors.

"You'd do it even if we weren't related. That's just who you are." She hugged me.

I would, too. And I wouldn't leave Alice with her intimidating friends, so I grabbed food and settled in beside her, declining the offer of champagne from Paris as Clay finished his tale of bravery again.

Less than an hour had passed, and I was rubbing my eyes and stifling yawns every five minutes.

"I have to admit defeat," I whispered to Alice. "I can barely keep my eyes open."

"Same here." She stood and tapped her champagne flute with her nails to get everyone's attention. "Ladies, and honorary gentleman, we've got a busy day tomorrow. Let's give the champagne a rest and start again in the morning."

"You're no fun," Paris slurred. "And where is everybody else?"

"Do you mean Delphine?" Alice said. "Emma took her upstairs because of her migraine. Don't you remember?"

"Ignore Paris. She's drunk almost a whole bottle of champagne to herself. She can't even see straight, let alone remember where she is or who she should be with," Verity said, sounding more than a little tipsy herself.

"You're just as bad," Paris said. "And I don't mean Delphine. I saw her wandering around the corridor when I went to the bathroom. I meant all the gorgeous, single men. And where is Rupert?"

That was an excellent question, and I'd be having a word with my absent husband. He'd left me and Alice to fend for ourselves. Although, I couldn't blame him.

This evening had felt more like an endurance sport than a fun, pre-Christmas activity.

"It's definitely time for you to get to bed, Paris." Alice helped her drunk friend to her feet. "Rupert left ages ago, and I've already told you the bad weather is keeping everyone else away. It's just us for Christmas."

"Did you tell me that?" Paris gripped Alice's shoulder as she swayed on her heels. "I'm sure you didn't. You must have been speaking to somebody else. I need to find a husband."

"Paris, I'd never mistake you for anyone else. You're far too beautiful. You're unique."

Paris planted a sloppy kiss on Alice's cheek. "You always were my favorite in the group. I suppose I could do with an early night. Then we'll find me the perfect guy."

A quick glance at my watch revealed we were fast approaching one in the morning. If this was early for Paris, I'd hate to see her late.

After many more rounds of air kissing, the party broke up, and we left the ladies' parlor.

I smiled at Emma as she walked past. "How was Delphine when you left her?"

"Almost asleep. She gets terrible migraines. I put it down to stress. I'll check on her before I turn in for the night and make sure she doesn't need anything. If she does, she'll only call me, which I try to avoid after midnight." Emma grimaced.

"Have you worked for Delphine for long?" I walked along beside her with Meatball as we headed to the stairs.

"Six months. We've known each other a lot longer than that, though. We went to school together. We're all friends."

"Oh! And now you work as Delphine's assistant?"

Emma shrugged. "It's a long story. I ran into a few difficulties, and Delphine helped me out. I know she can be catty, but under all the gloss, she's a good person. I don't know what I'd have done if it weren't for her."

I was intrigued to know more, but my eyes were having trouble staying open and I wanted to get back to Rupert and my comfy bed. "I'd like to hear that story sometime."

"Sure. It's not exciting, though. I'd better get to bed. See you in the morning." Emma headed up the stairs.

After Alice's friends were all upstairs, I let out a slow breath and turned in a circle. The large, decorated tree twinkled at me from the corner, and there was a faint smell of pine needles in the air.

Meatball looked up at me and gave a gentle woof.

"I know. It's past our bedtime. Maybe Chef Heston won't mind if we start late tomorrow. With all the snow, we won't be busy again." I wandered back to the ladies' parlor to find Alice staring out the window. "Everything okay?"

She turned and walked over, her expression tight. "You will keep quiet about my plans to propose to Campbell, won't you?"

"Of course. I mentioned it to Rupert. I figured you'd have talked to him about it."

"He's fine. I didn't mean him." She sighed. "I planned to propose on Christmas Day, but seeing how my friends are misbehaving, I might wait until they're gone. I'd hate for Delphine to ruin things."

"Whatever you think is best. There's no rush. Campbell's not going anywhere."

"There is a rush! I want a husband, children, and my own place. I can't live in this drafty old castle forever. And I want Campbell. I want him forever." Alice's big blue eyes glistened with tears. "I want my happily ever after with my grumpy super spy."

"Campbell wants the same. He's just bad at showing it."

A soul freezing scream rocketed along the upstairs corridor.

Meatball barked, and Alice squeaked and gripped my arm so hard I knew there'd be bruises tomorrow.

We raced up the stairs and discovered Paris outside Delphine's bedroom. Her face was drained of blood. "She's... she's..."

I dashed past Paris and into the bedroom.

Delphine was splayed out on the bed. And she wasn't moving.

Chapter 6

I sucked in a breath, my pulse pounding so hard my ears rang. I inched closer to Delphine and caught hold of her wrist. Although she was warm, there was no sign of a pulse.

Alice appeared beside me, her eyes wide. "What happened to her?"

I shook my head as I felt for a pulse on Delphine's neck. "I don't know. I don't see any injuries."

"Is that chocolate cake on her face and hands?" Alice said.

"Maybe. Switch on the overhead light so we can see better." Despite checking several times, there was no pulse. A sinking sensation landed in my stomach as I stepped away.

"Who screamed?" Alice flipped on the light, and I was dazzled for a few seconds.

"That was me." Paris leaned against the door. "I came in to say goodnight to Delphine, and I found her like that."

"Was anyone else here?" My gaze flashed around the room, but there was no one hiding in any corner to jump out at us. Even so, my nerves jangled. Delphine hadn't been dead for long.

"No! Please, tell me she'll be okay." Paris squeezed her eyes shut.

"What's going on?" Verity staggered into view, Emma, Tabitha, and Clay right behind her.

"You shouldn't come in," I said. "Something's happened to Delphine."

"Happened to her? What do you mean?" Verity seemed almost as tipsy as Paris as she peered into the bedroom along with the others.

"It's terrible." Paris sobbed for a few seconds before dragging in a ragged breath. "Delphine's dead! I touched her hand, and she didn't respond. OMG! I touched a corpse!"

"Good one." Tabitha shoved her in the shoulder and snort laughed. "Delphine claims to be immortal. She said she'll live forever. She was looking into cryogenic freezing only a month ago."

"This isn't a joke." Paris sounded more sober than she'd done in hours. "Look at her. Her pills are scattered over the bedside cabinet, and there's an empty bottle of champagne beside her."

I'd been so focused on checking for signs of life, I hadn't looked around the rest of the room, other than to make sure there was no direct threat. Paris was right. There were two open prescription bottles of medication and an empty bottle of champagne. There was also a plate with some chocolate cupcakes on.

"What should we do?" Alice said to me.

"Phone for an ambulance. We're probably too late, but we need help. And the police need to know about this, too."

"Who has a phone?" Alice turned to her group of friends.

"Mine's in my room. I'll get it." Emma dashed away and returned a moment later. "I can't get a signal. It keeps dropping out."

"It's the bad weather," I said. "We've had trouble making calls for days."

"The landline is downstairs. That'll work." Alice dashed away, almost tripping over her long dress in her haste.

"Is Delphine really dead?" Shock laced Verity's tone and her eyes were huge as she stared at her fallen friend.

I turned and nodded. "I'm so sorry."

Emma approached the bed. She gripped her phone as she stared at her boss. "Delphine was fine when I said goodnight to her. Woozy from the champagne, but I watched her take two pain pills and then put the bottle in her cosmetics bag. They weren't out like this when I left."

"Did she bring the cakes and champagne up with her?" I said.

Emma shook her head. "I asked if she wanted anything, but Delphine said she just needed to lie down and sleep it off. She must have left her room after I came back to the party and gotten them. But I didn't see her do it. Did anyone else see Delphine after she went to bed?"

"I did," Verity whispered. "I was up here with Paris. We came upstairs looking for the bathroom. Delphine was wandering along the corridor. She seemed lost. I called out to her, and she raised a hand, but then wandered away from us."

"And I was so desperate to go, I ignored her," Paris said.

"Did she seem in discomfort or pain?" I said. "She didn't ask for help?"

"She didn't speak to us. I didn't notice if she was in pain." Verity shot a guilty look at Paris. "We were laughing about something silly and didn't pay her much attention. Maybe if we had, we'd have realized something was wrong."

Clay, who'd been silent, nudged past me and dropped to his knees by the bed. "We were getting married. This can't happen."

I wanted to tell him to keep his distance, but I didn't have the heart to as tears trickled down his cheeks while he held Delphine's lifeless hand.

"What's going on?" Campbell's voice echoed along the corridor.

I looked at the door. I needed Alice here as backup. She was the only one who could control Campbell, and he'd need controlling when he saw this. His instinct to take control would kick in, and he was in no condition to deal with a body in the castle.

"Emma, would you mind finding Alice for me? The main house phone is in the hallway by the front door. Ask her to get up here as soon as possible. Tell her we have a Campbell situation."

"Of course." Emma dashed out of the room.

A few seconds later, Campbell appeared in the doorway. "Holly! What's happening?"

"We have a problem." I moved away from the bed, so he had an unobstructed view.

He flinched, but then his training kicked in and his gaze blanked as he observed the scene.

"Campbell! You shouldn't be out of bed." Alice appeared behind him in the nick of time. "The doctor ordered two weeks of complete rest."

"I couldn't stay in bed after hearing that scream." His stern gaze softened as he looked at Alice, but then his eyes lifted back to Delphine.

Alice sighed as she assisted him to hobble into the bedroom. "Paris screamed when she found Delphine dead on the bed."

Campbell nodded at me, but his attention was on the body. "What was the cause of death?"

I gestured to the pills and the champagne bottle. "At a guess, death by suicide."

"Delphine would never do that." Tears ran down Tabitha's cheeks. "Her life was idyllic. Everyone wanted to be her, or be around her so they could bask in her glory."

Paris sniffed. "She always took us to the best parties."

I held in my opinion about Delphine's popularity. If she was as mean to people as she was to me, she can't have been well-liked, no matter how many wonderful parties she got them an invitation to.

"Where's my team?" Campbell said. "I need to coordinate with them."

"Most have already gone home for the holidays," Alice said.

He pulled himself upright on his crutches. "I didn't authorize that."

"The Duke did. He called everyone together two days ago and said they could have an extended winter break. On full pay, of course," Alice said.

"He can't do that."

I shot Campbell a warning glance. "The Duke can do what he likes. You work your team hard, so they needed a decent break. And we didn't think anything like this would happen."

His eyes narrowed. "Who's left? Or did he send them all off to have fun and risk the entire family?"

"Saracen's still here," I said.

"That's it?"

"It's Christmas. The season of goodwill." I looked at Delphine and bit my lip. "Not for everyone, though."

"I don't see Saracen. He's probably in the kitchen, eating your gingerbread cookies." Campbell adjusted his grip on the crutches. "We need to keep everyone back, then I'll look at the scene."

"You need to return to bed," Alice said. "You're in pain."

"Give me a minute. I need to make sure..." He moved away from Alice, his gaze scanning from side to side.

I walked behind him with Meatball. "Make sure what?"

"Make sure this isn't more complicated than it looks," he muttered.

I leaned in close. "Murder?"

He kept hobbling.

Alice sighed dramatically and crossed her arms over her chest, but she stopped complaining as Campbell took his time checking the body, being careful not to move anything.

Clay looked up from his position on the floor by the bed. "I don't know what to do. Can I help? I want to do something useful."

"It's best if you stay back for now," Campbell said.

"I don't want to leave Delphine like this."

"We'll look after her."

Alice patted Clay's shoulder. "She wouldn't want you crying over her. Go be with your friends. Look after each other."

"She would want our tears," Verity mumbled. "Imagine the headlines when word gets out about this."

"Word won't get out," Campbell snapped. "No one talks about this to anyone outside the castle. Do you all understand me?"

Verity's eyes narrowed, while Paris seemed too stunned to move. Tabitha kept crying. After encouragement from Alice, Clay got to his feet and joined his friends, who comforted him with hugs.

"Holly, you're with me." Campbell slow-hobbled around the bed, taking in everything. "Those are the victim's pills on her bedside cabinet?"

"Yes. Her personal assistant, Emma, confirmed that."

"Where is Emma?"

"I sent her downstairs to find Alice. She must be trying to get through to the emergency services on the landline. The snow is messing with our phones again."

He nodded. "Do you know what the pills were prescribed for?"

"According to Emma, Delphine got migraines."

Campbell gestured at the bed with his chin. "That bottle of champagne is from the castle cellar."

"Delphine must have gotten it for herself. There were bottles in the kitchen."

He leaned over Delphine. "What's with the cake? Why is it smeared all over her?"

"No idea. Maybe she took too many pills and had an accident." I walked along beside him. "It looks like suicide, doesn't it?"

He nodded slowly.

"You're wrong," Tabitha said from the doorway. "Delphine wouldn't do that. She'd just secured a huge book deal. Everyone would know her name after it came out."

"What was her book going to be about?" I said.

"It was basically the same as her blog. Delphine specialized in exposing socialite scandal. Her blog gets a million hits a week. She planned on putting her most salacious posts into a book and promised an explosive new reveal. There's a buzz in the community about it. She wouldn't end her life when she was on the verge of something so amazing," Verity said.

"I don't like to disagree with you, ladies," Clay said, "but Delphine was worried about something. I asked her several times what was the matter, but she wouldn't reveal anything. It was partly why I visited here. I wanted to get her out of her usual surroundings in the hope she'd confide in me."

"Have you got any idea what she was concerned about?" I said.

"I thought she might be feeling pressure about delivering on this new book," Clay said. "She got an enormous advance, had already spent most of it, and she'd barely written a word of the book."

"Delphine was excited about that book. She said she'd got an amazing story to tell, and people would gossip about it for months," Verity said. "She wasn't stressed about making it a success."

Campbell took a final look around the room. "We need to close this bedroom and make sure no one else gets in until the police arrive."

Everyone dutifully backed out.

"What should we do?" Paris said.

"Everyone go downstairs," I said. "We'll join you in a few moments."

Although there was muted grumbling, everyone trailed off, and I assisted Alice to get Campbell back to his room. Meatball danced around us, wagging his tail and doing his best to trip him up.

"I need to speak to Saracen. Then I'll talk to the police," Campbell said once he was back in bed.

"That's enough work for you," Alice said. "You're putting on a brave face, but you're sweating and grinding your teeth. You must rest."

"There's been a suspicious death in the castle. It must be investigated."

"It will. But you'll be no good to anyone if you set back your recovery. The doctor said if you don't follow his orders and stay in bed, you'll be admitted to the hospital. The break was serious. You almost lost your foot. Please, for me, stay here."

Campbell swiped a hand down his face. "What about your dead friend?"

"I'm more worried about my beloved guy." Alice kissed his cheek.

Campbell let out a sigh, but his lack of resistance showed he was suffering.

He glared at me as Alice tucked the covers around him. "You know what this means?"

Meatball ruffed once and cocked his head.

Alice squeaked and clapped her hands together. "I do. It means we're in charge of solving a murder mystery."

Chapter 7

"Hold on! This might not be a murder," I said. "The pills and champagne suggest death by suicide. I didn't examine Delphine too closely, but there were no obvious injuries on her body, and no blood to suggest she'd been shot or stabbed."

Alice was shaking her head before I'd finished speaking. "I'm siding with Verity on this. Delphine was far too proud and in love with herself to end her own life."

"Both of you take a breath," Campbell said. "I didn't mean you two would be in charge of the investigation. You need to contact the police. As little as I think of Detective Inspector Gerald, he'll have to lead on this."

"Can't we do it?" Alice said. "Holly is great at snooping and learning people's secrets."

Campbell's expression turned caustic. "Don't I know it. But her snooping has always had me around for backup."

I couldn't help but grin at that comment, even though it would get me in trouble. "After all this time, you admit I'm in charge when solving mysteries."

He growled at me.

"Campbell is right," I said, as my grin faded. "We need the experts here. With most of the security team gone and Campbell confined to bed, we have to get the police involved."

Alice huffed out a breath. "I suppose so. But when I checked the landline, it wasn't working. I left Emma trying to get a dial tone."

"It's the snow." Campbell was looking at his mobile. "And there's still no wi-fi signal. The system may need a re-set after the power cut."

I peered into the inky sky as fat blobs of snow stuck to the glass. "Someone will get a signal soon. Then we'll make a call and get the experts here to figure out what happened to Delphine."

"I should send someone to the station," Campbell said. "You don't mind walking Meatball in the cold, do you, Holly?"

"Campbell! You can't send Holly out in weather like this." Alice thumped his arm. "And poor little Meatball will freeze."

"He's teasing. You are teasing, aren't you?" I could never tell with Campbell.

He shrugged. "You always say you're up for a challenge."

"In case you haven't checked, there's several feet of snow on the ground and a storm is threatening," Alice said. "Delphine's fiancé, Clay, almost froze to death getting here. And the station is miles away."

"It was just an idea." Campbell glared at his mobile as he jabbed the buttons. "But if this wasn't a suicide, then someone in this house is a killer."

I took a few seconds to let that unpleasant possibility sink in.

"And we're trapped inside with them," Alice said.

"With no help from the outside world, and no way of getting the police here quickly," Campbell said.

Alice perched on the edge of the bed, a hopeful look in her blue eyes. "Sweetie pie, we're good at this. And we need to know what happened. Even if we only find out Delphine took too many pills, it'll put everyone's mind at rest."

"And if she didn't..." I didn't need to finish the sentence. If Delphine's death hadn't been by her own hand, we were in trouble.

Campbell closed his eyes for a second. "Very well. Holly, I need you to work with Saracen. You've assisted in solving mysteries in the past."

"Holly's solved more murders than... well, more murders than Detective Inspector Gerald," Alice said. "And me. I must be involved, too. Delphine was my friend. I could have useful information."

Campbell looked like he was about to protest.

"Alice's information will be valuable," I said. "I can't do this alone."

"You'll have Saracen."

"I need all the help I can get." I leaned closer. "And Alice will only complain and beg if you don't let her help."

"I heard that!"

He sighed. "If you must. But I don't want Alice put in any danger."

"No danger. I'll be on my best behavior." Alice bounced on the edge of the bed.

"We should make sure no one is missing," I said. "If someone's done a runner, they're most likely the killer."

"Talk to everyone now. And then send Saracen up, so I can bring him up to speed and remind him his patrol duties lie beyond the kitchen," Campbell said.

"Then you must sleep. The doctor said sleep is crucial for a fast recovery." Alice smoothed a blanket over Campbell's legs. "Do you need a fresh glass of water? Or milk? I could bring up Holly's Christmas cookies."

Campbell shot me a pleading look.

Before they bickered over the benefits of sleep versus solving Delphine's mysterious death, I hurried Alice down the stairs with Meatball beside me, and we went into the ladies' parlor where everyone had gathered. The party atmosphere had been whisked away, and everyone was quiet.

Clay stared into the crackling fire, Emma sat in the corner seat she'd occupied most of the evening, while Paris, Tabitha, and Verity sat together on the couch.

"What's going on?" Paris said. "Are the police coming?"

"We haven't been able to contact them." My gaze went to Emma. "Did you get through?"

She shook her head. "The line is still dead. I got a couple of crackles, but nothing else."

"Same with my mobile," Verity said.

A quick scan of the room revealed everyone was accounted for, so if Delphine had been murdered, her killer was staying put. It was no surprise, since it was freezing outside and they'd make themselves an obvious suspect by vanishing into a snowstorm.

"It's late, so I won't keep you for much longer," I said. "I just wanted to know if any of you saw anything unusual. Anyone behaving oddly, or sneaking off to see Delphine after she'd gone to bed."

"We were all here," Verity said. "We spent the evening partying."

"Although we also all left at certain points," Paris said, a note of caution in her voice. "We went upstairs to use the bathroom, Clay went to find food, Tabitha was poking around the portrait gallery, and Emma went off to see if she could get a signal on her phone. And you and Alice ducked in and out. And I haven't seen Rupert all evening."

I pressed my lips together. Therefore, potentially, any of them could have done it. Even though I wanted to question them individually, first thing in the morning would do. By then, the police would be here, and Delphine could be taken away. "You must all be tired. Why don't you go to bed? I'll wake you when the police arrive."

"I won't be able to sleep," Verity said. "Not with a body laid out in a bedroom."

"Should we... put her outside?" Tabitha said.

"No!" Verity pursed her lips. "Should we?"

"Definitely not," I said. "Her bedroom is sealed to preserve evidence." I repressed a shudder at the thought of Delphine lying on that bed all night. I was glad I had my cozy cottage waiting for me and Rupert and Meatball to snuggle up to.

"Stay in my room," Paris said to Verity. "I've got a huge bed we can share, and we used to bunk together in boarding school. It'll be like old times."

"I... I don't have a room," Clay said. "I planned to stay with Delphine."

"I'll find you one," Alice said.

I looked at Emma, and she gave a small nod.

As everyone left the room, I spotted Saracen ambling along the corridor, munching on a gingerbread cookie.

I dashed over to him. "We need to make sure the external doors and windows are locked. No one is allowed out of the castle."

He stuffed down the last of his cookie and brushed crumbs off his fingers. "Why? What's going on?"

"One of Alice's friend's has died and Campbell thinks it's suspicious. Since he's stuck in bed with his broken foot, it's down to you, me, Meatball, and Alice to deal with this until the police arrive."

"A death? The police?" He glanced over his shoulder at the kitchen door. "I've missed a lot. Campbell will kill me."

"There won't be any more killing. I'll get you up to speed, and in the morning, the investigation begins."

❧❧⟫⟩⟩⟩⟩⟩ ⟨⟨⟨⟨⟨❧❧

"These were supposed to be scrambled eggs, but I put too much liquid in them." Alice placed a tray of watery eggs, burned toast, and rubbery bacon in front of Campbell. She looked at me and grinned, so proud of her cooking skills.

He stared at the plate, just managing to hide his mortification. "Breakfast in bed. What a treat. And you made it yourself."

"Of course. I wanted to show you how talented I am." She kissed his cheek. "I thought you could eat, and we'd discuss what to do about the corpse."

"You mean, the dear friend you grew up with, who sadly lost her life last night," I said.

Alice shrugged as she picked at a piece of burned toast on Campbell's plate. "It's easier to think of Delphine as just a body, then I don't remember who she was. Oh, I forgot the hash browns! I'll be right back." She dashed out of the room.

"Holly, please don't make me eat any of this. I'll get food poisoning." Campbell pushed away the plate.

"Are you sure you don't want it? It looks delicious."

"I love Alice, but her food is the worst."

"I suggested she wait for Chef Heston to arrive, but she was determined to look after you." I grabbed the plate of food and offered it to Meatball.

He whined and barked once, then backed away and growled at the offering.

"Even Meatball knows when something shouldn't be called food," Campbell said.

72

I emptied the contents into the waste basket in his attached bathroom and then piled tissues on the top to hide the evidence.

"I hope the hash browns aren't burned, or I'll starve." Campbell's eyes widened. "What if Alice makes me lunch, too? You must sneak me some of your mint frosted cupcakes."

"You won't starve. She's trying to make you happy." I returned the empty plate to his tray. "I made the coffee, so you know that's good."

He took a sip. "I've had worse. Any developments overnight?"

"Nothing new since Saracen talked to you. We went around the castle and made sure there was no way for anyone to get out. We even shut Lady Philippa in without her knowing, just in case someone braved the turrets, looking for an escape. I barely slept, though. I kept listening for people creeping past the cottage as they escaped through the snow."

"Have the Duke and Duchess been informed?"

"Alice told them. They were shocked but took it in their stride. You know how stoic the Duke is." I paused by the window to watch the snow falling in a speckled white wave. "Maybe this was simply a tragedy. Delphine was having problems no one knew about and couldn't cope any longer."

Campbell grunted. "I never met Delphine until yesterday, but Alice told me all about her. She was a troublemaker."

"I figured that out from my fortunately brief encounters with her." I turned away from the window. "Even though she was told several times I was married to Rupert, she kept ordering me around."

"You do have the air of a lowly servant about you."

"I'll tell Alice what you made me do to your breakfast if you keep talking like that." I returned to the side of his bed.

He smirked. "My knowledge of Delphine is why I'm doubting this was a suicide. She must have made enemies along the way to the socialite spotlight. Alice said she wrote some gossip blog exposing her friends' secrets."

"And she'd secured a book deal to publish even more," I said.

"So we have a good motive for someone wanting her dead. Someone whose secret she was about to expose."

"I haven't missed anything, have I?" Alice dashed in with a plate of slightly crispy but edible hash browns. "Oh! You've eaten it all. I'll go get more. You must be burning through extra calories while you heal."

Campbell jerked upright. "No, I'm almost full. Those hash browns look delicious, though."

Alice seemed thrilled with the compliment and handed over the plate. "So, what's the plan to solve this murder?"

"I was just saying to Campbell, I'm still not sure it was murder."

"Let's assume the worst. I posted Saracen in the main hall to be on guard and see if anyone behaved suspiciously," Campbell said.

"All night?" I said.

"He had nothing else to do."

"You should have told me. Saracen must be exhausted. And there's no need for him to stay there now we're up."

"He stays there until I say otherwise. He's got the keys to the main door and the motion detectors are set outside the castle. I've had him monitoring the cameras. When they've worked. The snow has been messing with them, too."

I snagged a hash brown off Campbell's plate and ate it, breaking off a piece for Meatball. Campbell was so hard on his team. I'd get Saracen a coffee and a big plate of eggs and sausage the second I got the chance.

"What about everyone's alibis?" Campbell said. "What did you learn after speaking to them?"

"Everyone was in the ladies' parlor during the evening. But after Delphine had gone to bed, all the suspects left the room for short periods of time. Bathroom breaks, food gathering, that sort of thing," Alice said.

"Including me and Alice. No one has a perfect alibi."

Campbell mulled over the information. "You all had the opportunity to kill Delphine, then. And we have a decent motive for murder."

"What's the motive?" Alice said.

"Delphine's scandal blog. And her new book deal," I said.

Alice wrinkled her nose. "That hateful thing. She's always putting horrible rumors on there. She'd pretend to be someone's friend, get their darkest secret, and put it all over the internet. She did a special on my broken engagement. It was humiliating. I didn't talk to her for a month."

"Maybe keep quiet about that, unless you want to become the police's prime suspect," I said.

"Keep digging into motives and alibis," Campbell said. "There could be other secrets to uncover. Or the blog may not be the only reason people wanted her dead."

"We'll question everyone as soon as possible," I said, "while the information is fresh in their heads. I asked last night if people had seen anything odd, but they were all too shocked or tired to be much use."

"Or tipsy," Alice said. "They got through gallons of champagne."

"I've been thinking about the scene," Campbell said. "And I can't work out why Delphine had chocolate cake smeared on her face and hands. Any ideas?"

Alice stood and walked to the window. "I can't tell you the reason she made such a mess of her last supper, but I know those cakes were mine."

"How do you know that?" Campbell said.

"I made them with Holly. They were covered in edible glitter, and I iced them myself with mint frosting."

I bit my bottom lip. "Is it a coincidence the cakes you made ended up smeared over a possible murder victim?"

Alice whirled around to stare at me. "Yes! What else could it be? Delphine got hungry after she'd gone to her room. Maybe she felt better, so came down to the kitchen. I'd left the cupcakes on the counter under a plastic cover. She must have seen them and taken them upstairs."

"Or they were planted at the scene," Campbell said.

"Why? What's the point of planting my mint frosted cupcakes in Delphine's room?"

"To put you at the scene of a potential crime," I said. "What if whoever did this wants the police to focus on you as the murderer?"

Alice's cheeks drained of color. She shook her head. "That makes no sense. Everybody likes me."

Campbell beckoned her to the bed and gently took hold of her hand. "They do. But sometimes, desperate people do damaging things to others. The police will ask this question when they learn you made those cakes."

"They can ask anything they like about the cupcakes. All I'll tell them is the last time I saw them, they were sitting on the kitchen counter. I'd forgotten about the cupcakes, otherwise I'd have brought them to the party. Delphine must have found them and decided she wanted them all. She was terrible at sharing when we were at boarding school. Some things never change."

There was a knock on the bedroom door, and Saracen appeared.

"You're supposed to be guarding the front door," Campbell snapped.

He stifled a yawn. "Everything is locked tight. No one's getting out, unless they smash a window, and that'll trigger the alarm."

"You still shouldn't have left your post unguarded."

"It's guarded. One of the Duchess's corgis has been keeping me company. The new one. Dottie. She's been sitting with me for hours."

Meatball's ears pricked at the mention of the other corgi. He dashed out of the room, and his little feet thundered down the stairs. Excited yipping followed as the pups were reunited.

"This had better be important for you to leave your post," Campbell said.

"I've been thinking, since we can't get hold of the police and the line is still down, we could use an estate tractor," Saracen said. "Those things get through anything. I can clear a path for the police to come back and investigate."

"That's a great idea," I said. "You should take the evidence with you, though, in case you get stuck in the village and can't get back."

"Going out is a risk. There'll be black ice under the snow." Campbell pointed at his injured foot.

"Those tractors don't slide. And I've driven one before. I'll take it slow."

"You should try," Alice said. "We can't leave Delphine in that room for much longer, or she'll start to smell."

I grimaced, but Alice had a gruesome point. "We could turn off the heating in that room and open the windows. That'll preserve things for longer."

"It'll also interfere with a crime scene," Campbell said. "Saracen, bag the evidence and take pictures of everything. Then go to the police station."

"They'd better not have already closed for the holidays," I muttered. Detective Inspector Gerald wasn't to be relied upon, and he liked long lunch breaks and short working weeks. And this close to Christmas, he could already have jetted off somewhere warm to escape the ice and snow.

"I'll get on it," Saracen said.

"There's a camera and plastic bags in the staff room," Campbell said. "Bag up the pills, champagne, and anything else you see that could be relevant."

Saracen saluted, then dashed out of the room.

Alice slumped onto the bed. "This is so unfair. Christmas has been ruined because my friend had to die. If this was a suicide, I'll be so cross with her."

"You'd better hope it is, otherwise we're all suspects," I said.

Alice chewed on her thumbnail for a second. "I should be a suspect. After all, my cakes were found in her room. I could have taken them to her, we got into an argument, and..."

"What is it?" Campbell said. "I know you didn't do this. I was only teasing earlier."

Alice huffed out a breath. "I didn't like Delphine. She bullied me at school and continued to do so even though we're adults. I've always pretended to like her, but she was a terrible person. She was snide and mean to everyone. And she was horrible to Holly. She kept treating her like a servant."

Campbell's gaze slid from Alice to me. "I suppose it's possible the two of you were in on it together."

"In on it together how?" I arched an eyebrow.

"It would have been easy to hide poison in one of your cakes." Campbell seemed to warm to the idea we were killers. "Alice confided in you about how much she hated Delphine, and, as her supportive sister-in-law, you got rid of her problem."

Alice swatted his arm. "You'd better be joking. Besides, if I was going to kill someone, I'd want to look them in the eyes and tell them why I was doing it. I wouldn't be sneaky and poison them. Where's the fun in that?"

"There's fun in murder?" I said.

"You know what I mean. If you have a mortal enemy, you want them to know you've defeated them as you plunge in the knife. Sneaking poison into a cake isn't the way to do it. Well, it's not the way I'd do it."

"You have a point, even though it's a deeply twisted one." I returned my glare to Campbell. "Where did I get the poison from?"

"You're always reading boring history books. Perhaps you found something devious in one of them to add to your baking. Some old toxic plant no one knows about. And you're friendly with the estate gardeners. Maybe one of them gave you rodent poison, or anti-freeze."

"I'm beginning to like Alice's idea. Looking your victim in the eyes and telling him how annoying he is before finishing him off has great appeal." I jabbed a finger at Campbell. "And you're an easy target, since you can't run away."

Campbell half-smiled. "I'm just covering all the bases. The police will do the same."

"If I didn't love you so much, I'd think you were a terrible person," Alice said.

While Alice grumbled at Campbell, and he looked vaguely embarrassed, my thoughts turned to everyone else in the castle. If this was murder, it must have been one of Delphine's friends. But which one?

"After Saracen has left, let's speak to the fiancé. Clay was quick to support the idea of death by suicide. Maybe he was deflecting, so no one looked at him as a possible killer," I said.

Alice tore herself away from Campbell's side. "Agreed. How exciting! Let's interrogate our first suspect."

Chapter 8

"Have you got everything?" Campbell yelled from the bedroom window.

"Get back into bed," Alice said. "If you catch a chill, you'll get even grumpier."

Meatball barked up at Campbell, then jumped into a huge snowdrift and vanished from sight.

Saracen, who sat in a small red tractor, raised his hand. He was huddled in a thick black jacket with a wooly hat pulled low on his head.

"We know what we're doing. So does Saracen." Alice turned to me and dramatically rolled her eyes. "He's such a worrier."

"He's a control freak." I tugged my scarf over my mouth. It was so cold, it felt like my teeth might freeze and shatter every time I took a breath. I pulled Meatball out of the snowdrift and hugged him.

He licked the underside of my chin and snuggled against me, seeming grateful for the warmth and the rescue.

"Campbell just likes everything to be done in the most efficient way." Alice looked up at Saracen. "You're so brave. Are you sure you want to do this?"

"Thanks, Princess Alice. I'm used to driving tanks through the desert in Afghanistan, so I can handle some snow." He patted the tractor's steering wheel. "I'm looking forward to it. And no offense to Campbell, but I'll enjoy a break from him snarling at me every time I get caught in the kitchen."

"I'm tempted to order you out so I can go in your place," Alice said. "I love the man, but he's the world's worst patient."

"You shouldn't hang around." I handed Saracen a large thermos of tomato and basil soup. "Those clouds heading toward us are full of snow."

He eyed the yellow clouds as they loomed closer. "I'll take my time and stick to the main roads when possible. I doubt many people will be out when the forecast is so bad. They'll be inside in the warm, enjoying festive food."

"There's bound to be a few. Make sure you don't kill them, or yourself," Alice said.

"I'll do my best not to. I've got the evidence safely in here. I'll let you know when I get to the police station."

"Provided the phone lines are working. The landline is still dead," I said.

"I got a signal for a couple of seconds this morning," Saracen said. "Something will work."

"Ask the police to hurry," Alice said. "I don't want to go back in the castle knowing there's a body in a bedroom, even if it is the body of a friend."

"Why isn't he moving?" Campbell yelled. "Can't you see the snow coming?"

"You'd better get out of here," I said, "or Campbell will come down and drive this tractor himself."

"I wouldn't put it past him." Saracen pulled the door closed and started the tractor. He let the engine rumble as it warmed up, then waved and headed slowly away from the castle, along what was most likely the gravel driveway, but the snow was so thick it was hard to tell where the proper road was.

"One of us should have gone with him," Alice said.

"Saracen is a big, tough guy. And we need to stay here and question suspects."

Alice bit her bottom lip. "By the time the police get here, we'll have solved this case."

"That would be the perfect Christmas gift." I leaned against her. "My toes are numb. Let's get inside, grab coffee, and then find Clay."

"You still think he did this?"

I turned back to face the castle. "There's only one way to find out."

Twenty minutes later, and after shedding our winter gear, defrosting our toes, and enjoying freshly made coffee from the kitchen, we headed to Clay's bedroom.

I left Meatball snoozing over a warm air vent in the hallway, so he could thaw out after his snowdrift adventure.

Alice tapped on the bedroom door. "Clay, are you up?"

There was no answer.

She tapped again, then slowly opened the door.

I poked my head in and looked around. The bed had been slept in but was currently empty. "Perhaps he's gone down to look for breakfast. We could have just missed him."

"That's a good idea. Breakfast! We could interrogate and eat at the same time."

"Less of the interrogation tactics. We're keeping this casual and asking questions because Delphine was your friend, and you're worried."

"Yes. That, too. But I mainly want to make sure there isn't a killer lurking in my castle."

We left the bedroom, headed along the corridor, and down the stairs.

"Everyone here must be thinking the same thing," I said.

Alice rubbed her arms. "That this place is colder than an igloo?"

"No! That someone staying here killed Delphine. Paris and Verity were quick to say it wasn't a suicide, so we aren't the only ones thinking it."

"Clay was keen on the idea. Does that make him guilty?"

"To figure that out, we need to find him. But the fact he's telling a different story to the others makes him stand out," I said.

We reached the bottom of the stairs and headed to the kitchen again.

"I don't know Clay well. Delphine talked about him a lot, and of course, there are pictures of them as the perfect couple all over social media. This is the first time we've actually met," Alice said.

"What's his background?"

"New money. His parents made a fortune in the mobile app field. Clay works for them. Delphine was often talking about the latest app they launched and how much money it made him."

"Did she ever talk about any trouble between them?"

"According to Delphine, their life was perfect. Looking at her online pictures, you could well believe it."

"Nobody's life is perfect. Not even a princess living in a beautiful castle and dating a scary James Bond look alike."

She thumped my arm, a smile on her face. "Mine is pretty perfect. All I need to do to make it idyllic is to get Campbell to marry me."

"Maybe ask him when he's less grumpy. He looked like he was about to burst a blood vessel when he was yelling at Saracen."

"I'm still thinking about how to do it," Alice said. "That's the one thing that'll make my life exactly how I want it. I've got everything else."

84

"If you need a hand making plans for your big romantic gesture, let me know. I could make a special dinner, or a cake—"

"Ooh! What a great idea. I could surprise Campbell by bursting out of a cake and proposing."

"Um... maybe something more understated would work better."

"Why? He loves cake. I love cake. And you make amazing cake."

"Alice! I'm not making a giant cake for you to destroy by bursting out of it like that brain eating creature from the alien movie. And perhaps we should solve the mystery of what happened to Delphine before tackling your almost perfect love life?"

Alice sighed. "It's just like her. Delphine loved taking the limelight in any situation."

"It's not as if she died to scupper your plans for a romantic proposal."

"I wouldn't put it past her to do just that."

I pushed open the kitchen door. Chef Heston had his back to us and was muttering as he studied some paperwork.

"Morning, Chef," I said.

He turned. "I could have done with you here half an hour ago."

"It's my day off. Is there a problem?"

"I'm closing the café. We've had barely any visitors in this week, and with the guests arriving last night, I'm having to tend to their needs." He glanced at Alice. "Not that I mind doing that."

"Of course you don't. You're wonderful." Alice skipped over and kissed his cheek. "And I know how high maintenance my friends can be. Tell them they'll get the basics and have to put up with it."

Chef Heston puffed out his chest. "I never serve basic food. I'm happy to cater for them, but I'm down on

85

staff, and I can't run the café on my own while looking after the family and your guests. I hope you understand, Princess Alice."

"If you need me to work, I can lend a hand," I said.

Chef Heston waved away my comment. "There's no need. I'll do it all myself, as usual."

I was about to protest when the kitchen door opened. Clay walked in with a mug in his hand. His hair was tousled, his shirt misbuttoned, and his eyes were red.

I nudged Alice. "I'll grab coffee. You take Clay and find somewhere quiet for us to talk."

Alice hurried over to him, and after they spoke quietly for a moment, they left the kitchen, and she lobbed me a thumbs-up behind her back.

I dashed around and made more coffee.

"What are you up to?" Chef Heston loomed over me.

I gave him my most innocent expression. "Nothing bad. But I have a few questions about what happened last night. You've heard about Delphine?"

"The Duchess was kind enough to inform me when I arrived this morning." His gaze lifted to the ceiling. "Gruesome business."

"It is. And we've been unable to contact the police or get an ambulance here to take Delphine. Saracen's left in a tractor to let them know what's going on, so they'll get here soon, but..." I gestured at the kitchen door.

"You're poking around, as usual."

"I need to make sure it was an accident. Well, death by suicide isn't an accident, but you know what I mean."

Chef Heston hesitated. "You're thinking foul play?"

"Exactly. Well, it's a possibility. And Delphine was an interesting character."

"I know." He helped himself to a mug of coffee. "I follow her blog."

"You do?"

Chef Heston smirked. "Delphine was one of the most well-connected socialites around. She knew everyone who was anyone, and most of them move in the same circles as Princess Alice and Lord Rupert. It pays to stay informed. If any of them dropped by, I'd know what they liked to eat."

"You don't read it for the scandalous gossip and fashion tips?"

He pointed at the door. "Don't come back unless you want to bake. And even then, I may not let you in."

"You have to. I'm a lady of the castle these days."

"Out!"

I grinned as I collected the coffee things on a tray and hurried out.

Meatball looked up from his curled position on the floor in the hallway and yawned.

"You joining us?"

He lowered his head and closed his eyes.

Hmmm, that wasn't like him. He usually loved to poke and sniff around the castle. I gave him a quick pet, being careful not to spill the coffee, then followed the quiet talking, discovering Clay and Alice in the library.

"Here's Holly with our coffee," Alice said. "That'll make you feel better."

Clay glanced up at me. "Thanks. I barely slept. I kept thinking about Delphine in that room, all alone." He pinched the bridge of his nose.

"I'm sorry for your loss." I settled in a high-backed leather seat opposite him and handed around the coffee.

"We had our whole future ahead of us. There was so much to look forward to. And now... it's gone."

"It's so sad." Alice stirred her coffee.

"Delphine was sweet. Everyone saw her sharper side in her blog, and she over-stepped occasionally when reporting people's secrets, but she was good to me. She could be kind."

"How long had you known each other?" I said.

"Our parents introduced us as babies," Clay said. "They used to say we were destined to be together. We even shared the same birthday. That's how our families met. We were born in the same hospital. Although, when we were children, we hated each other. I used to pull her hair, and she'd scream at me. But even through all that, we had a connection. We dated a few times when we were teenagers, but then lost touch."

"I remember Delphine saying she met you again at a Silver and Gold party," Alice said.

"That's right. We reconnected on a yacht as it glided around Italy and have been happily together ever since. I can't see a future without Delphine in it." He raked a hand through his hair. "I had been worried about her, though. There was something troubling her. She'd been going to a weekly therapy spa to lift her mood and seeing a therapist."

"Did she talk about what was troubling her?" Alice said.

"No. Delphine had this wall around her. I got the impression she feared showing the world that everything wasn't perfect. I suggested her fans would like to see her vulnerable side, but she wasn't prepared to take the risk." Clay stared into his coffee mug. "She must have been more troubled than I realized to do this."

"She seemed her usual self," Alice said. "I wasn't worried about her."

"Delphine had been getting headaches," Clay said. "Sometimes, the only thing that would get rid of them was pills and a dark room. That was getting her down. And despite what her friends say, she was worried about that book. She had a big expose planned, but it was about someone close to her, and she was worried it could ruin them."

"A family member?" Alice said.

88

"I don't think so. She never told me about the secrets she uncovered. Delphine was amazing at keeping secrets. But look where it got her. She died alone." His voice cracked on those last words.

Alice exchanged a look with me, and I nodded at her.

"I'm not so sure it was suicide," Alice said gently. "Neither are Paris or Verity."

"Don't believe anything they tell you. And those ladies were a big part of the troubles in Delphine's life," Clay said. "Of course, I exclude you in that, Alice. But they were a bad influence."

"What makes you say that?" I said.

"They didn't want her to change. They still wanted the parties, to date the eligible bachelor of the month, and have pictures taken quaffing champagne in the latest designer outfits they'd been sent."

"Isn't that what Delphine wanted, too?" Alice said.

"Maybe, for now. But we can't live the party lifestyle forever, no matter how much fun it is. And it wouldn't have been long before we married and started a family. Everything would have changed." Clay drained his coffee mug. "I don't know what to think. The sooner the police get here, the better. They'll know what happened."

"Try not to worry," Alice said. "And I'm sure you're right. They'll figure it out."

"You always were a good friend to Delphine, even when she didn't deserve it." Clay set down his mug. "I should leave you ladies to it. I've been trying to get a phone signal so I can arrange a ride out of here, but the reception drops out after a few seconds."

"You can stay for as long as you like." Alice shot me a worried look. "You should."

"The police will want to talk to you," I said.

"Me? Why?"

"You knew Delphine. They'll want to tidy up any loose ends."

"Oh! I suppose so. There seems no point in me staying, though. Now Delphine's gone... If you'll excuse me, I need some time on my own." Clay stood, nodded to us, then left the room.

Alice waited until the door closed before speaking. "Is Clay making a plan to escape?"

"Maybe. I can understand him not wanting to be here, but it does seem suspicious. He must realize he can't leave."

Alice pulled out her mobile and gasped. "I've got a signal. Quick! I want to find out everything about Clay Osbourne." She typed in his name, and after a slow minute of the search loading, dozens of articles flashed up.

I took out my mobile and tried calling the police. The line wouldn't connect.

"They're so gorgeous," Alice said. "These pictures of them suntanned with their perfect smiles must be fake. I'm sure those are veneers. Delphine's teeth were never that good in school."

"They made an attractive couple."

"Look at this! It's from another gossip site." Alice leaned over so I could see her phone. "Trouble in paradise. Bachelor of the month, Clay Osbourne, and Delphine Augustus were seen arguing outside Chantilly Dreams in the early hours of yesterday morning. Before that fiery encounter, insiders reported seeing Delphine throw her drink in Clay's face and run off. The drink was pink champagne. The dress was by Dior. The diamonds by Cartier."

"That doesn't sound so idyllic. When did that happen?" I said.

Alice scrolled up the page. "The post is dated a month ago."

"So Clay wasn't being truthful about their relationship."

"Which means he's still a suspect."

"He has to be. And just like everyone else, he left the party during the evening."

"And if their relationship was troubled, it gives him a motive," Alice said.

"Maybe they were having problems, and he felt trapped. Delphine had a domineering personality. Clay may have felt he couldn't back out of their relationship for fear of becoming the next hot topic on her blog."

Alice sat forward in her seat. "Clay stays on the suspect list. Who should we target next?"

"Verity?"

"Sure. She's as good as any. But before we do that, I'm famished. Let's have some of your delicious cranberry cupcakes. We need fuel to tackle this mystery."

"You're willing to risk Chef Heston's wrath to get cake for breakfast?"

"No, silly. You are!"

Chapter 9

I'd just returned the plates and coffee mugs to the kitchen after a large breakfast of festive muffins, and Alice had gone up with more coffee for Campbell, when I spotted Emma trudging through the snow, holding up her phone.

I grabbed my jacket and snow boots and opened the back door. Meatball yipped and raced into the snow before I could put on his leash. I wasn't worried about him escaping, since the snow would soon slow him down.

"Emma, is everything okay?" I raised my hand as I plowed through the snow to join her.

"Not really. I'm desperate to get a signal. Delphine's family don't know what's going on. And her fans will wonder what happened. She never goes more than a few hours without posting an update on her life. There'll be thousands of comments and theories online."

"I didn't think about that." I checked the sky. Fresh snow was about ten minutes away. "You should get inside, though."

"I've walked most of the castle looking for a signal. I figured the thick walls could be messing with the reception, so I came out here. I got a bar a few seconds ago, but then nothing."

"This'll be a small comfort, but no one's been able to get much of a signal. It's the atmospherics. Maybe Delphine's fans will theorize about that. Did they know she was coming here for Christmas?"

"She kept dropping hints about her fabulous castle getaway." Emma tugged on her bottom lip with gloved fingers. "I'm in charge of Delphine's social media posts, though. It's scary how quickly these things get out of control. And I must let her parents know. They'll know something is wrong. Delphine didn't get home much, so her family followed her blog to keep up to date with her life."

That seemed tragic. Why wouldn't their daughter visit or call them more often?

Emma must have seen something in my expression. "Delphine did her best, but she was busy. Her parents understood. They wanted the best for her and were proud of how hard she worked."

"I'm sure they were. And they'll know soon. Saracen, a member of the castle's security team, went to the police station this morning. Once they know what's going on, they'll contact Delphine's family."

Emma lowered her phone. "That's a relief. But I still have so much to plan." She glanced at me. "You might think this is strange, but Delphine had a strategy for what would happen in the event of her death."

"A funeral plan?" I walked beside her, Meatball hopping through the snow to stop from sinking.

"It was more than that. It's something most people in the public eye have in place. They put together a plan to make sure their final celebration or party is one people will remember. Delphine's agent suggested it soon after her blog got popular. Well, she did before they parted company, and Delphine decided she didn't need anyone taking fifteen percent of her earnings."

"She had a falling out with her agent?" Did I need to add another name to my list of suspects?

"It was the fourth agent she'd fired. None of them lasted over six months. Delphine had a particular way of doing things."

I could imagine it involved talking over people, sneering, and being unpleasant if she didn't get her own way.

When I didn't comment, Emma tilted her head from side to side. "In the event of her death, there are plans in place, and I must make sure they're carried out. There are posts to schedule, an online memorial wall, the donations page to go live, and then the funeral. Delphine knew what she wanted. It'll be the biggest and best party anyone has ever been to." She checked her phone and sighed. "You forget how reliant you are on these things until they stop working."

I touched her arm. "Delphine would understand if you couldn't make it happen right away. We're stuck in extreme circumstances." I crouched and pulled Meatball out of a deep mound of snow.

Her gaze was rueful as she watched Meatball shake, sending snow flying in all directions. "No offence, but if you think that, you didn't know Delphine. I'm almost afraid she'll come back and haunt me because I'm not carrying out her last wishes fast enough. She'd hate to be forgotten."

"What kind of boss was she?"

Emma was silent for a few seconds. "Delphine had high standards. She expected everyone to be the same. Everything had to be perfect and done Delphine's way or it was wrong. That offended some people."

"That doesn't sound like the easiest job. Did you enjoy your work?"

"It had its moments, but the good times outweighed the bad. Not everyone understood Delphine, but I had no issue with her, as a friend or a boss. When she wanted results, she got them."

"Wait for me!"

I turned and discovered Alice wading through the snow. She wore a pale pink wool coat and a matching hat with a white fluffy bobble on the top.

Meatball barked his joy and made a valiant attempt to reach her.

"You should have told me you were going for a walk." Alice scooped Meatball up and kissed his nose.

"I saw Emma and thought I'd join her." I discreetly winked at Alice.

"Oh! Of course. I was with Campbell when I saw you. I didn't want to miss the fun." Alice tripped and landed in the snow.

Meatball gave an annoyed sounding bark as he hit the ground, then waddled away to investigate an interesting smell.

I helped Alice up and leaned in close. "Gentle questioning only."

She brushed snow off her coat, her expression tart as she leaned around me. "How are you holding up, Emma?"

"I'm okay. Thanks for asking. Obviously sad about Delphine, but I've got a long list of jobs to get through. Maybe being higher up would help me get a signal. I tried to go up one turret, but the door was locked."

"Don't go up there. My granny lives in one of the turrets, and she's a little... odd," Alice said. "And the southern turret is haunted. Go in there, and your hair will turn white."

Emma's expression grew alarmed. "I'll stay away. But I still need a phone signal."

"We got a signal in the library. You could try there."

"I've been in there. No luck." Emma turned and shielded her eyes.

"How are things with your parents?" Alice said. "I was sorry when I heard about their business going under."

Emma shrugged. "Thanks. They're getting by. They had to sell everything, though, and start again. They keep a tiny place in the Welsh countryside. I see little of them, since it's so far away."

"What happened?" I said. "If you don't mind me asking."

"I'm surprised you didn't read about it," Emma said. "They got caught in a Ponzi scheme. Invested most of their money and lost it when the scammer cleared the accounts and vanished."

"It happened a year ago," Alice said. "Several notable names got burned. It was quite the scandal."

"My family lost everything. I had to give up my trust fund, and there are still creditors on my parents' backs. I think that's why my dad's been unwell. Stress is so damaging."

"I'm sorry to hear that," I said. "Is that why you took a job with Delphine?"

"She was the only one who returned my calls when I needed help." Although Emma's tone was neutral, bitterness traced across her face.

"You should have called me. I'm always available for a chat," Alice said.

"I didn't want to impose on an old friend. And we lost touch after I went traveling. I thought you'd think it weird if I called and begged for work."

Alice's bottom lip jutted out. "We didn't deliberately lose touch. And you sent me postcards. I loved receiving them. You've been everywhere. Egypt, the Antarctic, France, Sweden. I lost track of you after a while."

"I had a great time. I've always loved exploring. You get to meet amazing people. But some of those places don't have great postal networks. I wanted to stay in touch, but you know, life happens."

"It wouldn't have been an imposition if you'd made contact," Alice said. "We've known each other since we were children."

Emma's gaze dropped to the snow. "I was humiliated. I'd called around a few friends to see if any of them would help. My parents always paid my mortgage, but when they lost everything, the money dried up. The bank foreclosed on my apartment and I was about to become homeless. I reached out to the people I was closest to, and I got silence or embarrassed excuses. After a dozen of those calls, what little pride I had left stopped me from calling anyone else."

"Oh, Emma, I never realized things were that bad. I'd have helped. You could have stayed in the castle. We have more rooms than we know what to do with."

"And I appreciate that offer, but at the last minute, Delphine stepped in and saved the day. I'd called her and left a message, and she got in touch. She said how sorry she was to hear of my situation and offered me the job as her assistant. I was so grateful, I cried."

"You seem perfect in the role," Alice said. "Delphine goes through her assistants faster than I do Holly's mint frosted cupcakes."

Emma smiled. "I had a few people warn me Delphine was difficult to work for, but I never found that. It helped that I knew what to expect. Sure, she was demanding, and the long hours could get tiring, but provided I did what she wanted when she wanted, we didn't have a problem."

"You must have become close," I said.

"We were together every day. I'd sometimes stay at her apartment when we worked late. We'd often be at clubs or parties, hunting for new information to put on her blog until the small hours."

I gestured toward the castle, aware my toes were numb and Meatball wasn't properly dressed for being

97

outside. "Did you see any signs to suggest Delphine was unhappy?"

"No. I mean, she got frustrated, but only when people let her down or didn't do what they said they would." Emma stared out across the snow as she walked slowly beside me with Alice. "I can't believe she ended her own life, though."

"What about the medication she was on?" I said. "Could that have made her depressed?"

"Not depressed. Never! Delphine was highly strung, though, and she'd been getting migraines for six months. The doctor told her to clean up her diet and stop drinking. She was fine with changing her diet, but insisted on having champagne most days. I'm certain that was what triggered the migraines. The pills helped."

"Was she on any other medication?" Alice said.

"Mild sedatives. She had trouble sleeping. The doctor said the alcohol was the problem there, too. But once she got the medication for her migraines and her insomnia was under control, she was fine. Delphine wasn't unhappy. Why would she be? Her life was one long party."

"It may have appeared like that on the outside, but life in the public eye is tricky," Alice said.

Emma pursed her lips. "You're right. I didn't mind having my picture taken when attending a fancy party, but when everything went wrong for my parents and the press lurked outside the house to get unflattering photos, I realized life in the public eye was only good when you're not surrounded by scandal."

"You don't think that's what happened with Delphine, do you?" I said. "Perhaps the media got hold of a story about her and planned on publishing it."

"I can't imagine what it would be. Delphine loved to party, but she did nothing scandalous. She was too media savvy for that."

"What about her relationship with Clay?" I said. "How were things between them?"

"Usually good. And when they were in public, you'd never know they fought."

"What did they fight about?" Alice said.

"This and that. All couples bicker, but Clay and Delphine had been arguing more recently. Clay wanted to buy a place in the country, but Delphine wasn't ready to give up the party lifestyle."

"Did they resolve the argument?" I said.

"Not as far as I know. Delphine said if she lived in the country, all she'd be able to report on was muddy stilettos and hay bales. Her career would be over, and I'd be out of a job."

"Were you surprised when Clay showed up last night?"

Emma wrinkled her nose. "Not really. He's always one for big, romantic gestures. Delphine loved that sort of thing. He once hired an ice rink for the day. They had the place to themselves, even though Delphine doesn't skate. I was there to take pictures." She looked over at me. "You don't think Clay had anything to do with this, do you?"

"Well, a few hours after him showing up, Delphine died," Alice said. "I don't think it was suicide. Neither do you, so..."

Emma sucked in a breath. "I've been so caught up in Delphine's last wishes, I didn't think about that. Of course, she didn't do this to herself. I'd stand up in court and swear to that. So... someone here did it to her." She stopped walking and looked at the castle. "Someone in there."

"That's what we're thinking," I said, uncertain we should share so much with a possible suspect.

"Where are the police? Why aren't they asking questions and arresting someone? And Delphine is up there in that room..." Emma looked away and wiped her eyes.

"They'll be here soon." Alice looked at me and grimaced.

Emma's hand went to her chest. "How did they do it? Did they force Delphine to take too many pills? I saw them on her cabinet. I know they weren't there when I said goodnight to her."

Neither of us had an answer to that question.

"When you went up with Delphine last night, did you see anyone else around?" I said.

"No! But I wasn't looking for anyone. I got Delphine her cosmetics bag and laid out her nightwear. Then got a glass of room temperature water, so she could take her pills. I didn't see anyone when I left."

"What about the cakes and the champagne?"

"I don't know how they got in there. When I left her, there was no cake or alcohol. The doctor doesn't like her to drink when she takes those pills. Not that she listens to his advice."

"Perhaps the killer brought her my cakes," Alice said.

I raised my eyebrows and shook my head at her.

"Your cakes?" Emma said.

"Oh! Yes! I made them," Alice said. "If not the killer, perhaps Delphine snuck down and took them from the kitchen."

Emma considered that option. "It's possible. I didn't see her do that, though. But I always tuck myself away at parties. Delphine liked me to be on hand in case the gossip got juicy, so I'm always discreet."

It was possible Emma was the last person to see Delphine alive, but I couldn't figure out her motive for wanting her dead. Delphine had helped Emma when she was in an awful situation. Why kill someone who'd been so supportive?

"Why would the killer give Delphine your cake?" Emma's phone buzzed, and her hand shot up and she stared at the screen. "I've got a signal! Oh! I have so many messages. I'm sorry, but I need to get on."

"Mine is working, too. It's buzzing in my pocket," Alice said.

"If you'll excuse me." Emma hunched over her phone and started typing as she walked back to the castle entrance.

I caught hold of Alice's elbow as we trailed behind Emma. "What do you think of Emma as a suspect?"

"I'm not sure. I like her. She was one of the more decent girls at school. And it's true what she said. Delphine helped her out of a hole."

I had my phone out, trying the number for the local police station. It connected, but there was no reply. "If Delphine was the only person to help Emma, it seems unlikely she'd want her dead."

Alice was also looking at her phone. "That makes sense. Now Delphine is dead, Emma is unemployed."

"Although she had an opportunity, there's no motive."

Alice glanced up from her phone. "Scrub her off the suspect list?"

"Emma stays on for now, but I don't think she's the prime suspect. Unless we learn anything new about her, there's no reason for her to have killed Delphine."

Alice looked back at her phone. "What do we do next?"

"Hope the police get here soon. And while we're waiting, we question another suspect."

Chapter 10

Once we'd gotten back inside the castle, Alice had been called away to visit Lady Philippa on the important matter of Christmas present wrapping. I'd run around the corridors with Meatball a few times to give him exercise, and then spent the morning with Rupert going over the Christmas gifts we'd gotten everyone.

I'd just had lunch with Rupert and Alice, and we were walking along the hallway toward the kitchen to see if Chef Heston needed a hand with anything, when the landline rang. It scared us, since the shrill ring sounded so strange after the line had been dead for such a long time.

It even made Meatball bark.

Rupert dashed over and picked it up. "Audley Castle. Lord Rupert Audley speaking." He listened for a few seconds and gestured us closer. "It's the police. Saracen crashed the tractor on the way to the station."

"Is he hurt?" I said.

"Let me put this on loudspeaker, so everyone can hear. Detective, my sister Alice is here, along with my wife, Holly. If you have no objections, I'd like them to listen to this conversation."

"Of course." Detective Inspector Gerald's voice boomed from the loudspeaker. "As I was saying, the tractor crashed a mile from the station. Your man injured his arm when it pitched into a ditch. He was lucky that was his only injury. Although at first sight, I thought he was covered in blood. It turns out someone gave him a thermos of soup that exploded during the crash."

"What about the evidence he had with him?" I said. "Did that get damaged?"

"Who's that?"

"Holly. Saracen had evidence from the room where Delphine was found. We thought it might be important to the investigation."

"It's intact. He brought it with him."

"And Saracen? Did he need to go to the hospital?" I said.

"His injury wasn't severe, and nothing is broken. The doctor was kind enough to walk to the station and examine him."

"What about Delphine?" Alice said. "This is Princess Alice Audley, by the way. She's still here. We haven't moved her. Although I don't like the thought of her being on her own. It doesn't seem right. Are you sending someone to collect her?"

"Ambulances are only coming out in extreme emergencies," Detective Inspector Gerald said.

"This is an extreme emergency. There's a body in our castle!"

"I appreciate that, but we can't risk trained personnel in these conditions. We'll get someone out soon. There should be a plow coming through the village today. The second we can get through on the roads, we'll be with you. In the meantime, don't touch anything else in that room."

"Nothing will be disturbed," I said. "We have concerns about the cause of death, though. It was why Saracen brought the medication and cakes with him."

"He's explained everything, and we're rushing through tests on both items. Saracen was most insistent. What makes you suspicious this was more than a suicide?"

I exchanged glances with Rupert and Alice. I'd never been on good terms with Detective Inspector Gerald, so needed to handle this conversation delicately. We'd first encountered each other when I'd owned a café in Audley St. Mary, and I hadn't formed a high opinion of him when he'd been more interested in examining my cakes than the suspects in another murder.

"We've been talking to people here," I said cautiously, "and nearly everyone thinks it unlikely Delphine would end her own life. She had a flourishing career and support from friends and family."

"Don't poke around and ask too many questions," Detective Inspector Gerald said. "You don't want to alarm anyone when there's no proof of misadventure."

Rupert cleared his throat. "While we appreciate the advice, as you know, Audley Castle has a special relationship with the village police. Our security team is trained to investigate all issues, including murder. If they believe there's more to this death than meets the eye, I'm inclined to trust them."

Rupert wasn't always masterful, but when he had to be, he stepped up to the mark, and I appreciated it. I also appreciated his belief in me. It was one of the many reasons I loved him.

"Of course. And I understand that. Saracen was kind enough to point that fact out to me, too." Detective Inspector Gerald's tone turned sharp.

"And since these circumstances are as extreme as extreme can get, it would be unwise to not ask questions. After all, if this wasn't a suicide, there's a killer in my family's castle. That's unacceptable," Rupert said.

There was silence on the line for several seconds.

"Hello? Are you still there? The line hasn't died again, has it?" Alice said.

"I'm still here. The tests on the champagne bottle, pills, and food will be done by the end of today. There's no other work for my people to do, since the snowstorm is keeping everyone trapped inside. Providing the lines hold up, you'll know the results as soon as I do. Then we'll know what action to take."

"We appreciate your speed in this matter," Rupert said.

"Make sure you take the best care of Saracen," Alice said. "He was so brave to make the perilous journey to your station."

"He's being looked after," Detective Inspector Gerald said. "I have a question you could help with, though. From what I've learned, the medication found by the body belonged to Delphine."

"That's right," I said. "I spoke with her personal assistant, Emma, and she said Delphine got migraines."

"Her doctor confirmed that with me. And although it's too soon to say, I have concerns about the cakes. Where did they come from?"

"From me. I made them," Alice said. "They were supposed to be for everybody, but Delphine could be greedy when she saw something she wanted."

"What are your concerns about the cupcakes?" A knot of worry wound around my stomach. Detective Inspector Gerald was known for jumping to the wrong conclusions, and I had a feeling he was heading for a gigantically bad leap toward Alice.

"Delphine wouldn't have made a mistake with her medication. Her doctor confirmed she'd been on the pills for months and was stable."

"That's good to know," I said. "What does that have to do with Alice's cakes?"

"It led me to believe there was something in the cupcakes that made Delphine unwell. Possibly another drug. Or a poison."

"Poison!" Alice said. "You think someone poisoned my cakes?"

I gave her arm a reassuring squeeze. "Impossible. I helped Alice make them, so I know exactly what was in them."

"You're involved, too?" Detective Inspector Gerald said sharply.

"Involved in making delicious cupcakes for a Christmas party, but that's all," I said. "Why not focus on the champagne?"

"We're looking at both items. But I've seen the pictures taken of the scene. Cake was smeared over Delphine's hands and face, and there was a large amount inside her mouth as well. It looks as if someone put it there deliberately after she died."

I tilted my head. That was odd. Why would someone feed a dead person cake?

"It wasn't me, if that's what you're suggesting," Alice said. "I wouldn't waste perfectly good cupcakes on Delphine, especially not after she'd shuffled off this mortal coil."

I caught hold of Alice's elbow and shook my head.

"You weren't fond of her?" Detective Inspector Gerald said. "Was there trouble between you two?"

"No! I mean, no more than usual. We... we were fine." Alice bit her lip and hitched her shoulders.

"Alice and Delphine were childhood friends," I said. "She wouldn't have invited her to the castle if they didn't like each other."

Detective Inspector Gerald snorted. "Perhaps she had an ulterior motive for sending the invitation. Do you usually spend time in the kitchen, Princess Alice, or was this a special occasion?"

"Detective Inspector, I must object," Rupert said. "My sister can be eccentric, but she doesn't have a spiteful bone in her body."

"That's for me to investigate," Detective Inspector Gerald said. "Now, I'll need—" There was a hiss and a buzz.

"Hello? Are you still there?" Alice said. "I'm not the killer! You're looking in the wrong place."

There was rustling on the line, and then silence.

"What did he mean?" Alice turned to me, her face pale. "He's talking as if I killed Delphine."

I picked up the phone and listened for a few seconds. "Maybe he'll ring back." I placed the phone in the cradle.

"Holly! He thinks I'm a killer." Alice grabbed me by the shoulders and shook me. "We need to figure this out fast. I refuse to spend Christmas in prison."

"Or the next thirty years, if it turns out you did it," Rupert said.

Alice glared at him. "If you can't be helpful, go away. What do you see in him, Holly?"

"Take a breath. Detective Inspector Gerald is just poking around to see if anyone reacts. Don't give him the satisfaction. Although you need to stop talking about how much you disliked Delphine, or you'll shoot to the top of his suspect list."

"I'm not lying to him. I thought little of her. If it hadn't been for our school connection, I'd have cut her out of my life a long time ago."

"Saying that in front of the police, especially to Inspector Detective Gerald, who loves to jump to the wrong conclusion, won't be helpful." I eased her hands off my shoulders. "And, of course, none of us think you poisoned Delphine."

"The cake in Delphine's mouth is strange, though," Rupert said. "Some sort of message from our killer?"

"What message?" Alice paced across the hallway. "Campbell even said I could have done something to those cakes. He also mentioned poison and accused us of being involved."

"Campbell has worked with Detective Inspector Gerald for years, so knows him backward and forward. Of course, he'd know he'd ask those questions," I said. "It doesn't mean he thinks you're guilty."

She huffed out several breaths. "I should have been prepared with a better answer. Now, Detective Inspector Gerald thinks I'm a killer."

"You did the right thing," Rupert said. "There's no point in hiding things from him. That really would make you look guilty."

"Once the police get here, they'll want to talk to all of us," I said. "Just like we're doing with the real suspects."

"I should get my story straight. I refuse to be arrested. That would be the worst Christmas present ever."

Rupert shook his head at me, exasperated by his panicking sister. "It's cold in the hallway. Go to your parlor, Alice, and relax."

"I'm relaxed!"

"You seem tense," I said.

She threw up her hands. "Of course! I've been accused of a crime. You must come with me and help me make sense of this."

"Sure. Will you come, too?" I said to Rupert.

"Sorry, but the Duke needs me. I won't be long."

"It's fine. You go." I kissed his cheek. "I'll make sure Alice doesn't explode in a puff of Christmas glitter from all this stress."

"You're an angel. Only you know how to deal with her when she's like this." He hurried off.

"This is so annoying. I feel guilty, even though I'm innocent," Alice said as I turned to her. "And what a

108

rotten thing to say to me. Detective Inspector Gerald has ruined my festive fun."

I looped my hand through Alice's elbow and guided her toward the ladies' parlor, Meatball trotting beside us. "Forget him. We'll get a fire roaring, toast marshmallows, and figure this out."

"With hot chocolate?"

"Whatever you like to make you feel better." I slowed as we reached the door to the ladies' parlor. "Can you hear that?"

Soft crying filtered through the air.

Alice poked her head around the door. "Tabitha! What's the matter?" She hurried over to her friend, whose pretty, heart-shaped face was red and blotchy.

Tabitha dabbed her nose and eyes. "Sorry. I didn't realize anyone would want this room. I'll go."

"It's fine. You can stay here. What's wrong?"

"Delphine is dead!"

Alice sat beside Tabitha on the pale blue couch and patted her hand. "I know. That was thoughtless of me. Of course, you must be sad. We all are."

I settled on the chair opposite them with Meatball on my lap, and we waited a moment as Tabitha composed herself.

"I don't know what to do with myself. One minute, I'm fine, and the next, I burst into tears. Paris told me to pull myself together. How am I supposed to do that? She seems so blasé about the fact one of us is dead."

"You know what Paris is like. She's either obsessing over her next macro approved diet meal or scrolling her social media posts and blocking anyone who puts a mean comment on them. She's practical about these things."

"But Delphine is gone! She's never coming back." Tabitha broke into more sobs, and Alice and I could do nothing but wait for them to subside. "Sorry. I look a mess. I'd do anything for this to be a nightmare. This was supposed to be a fun Christmas get-together, and Delphine was so excited about her book. Now, everything's gone wrong."

"What do you think happened to her?" I said as gently as I could.

Tabitha glanced at me. "It wasn't suicide, despite what Clay says. Something happened in that bedroom. Maybe it was an accidental overdose, but she wouldn't make a mistake like that. It makes no sense."

"We've just spoken to the police," Alice said. "Delphine's doctor had no concerns about her state of mind or her medication, so it seems unlikely it was an accident."

Tabitha's bottom lip trembled. "I sort of hoped it would be. Then this would be easier to accept. But I don't think she'd be so careless. You knew Delphine almost as well as I did. She planned everything. She left nothing to chance, and she'd never be foolish enough to take too many pills."

"You'd all had a lot to drink that night," I said. "And Delphine kept drinking when she went to bed."

"We were enjoying ourselves, but we weren't doing anything to excess. We all know how to behave. We've been raised properly." The look Tabitha gave me was sharp. "I was surprised Delphine had come down to get more booze and not poked her head in to see us. Social events are where she scores her best gossip. At least, that was how she used to do it." More tears trickled down Tabitha's face.

"You used to live with Delphine, didn't you?" Alice said.

"Until Clay muscled in, put a ring on her finger, and made me feel like the unwanted third wheel," Tabitha said. "We used to have such fun until he got serious and talked about weddings, babies, and mansions in the countryside. I hated the idea and made Delphine promise if neither of us were married by the time we were forty, we'd become spinsters, buy a dilapidated castle in France, and do it up. She thought it was a great idea, especially after arguing with Clay."

"They often argued?" I said.

"Sometimes. Clay didn't like Delphine partying. Not that she did all that often. Well, we'd go to the parties, but only so she could get gossip, not to meet another guy or get wasted. Clay got jealous, though. It was pathetic. He didn't trust her."

"I've heard from other people, they argued," Alice said. "How bad were things between them?"

"Delphine liked to throw things. I think that's part of the reason she asked me to move out. She didn't like anyone seeing a side of her life that was less than perfect. I didn't want to go, but it was her penthouse and I was only lodging with her, so I had no choice. And I suppose I couldn't have stayed once she married Clay."

"From the way you're talking, I doubt they'd ever have made it up the aisle," Alice said.

"They would. It was the most talked about upcoming society wedding for a generation. Of course, it won't happen now." Tabitha sniffed back tears. "I expect her funeral will be almost as beautiful as her wedding. Although you don't have bridesmaids at a funeral, so I won't get to be a part of it."

"You could offer to be a pallbearer if you want to be involved."

Tabitha gave a little squeak, so I hurried on with my questioning. "When was the last time you saw Delphine alive?"

Her eyebrows rose. "When she left the party. But I spoke to her when she was in her room. I went upstairs to get a wrap from my suitcase because I was cold, and knocked on Delphine's door to see if she wanted anything."

"What time was that?"

"Around midnight. Maybe a bit later."

"What did she say?" I said.

"Not much. Delphine was quiet, and I could barely hear her. I asked if she wanted anything or needed company, but she said no. Her head was still hurting and she'd see me tomorrow. That was it. I didn't press because she had a temper, and I didn't want to make her angry if she wasn't feeling well. I keep thinking I should have gone in. If I had, I could have done something."

I sat forward in my seat. Delphine had been alive after Emma left her that evening. I'd assumed Emma had been the last person to see Delphine alive.

Tabitha sighed dramatically and slouched in her seat. "I can't figure out why anyone would want her dead. Someone did this to Delphine, I'm certain of that, but I don't know who, or why."

"Delphine could be prickly," Alice said. "Her blog didn't make her friends."

"Oh, that! Everyone is bitchy online. It's what people do. And we can all be catty when we want to, but we're still alive." Tabitha's gaze went to the door. "At least, for now. It gives me the chills to think someone is wandering around with Delphine's blood on their hands."

I'd had the same spine shuddering thought more than once.

Tabitha dabbed at her nose and grimaced. "I need to make myself presentable. If Delphine were alive, she'd despair at my appearance. If you'll excuse me." She stood and left the room.

"I'm not catty, am I?" Alice said as I moved to join her on the couch, Meatball tucked in my arms.

"No. You're a different breed to Tabitha and the rest of your gang. It was interesting to learn Delphine was still alive so late in the evening."

"Maybe she wasn't after Tabitha had talked to her," Alice said. "Could Tabitha have gone into her bedroom and done something to her? Tampered with the champagne, or given her those pills?"

"That idea brings us back to the same problem. Motive. Tabitha is distraught over Delphine's death, much more than your other friends."

"Guilty conscience?"

"It's possible. She was alone with Delphine shortly before she died. Although, if we're to believe Tabitha, she only spoke to her through a closed door. Do we believe her?"

"It can't be Tabs. They were close. Tabitha was always sticking up for Delphine, even when she was being awful to people."

I slid back, letting Meatball lounge across my belly. "Although Tabitha had an opportunity, she has no motive. She was Delphine's ally and her roommate. Unless something went wrong between them we don't know about."

"I remember Tabitha being sad about having to move out of the penthouse, but she's got a charming little mews place. There were no hard feelings. And they were always chatting online."

"There were no hard feelings that you know of." My gaze went to the open fire. It sent a welcome blast of warmth into the room and made the tinsel flutter. "Maybe we're looking at this wrong."

Alice slumped next to me and reached over to tickle Meatball's head. "You want to give up?"

"What if this was a tragic accident or a suicide? We're seeing murder when there isn't one."

"Maybe it was, but until we know for certain..."

I nodded. Until we knew for certain there wasn't a killer in the castle, we weren't giving up. Even though the more we dug, the more confusing it became.

Chapter 11

Alice yawned loudly as she walked me to the main door of the castle. We'd spent the afternoon and the whole evening together, going over people's motives and opportunities, and ended up going around in circles. Clay was still at the top of the suspect list, given he'd hidden their relationship was less than idyllic. But was that enough of a reason for him to kill Delphine?

"Although it's a nuisance not having any mobile signal, I'm enjoying not being buzzed or getting ping notifications all the time," Alice said. "I haven't missed it one bit."

"Same here. Although I expect Rupert sent me a message asking where I am. I didn't expect to stay here so late."

"He'd better not be hassling you. No one likes a possessive husband."

I arched an eyebrow at her. "Alice Audley. You want to marry the most possessive man I've ever met. You'd better get used to always been checked on."

"Campbell isn't possessive."

I gaped at her.

She giggled. "Well, I like the alpha male type. He makes me swoon when he gets gruff and surly."

"I'd find it stifling."

"We like what we like. I like my alphas, and you like your, well, I'm not sure how to describe Rupert. A messy-haired romantic who spends his life thinking about poetry and tripping over his feet?"

"Rupert is charming, considerate, and all about equality."

She wrinkled her nose. "Whatever floats your boat."

I was reaching for my coat and hunting for Meatball's leash, when laughter drifted out of the games room.

"I didn't realize anyone else was up so late," Alice said. "That laugh belongs to Verity. She cackles when she's had a few drinks."

"We should go say hello." I waggled my eyebrows.

"You're wicked! You mean covertly interrogate them."

"We can ask a few casual questions. They've just lost a good friend, so I'm surprised they have anything to laugh about."

We headed into the games room. Every surface sparkled with decorations and tinsel. Alice had decorated this room herself, and she'd gone for a glitter explosion in Santa's grotto theme.

Verity and Paris were splayed on a couch, two bottles of champagne on the table in front of them, and several trays of treats. Paris was wiping her eyes, but she wasn't crying in sadness, she was laughing.

"Alice! And her little baking friend. Come, join us." Verity patted the seat next to her.

"You look like you're having fun." Alice approached them. "Where's Tabitha?"

Paris rolled her eyes. "Moping in her room. Verity was telling me the story of how she accidentally knocked the Duke of Buckingham's eldest son into the pool at a toga party. His toga went see through when wet."

"And he wasn't wearing underwear," Verity said. "I didn't mean to do it, but I bent over and caught him with my hip. He'd had too much to drink, lost his balance, and in he went. Then his fiancée tottered over on her heels and shrieked at me. She said I'd done it deliberately to ruin her evening. The nerve of the woman!"

"I remember that." Alice perched on a chair. "Didn't Delphine write about it on her blog? There were pictures, too."

Verity grabbed her champagne flute. "Of course she did. Although she made out, I'd been in a passionate embrace with the drunken buffoon. According to a made up source, he got handsy, so I shoved him in the pool to cool his passion. His fiancée saw us smooching, which was why she shrieked like a harridan in a windstorm. It was all lies. I didn't speak to Delphine for days after she published that scandalous bit of twaddle."

"I was the same after she wrote those articles about my failed engagement," Alice said.

"Which one?" Paris said.

Verity touched her glass against Paris's. "I learned not to take it personally. Delphine saw an opportunity in everything. Someone's scandal was her payday. I have no idea where we'll get our gossip now she's dead."

I exchanged a glance with Alice. Neither Paris nor Verity seemed sad about Delphine's demise. It was probably a relief not to have a so-called friend snooping into your less than exemplary behavior at parties.

"You must miss her not being around," I said.

Verity looked startled that I'd directed a question at her. "Well, of course. No one wants to go out like that."

Paris smirked. "If Delphine is looking down on us—"

"You mean looking up at us from the burning, fiery pit she deserves to be in?" Verity said.

Paris chuckled. "Wherever she is, if she's anywhere, she'll be furious. She had everything planned for her marriage. In the month leading up to the big day, she was planning a daily exclusive about the wedding. Her followers were drooling in anticipation. Now, all that planning and plotting has gone to waste."

"Perhaps you could write memorial blog posts for her," I said. "Something nice to remember her by on her site."

"Delphine let no one else near that blog. If we messed with it, she'd come back and haunt us. Even Emma was only allowed to do the basics," Paris said. "That blog was Delphine's baby."

Verity sat up straight and slapped her hands on her thighs. "We all know if it had been any of us on that bed, Delphine wouldn't be mourning. She'd see it as an opportunity to create a killer blog post and gather a heap of social media likes and new followers. She wouldn't wallow like Tabitha. She'd maximize the opportunity."

Paris pulled a face of mock surprise. "Was our dear friend really so shallow?"

Verity picked up a slice of iced fruit cake from a plate on the coffee table and peeled off the paper case. "She was. I'm just glad we were in her friendship circle. Imagine what would have happened if she'd exposed all our secrets?"

Paris grabbed a stick of celery from another plate and chewed on it, looking at the cake Verity nibbled on with no small degree of lust. "She knew enough secrets to ruin a lot of people."

"Could one of those secrets have gotten her killed?" Alice said.

"By whom?" Verity held out the cake to Paris, but she shook her head and pushed it away. "We all liked Delphine in our own way, even though she could be vicious. That was how she was."

"I don't know if you've heard, but the police are finally beginning an investigation." Would this news prompt a reaction from one of these ladies if they were involved? "We got some evidence to them, and they're running tests on Delphine's medication and the cupcakes found in her room."

"Why test the cakes?" Paris said.

"They're looking for murder weapons," Alice said.

"Delphine was murdered with a cupcake?" Verity grabbed another piece of iced fruit cake and dumped it on Paris's lap. "You're drooling, watching me eat. Have a slice."

Paris knocked the cake onto the floor as if it had bitten her. "I have a photoshoot the day after Christmas. The dresses have already been fitted. I can't afford to gain an ounce."

"You can afford to let go over Christmas," Alice said. "Our chef does an amazing festive menu. He'll be sad if you don't enjoy his food."

"Then he'll have to be sad. And you know I have a sensitive stomach. I'll need something light. Salads and broth will be fine." Paris watched Verity sink her teeth into the cake. "What's Delphine's death got to do with cake, anyway?"

"You're obsessed with cake," Verity muttered.

"The police think it's odd she had it smeared on her," I said.

"She always was a messy eater," Paris said.

Verity arched an eyebrow. "At least she ate."

Before the bickering continued, I leaned closer. "From what you both said when we discovered Delphine, neither of you think she did this to herself. Something must have been used as the murder weapon."

"Well, no. Why would she end her own life?" Verity said.

"Exactly. So someone did this to her," I said.

They were silent. Paris nibbled her celery while Verity took another piece of cake.

"Maybe the wonderful Delphine made a mistake," Verity said quietly. "She worked so hard to show the world how great everything was, but we all have problems. We're all hiding something, aren't we?" She nudged Paris with her elbow.

Paris shrugged. "Just like Tabitha."

"What's Tabitha hiding?" Alice said.

"Isn't it obvious?" Verity said.

"She was upset this morning when we spoke to her," I said. "And she seemed the closest to Delphine."

"She'd liked to have been very close to her. It broke her heart when Delphine kicked her out of the penthouse." Verity set down the cake.

"I don't understand," Alice said. "Tabitha moved out because Delphine was getting married. She didn't want to get in the way of the happy couple."

"Which was another stab to the heart," Paris said. "Tabitha didn't just like Delphine. She was in love with her."

I nodded slowly. It made sense why Tabitha had been so distraught. The woman she was secretly in love with was dead, and she couldn't tell anybody how heartbroken she was. I glanced at Verity and Paris. It was no surprise she didn't want to share her misery with them. They weren't warm and friendly types.

"You mentioned seeing Delphine out of her room when you went upstairs on the night of your arrival," I said.

Paris nodded. "That's right. Why?"

"We're trying to figure out exactly when Delphine died," I said. "Tabitha knocked on her door around midnight and she was still alive then. Do you remember what time you saw Delphine in the corridor?"

Paris tapped her nails on the couch. "It was definitely after eleven thirty."

"It was closer to midnight," Verity said. "Maybe later. Why does the time matter?"

"We want as much information as possible for the police," Alice said. "We were hoping they'd get here today, but with all the fresh snow, they haven't made it."

"So, you're playing private eye?" Verity cackled a laugh. "Alice, you need better hobbies. Living in the countryside is terrible for you."

"I love living here. I've got my family and friends with me. And I've got Campbell. What more could I want?"

Verity pursed her lips. "I'm sure your country life is fun, but take a look at yourself. I can tell you've gained weight, and you do nothing useful with your time." Her gaze cast my way. "You've also developed an unusual choice in friends. And, let's be blunt. Your choice of boyfriend is eccentric. Some may say ridiculous."

"Someone's channeling Delphine," Paris muttered.

I sucked in a breath to come to Alice's defense, but I needn't have worried.

Alice stood slowly and smoothed down her dress. "There's nothing wrong with enjoying my food. I'm a healthy weight for my height. And I spend my time improving myself. I've been learning to play the harp, and my Spanish is *competente*." She reached over and caught hold of my hand. "And my choice of new friends is excellent. Much better than it was when we were stuck in boarding school and had no option but to like each other. And as for Campbell, he's decent, honest, and would lay down his life for me. He adores me and tells me so every day. And I adore him right back. I have a wonderful life, wonderful friends, and an incredible boyfriend. And I have every intention of asking him to marry me and keeping him forever. Now, if you'll excuse us, we're going to bed." Alice yanked me out of the seat and stormed off, leaving me with no choice but to follow her, since she still held my hand.

Meatball barked several times, then raced after us.

I glanced back into the room to see Verity and Paris staring at us with open mouths. "Well done, Alice."

"Those two can be viperous when they're together," she said. "You don't think I'm fat, do you?"

"Alice, you're perfect. You're amazing. I love having you as a friend."

She threw her arms around me and hugged me tight. "Don't forget, I'm a perfect sister-in-law, too. I didn't go too far, did I? Do you think they'll still speak to me?"

"You got it spot on. You showed them you aren't a pushover. And if they stop speaking to you, it's their loss."

Alice stepped back and her hand went to her mouth. "Oh, dear. I revealed my plan to ask Campbell to marry me. They'll tell everyone. What if Campbell hears about it before I make the proposal? I shouldn't have said anything, but I got carried away."

"I wouldn't worry about that. The phone line is still not working, the wi-fi is down, and there's no-one to tell other than the people in the castle. Your secret is safe for now. And Campbell is too intimidating for them to seek him out and spill the beans."

She huffed out a breath. "True. But it doesn't leave me much time to figure out my perfect proposal."

"It's not the only secret uncovered, though," I said. "Did you know Tabitha was in love with Delphine?"

"No! How could I miss that? I thought they were just good friends."

I nodded. "And now we know there was more to their relationship than friendship, we have a new prime suspect to question in the morning. Tabitha suddenly has an excellent motive for wanting Delphine dead."

Alice bit her bottom lip. "The spurned lover. I can't wait."

Chapter 12

The view from my cottage window looked like I lived in the middle of a midwinter scene from a Christmas card. The snow was beautiful as it glistened under the weak winter sun. But as beautiful as it was, this snow couldn't have come at a more inconvenient time.

With Delphine's body still in the bedroom, all the suspects free roaming, and no sign of the police, we were in trouble.

Rupert walked into the room, rubbing his hands together. "Is it just me, or has it gotten much colder since last night?"

I touched the radiator underneath the window and frowned. It was icy. "The heating hasn't come on."

"There's oil in the tank. It was only topped up last week. We got a delivery the same day as the castle."

"Let's head to the castle. They'll have heat, so it'll be warmer over there. We can get breakfast and check in on Alice."

"I'm not sure about it being warmer. It's hard to keep that place warm. Audley Castle is beautiful to look at, but impractical to live in." Rupert took down our coats and sorted through a pile of hats and gloves.

"Which is why I love our cottage so much. That is, when the timer hasn't broken on the boiler." If that was the problem. I kneeled and petted Meatball.

Unusually for him, he paid me barely any attention, his gaze fixed on the door.

"He's still got a case of puppy love," Rupert said.

"I think so." I scratched between Meatball's ears. "You'll see Dottie soon. Stop making me feel guilty for keeping you two apart."

He whined and gently leaned his head on my hand. Poor Meatball. He was lovesick. All he wanted for Christmas was his cute little fluffy corgi friend.

"What's the plan for today?" Rupert asked after we'd gotten our coats on and locked the cottage door behind us.

"More sleuthing." I'd told Rupert what we'd learned about Tabitha last night, and he agreed she had an excellent motive for wanting Delphine dead. "I'm tackling Tabitha. She must be desperate to talk to someone, and I don't think she gets a sympathetic ear from Paris or Verity."

"Unrequited love makes people do terrible things," Rupert said. "I always thought Tabitha was one of the sweetest in the group, though."

"That's not saying much if you compare her to Delphine. Or Verity. And Paris has a sharp tongue," I said.

He chuckled. "True. Those ladies are scary."

"They are. And I haven't forgiven you for not coming back to the party on the night they arrived. You left me with those hyenas, and it didn't take them long to start making jibes."

He winced. "There's only so much gossip and giggling I can handle. And the Duke was having trouble figuring out what to give Alice for Christmas. It was a choice between a rifle with a pearl handle or a set of riding gear."

"Please tell me you went for the riding gear." Alice wielding a rifle, even a pretty one, would be risky.

"I suggested a gift voucher to her favorite store. Alice hasn't ridden in months, and I can't remember the last time she went clay pigeon shooting. We were able to order it online before the connection failed."

"Phew! At least we won't have to worry about being accidentally shot on Christmas Day when she unwraps her gifts."

"You never know in this place." Rupert took hold of my hand. "You're not angry I avoided the party, are you?"

"No. If I'd been given an excuse to sneak away, I'd have taken it. I tried to get away several times, but Alice insisted we saw things through to the bitter, champagne soaked end."

"And what an end. Tabitha killed Delphine! We just need a confession and then can hand everything to the authorities. Any message from the police about when they'll show up?"

"Nothing. And each time I've tried the main line or my mobile, they're still not working. We have to get the police to see sense and make sure Alice isn't in the frame for this murder."

"From the way Detective Inspector Gerald talked, he suspects her. He probably hasn't forgiven Alice for evading capture the last time she was accused of killing someone."

I huffed out a laugh. "You make Alice sound scary."

"She can be terrifying." Rupert grinned at me. "I'm allowed to say that since she's my sister. Just don't tell her I told you, or she'll come after me."

We walked briskly through the deep snow, Meatball leaping like a winter hare to keep his head above the drifts.

"It's a shame Campbell can't be in charge of this investigation," Rupert said. "He's always so capable."

"You don't think I am?"

"You're capable of anything you desire. It's just he's like a tank. He keeps moving until the job gets done."

"I'm like a tank, too. Just a smaller one."

Rupert kissed the side of my head through my woolen hat. "You're an adorable tank. My dream tank."

It was an odd compliment, but I'd take it. "It's best Campbell is out of this. If Alice is considered a suspect by the police, he won't keep a level head. Although Campbell does an excellent job of concealing his emotions, they run hot and true for Alice."

"True. And the last time she got in trouble, it felt like I was in the middle of a romantic thriller movie," Rupert said. "The bodyguard absconding with the princess to protect her innocence. It's got box office smash written all over it."

"With me as a side character. The level headed best friend who solves the murder and saves the day."

"Along with her furry sidekick and her roguishly handsome boyfriend providing backup. Although you were the true heroine in that adventure."

Meatball barked his approval at being included in the escapade.

I laughed. "It was a joint effort to keep Alice out of jail. And it looks like we'll be repeating our mission to make sure she stays on the right side of the bars if we don't figure this out."

As we entered the castle, Alice was rushing up the stairs with a tray of food in her hands. She glanced over her shoulder. "Tabitha has just come down for breakfast. Campbell's complaining about being hungry, and you know what he's like when he's got an empty stomach. I'll be quick. Don't start without me."

"I'll go up and say hello to Granny," Rupert said. "I won't be long."

I was about to head into the dining room to talk to Tabitha when Emma walked toward me, wrapped in a chunky dark brown sweater. I lifted a hand in greeting. She must have spent time with Tabitha since she'd worked so closely with Delphine. Perhaps she'd overheard Tabitha revealing her romantic intentions, or maybe an argument.

"How's your phone behaving today?" I said.

"Not great. I got fifteen minutes on it the other day before the wi-fi dropped out again. As much as I love the countryside, I couldn't handle the inconvenience of being so out of touch."

"It's not usually like this."

"Glad to hear it. And it's freezing in here. My room didn't have heat this morning. I twisted the control knob and thumped the radiator, but nothing worked. I also couldn't get hot water for my shower."

"Oh! It isn't just our cottage, then? We didn't have heat either."

"I had to sleep with three duvets on my bed last night."

I winced. "Sometimes, the heating system goes wrong. It's ancient. And with the weather so bad, it might not cope with the demands on the system."

"Don't think I'm complaining. This place is stunning. Spending Christmas in a cold castle won't be the worst thing I've ever done." Emma smiled at me. "Are you going in for breakfast?"

"In a minute." I glanced at the closed door leading into the dining room. "I wanted to ask you a question about Tabitha."

Emma cocked her head. "Sure. What about her?"

"I've heard it mentioned she was fond of Delphine."

"They were close. They even lived together for a while."

"I know they were good friends, but I wondered if there was more to their relationship than that."

Emma pressed her lips together. "I'm not sure what to tell you."

"The truth? Did Tabitha and Delphine ever have a romantic relationship?"

Emma's gaze lowered. "No, but Tabitha cared deeply for Delphine. It was much more than a friendship for her. And... well, Delphine exploited that. She led Tabitha on."

"Why would she do that?"

Emma shrugged. "Tabitha is the daughter of an oil baron. The family live in Dubai, and they're crazy rich. Tabitha has a role in the office based in this country, but I don't think she works much for the generous salary she gets."

"Okay. But what does that have to do with Delphine?"

"Tabitha's rich, and Delphine loved nice things. She'd innocently say she'd seen a new dress or a designer purse she liked, and Tabitha always went and got it for her. She was desperate to make Delphine happy. I wonder if she thought buying her things would win her affection." Emma shook her head. "That would never have worked. It was just Delphine being greedy. I thought it was cruel."

"Did you ever tell her that?"

Emma's eyebrows shot up. "Of course not. Delphine looked out for me. She gave me a job and security when no one else would open the door to me or answer my calls. I owed her big time. I wasn't calling her out on her less than angelic behavior toward Tabitha. Although..."

"Although what?"

She tilted her head from side to side. "Tabitha often sent Delphine gifts. Sometimes, I made sure they didn't get to her. I'd give them back and tell her Delphine didn't like it, or it was the wrong color, or she already had that purse. And I talked to Tabitha to get her to see sense. Delphine had been dating Clay for ages. She couldn't have started a relationship with Tabitha."

"Tabitha couldn't see she was being used?"

Emma sighed. "Love is blind."

"When was the last time Tabitha got Delphine a gift?"

"You mean her Spring Break surprise?"

"I didn't. What was that?"

"It was her most outrageous gift. Tabitha was so excited when she told me what she'd done. She booked passage on an all-inclusive, month long Caribbean cruise that sets sail in three months. Just the two of them. She said she'd make sure Delphine realized how much she cared for her. She knew the time away together would make Delphine see her relationship with Clay was wrong, and there were other options."

"Tabitha must have realized how inappropriate that was," I said. "She was trying to steal someone's girlfriend."

"I don't think she did. I convinced her not to say anything about it until after we'd celebrated Christmas. I said it would be a nice New Year's surprise for Delphine."

"Delphine didn't know about the trip?"

"As far as I know, Tabitha kept her word and said nothing. Why the interest in her?"

"I'm still looking into why anyone would want Delphine dead."

Emma was quiet for several seconds. "Why would Tabitha kill the woman she loved?"

I couldn't answer that question. But it was something I intended to find out.

"Emma, where are you?" Verity called from the top of the stairs.

Emma frowned. "I'm just going in to breakfast."

"I need help with my dress. The zipper's stuck. Be an angel and come up. It won't take long."

Emma scowled at me. "You'd think I worked for all of them the way they boss me around. I'd better fix this, or I'll get bitched at for the rest of the day." She turned and hurried away.

I slid into the dining room and was pleased to discover Tabitha sitting alone at the table. She looked glum as she sipped on a black coffee.

She nodded at me as I collected a plate and helped myself from the small buffet Chef Heston had set out.

"Would you like anything?" I said to Tabitha as I piled fresh crumpets on my plate, along with a side serving of stewed apples and raisins.

"I've got no appetite this morning," she said.

"Still feeling down?" I joined her at the table.

She dabbed at her eyes with a napkin. "I know it's silly, but I can't stop crying."

"You should eat something. It always makes me feel better when I'm sad."

Tabitha sniffed back more tears. "Those crumpets look nice. May I?"

I pushed my plate over to her. "Help yourself. I can always get more."

"Thanks. You'll think I'm ridiculous, but I can't even manage the most basic of things. It feels like my world is falling apart. I stood and stared in the mirror for ten minutes this morning, before remembering I was supposed to be brushing my teeth."

"Grief makes you do odd things. It hits you hard when you lose someone you love." I studied Tabitha carefully for her reaction to my words.

The crumpet she was about to bite froze by her lips. "You mean, Delphine?"

"You did love her, didn't you?"

"We were best friends. Of course I loved her."

"As more than a friend. I couldn't help but compare your reaction to the news about Delphine's death with your friends. They got drunk on champagne and joked about how Delphine would look down on them and complain. You keep bursting into tears and won't eat."

"They've been gossiping about me, haven't they?" Tabitha set the crumpet back on the plate. "Those two are hags. They can't keep anything secret."

"They may have mentioned something about how fond you were of Delphine. And I believe you've been sending her gifts to win her affection."

"Is nothing a secret around here?" Tabitha grabbed her coffee mug. "What's that got to do with you, anyway?"

"I want this puzzle solved as much as you. Audley Castle is my home, and it's wrong something so terrible happened here. I want to find out why Delphine died."

Tabitha's breath came out shaky, and her eyes hazed with tears. "Sorry, I didn't mean to snap. So do I. And, yes, perhaps I cared for her more than I should. There was something about Delphine, something special. When she paid me attention, I felt so good. Like I could take on the world and win. But then, she'd turn her light away, and it felt like everything was over. I just wanted her to notice me. We could have been so happy together." She grabbed the crumpet and ate it in three bites, leaving a smear of strawberry preserves on her chin.

"You mentioned you went to see Delphine after she went to bed with her migraine."

Tabitha nodded as she chewed on her crumpet.

"Was there more to the conversation than you've already told me? Did you argue about something?"

She reached for another crumpet. "I... I asked if she wanted company. I tried to get into her bedroom, but the door was locked."

"You definitely spoke to her, though?"

"Yes. Delphine was in the room. I said I wanted to look after her, but she laughed at me. I got upset and told her she was being mean, but she kept laughing. She sounded odd, though. Not herself. I told her I hoped it was the worst migraine she'd ever had and then stomped away."

She shrugged. "Not my proudest moment. I took a few minutes to calm down in the bathroom and then went back to the party."

"And the bedroom door was definitely locked?"

"It wouldn't budge when I tried the handle. Why? Is that important?"

"No. I mean, I'm not sure. Perhaps." How had Paris been able to open the bedroom door and discover Delphine? Had Delphine locked herself in earlier in the evening but then unlocked the door? Maybe she forgot to lock it after getting the cupcakes from the kitchen.

"Even though I was angry with her that night, I still cared for her. As much as Delphine frustrated me, I'd never hurt her. I... I loved her." Tabitha blew out a breath. "It feels good to say that. I've been keeping it inside for so long."

"I'm sorry you're going through this," I said. "It must be difficult when you don't have anyone to talk to about how you feel."

"You mean, I can't talk to the Witches of Eastwick about this?" Tabitha smirked. "Don't worry, I've called them worse to their faces. Verity and Paris view this as an adventure. Something fun they can gossip about with their online friends and followers. If it weren't for the lack of wi-fi, they'd be live streaming this whole thing, taking photographs, and turning Delphine's death into a sordid circus for people to gawp at and comment on."

"If the tables were turned, wouldn't Delphine have done the same?"

Tabitha sighed. "Yes. I loved a terrible person. She could be so shallow. But when she let down her guard, she was sweet."

I held my tongue over that suggestion.

She pulled herself upright. "I'm done with those society witches. I'm cutting contact once we're out of here. I tried to talk to them about my feelings for

Delphine a few times, but they made a joke of it and suggested I needed to find a real man. They didn't understand."

"Have you spoken to Alice? She'd understand. She never judges people based on who they love."

"Not really. We're not that close anymore. Perhaps I could. Delphine used to joke about Alice turning into some crazy spinster, floating about in an old castle with only the ghosts for company and some weird kitchen assistant as a friend." Her cheeks flushed. "Sorry! That was you, wasn't it?"

"I'm happy to be her weird kitchen friend." I sipped my coffee. "And Alice may not have chosen a life like Delphine's, but that doesn't mean she's unhappy."

"Alice is always happy. And I see why now I'm here. She's got everything she needs." Tabitha pushed a crumpet my way. "Sorry about saying you're weird. I think you're great for Alice."

"And she's good for me. Alice has a unique perspective on things. You might like to rekindle your bond. It'll help you remember what a true friendship should be like. It isn't all about getting the perfect picture in the perfect place while wearing the perfect dress."

"I... yeah, I know that. Thanks. I'll give it a try." Tabitha ate another crumpet. "Part of the allure with Delphine was her air of mystery. Although, I could never get my head around why she got engaged to Clay. She should never have accepted his proposal."

"You didn't think they were right for each other?"

"They looked perfect together, but he believed socialites were pointless."

"I didn't know that."

"Maybe he's grown up since he made that dumb comment, but Clay always reckoned he'd marry someone with a brain and not just a family fortune to live off."

"So, why were they together?"

"They had little choice. Their parents always wanted the match."

"They were happy together?" I said. "I know there'd been arguments between them, but they wouldn't carry on the engagement if they didn't love each other, would they?"

"Tradition, the right social status, and an appropriate marriage partner are always important, no matter what century we live in." Tabitha's gaze skimmed over me. "Although I think Rupert did the right thing by marrying you. It helps to shake things up."

"Thanks. I think he made the perfect choice, too."

Tabitha grabbed the last crumpet off my plate and sank her teeth into it. "Ugh. I'm a disgusting mess. I need a shower and to pull myself together. And I must stop crying. All it's doing is giving me a headache and red eyes."

"And maybe talk to Alice, too?"

"Yes. It would be good to talk to someone who doesn't judge me. Thanks, Holly. You're not half as odd as Delphine claimed you were. See you later." Tabitha stood and strolled out of the room.

She'd only been gone for a few minutes, and I'd just refilled my plate and was enjoying a more relaxed meal as I mulled over our conversation, when Alice dashed in, her cheeks flushed.

"Is something the matter?" I said.

"Saracen got through to Campbell for a few seconds on his phone. The test results are back on Delphine's blood work. It wasn't a suicide."

Chapter 13

After abandoning my breakfast, I'd dashed up the stairs with Alice, Meatball beside me, and into Campbell's bedroom.

He was sitting up in bed, dressed, and with a plate of untouched burned toast beside him. Poor Campbell. He really must love Alice to endure her dreadful breakfasts.

"Alice just told me the news," I said. "It was definitely murder. What did the results show?"

"You'd know everything if Alice hadn't rushed out of here the second I got the call," Campbell said.

"Holly needed to know. She's our lead investigator," Alice said. "I'm sure I missed nothing important."

"You missed plenty. Delphine overdosed on the sedatives she was prescribed," Campbell said. "There was a massive dose found in her system."

"Enough to kill her?" I said.

"More than enough."

"That suggests she did it to herself."

"There's more. The cupcakes. My cupcakes! They're involved." She waved a hand at Campbell. "Tell Holly!"

"I was about to. Unfortunately, the cupcakes are significant." Campbell's expression was thunderous, but he wasn't directing his anger at Alice. He was glaring at his phone. "When Delphine was found, we thought it strange chocolate cake was smeared all over her."

"And some of it stuffed in her mouth, too," I said.

"Exactly. I didn't see that at the time, but Saracen did an excellent job of photographing everything, including taking pictures of the inside of Delphine's mouth. A huge lump of cupcake had been stuffed in there, and some even forced down her throat."

"Delphine suffocated because she had too much cake in her mouth?" I said. "Someone force-fed her until she died?"

"No, the police are certain Delphine was dead by the time the cupcake was put in her mouth. Someone did that to her."

"What's so special about the cupcakes?" I said.

"It's the worst news. They had aconite in them," Alice said. "It's a poisonous plant."

I placed a hand on my stomach. "How did poison get into your cakes?"

"That's what we need to find out. And quickly," Campbell said. "The police are focused on the poison now, not the pills."

"But the pills killed her," I said.

"You don't think... well, you don't think we were all supposed to be poisoned?" Alice said quietly. "I made those cupcakes for my friends, but then forgot about them. If I hadn't, I'd have presented them at the party and we'd have eaten them. You, too, Holly. And I'd have brought some up to Campbell. We'd all have died."

"Who would want us all dead?" A shiver ran through me. Was someone plotting to kill everybody in Audley Castle?

"The police will think Alice did it," Campbell said darkly. "Before the line died, Saracen was saying they were running a background check on her."

"They won't find anything on me!"

"Of course not." He caught hold of Alice's hand. "But Detective Inspector Gerald isn't a fan of the Audley family. He's always held a grudge because of your special relationship with the village. This is his way of showing you who's in charge."

"By making Alice look guilty of murder?" I shook my head. The man was an idiot.

"Which is why we have to act fast, or Alice will be in the spotlight for Delphine's murder, and potentially the attempted murder of everyone else."

"I'm eccentric, not insane," Alice said. "And don't be mean. Of course, I don't want my friends dead. Nor you, despite how horrible you're being by suggesting I'm a poisoner."

Campbell sighed. "I don't think that, but you once described your friends as a pack of ravenous hyenas at an all-you-can-eat rib party."

"Well, Verity cackles like a hyena when she's been drinking. And Paris—"

"Alice, this isn't a joke. If you've complained about them to me, you've complained about them to other people. That'll get back to the police. It gives you a motive."

"You have said to me once or twice you wished you'd never met them," I said. "Of course, I don't think you poisoned your cupcakes in the hope they'd die. But, to an outsider, it looks suspicious."

"And as I've already explained, and will be happy to do so to the police, poison is sneaky. It has no place in my murderous plans for anyone."

"Please, stop talking about murderous plans. You're giving me palpitations." Campbell rubbed his chest with his free hand. "We both know you didn't do this. But somebody did."

"Alice is teasing about her murder plans. You are teasing, aren't you?" I said.

She tugged her hand free from Campbell and crossed her arms over her chest. "I just don't want to be underestimated. I could kill if I had to."

"You're focusing on the wrong thing," Campbell snapped. "The police found vast quantities of aconite in those cupcakes. It didn't get in them by accident."

"It wasn't put in the cupcakes to make people sick, but to actually kill whoever ate them?" I said.

"It would appear so."

"My poisonous plant knowledge is lacking," I said, "but wouldn't that amount of aconite have been noticed? It must have a particular taste."

"It does. I had Chef Heston bring me a book on plant poisons from the library. Aconite tastes bitter. It would have made the cupcakes inedible."

"Which was why the killer had to force it into Delphine." My mouth twisted to the side. "Even though she was dead."

"How did the killer get it into the cakes?" Campbell said.

"The kitchen is open to anyone at night," I said. "It would have been easy to sneak in. They could have injected it into the cakes and then covered the hole with the mint frosting. It was soft set icing, so no one would have noticed."

"They must have seen them on the counter and assumed they were for the party," Alice said. "I was right! That poison was meant for all of us. Delphine wasn't the target, she was just unlucky. This is awful!"

I shared a look with Campbell. From his tight expression and the way he gripped the bedsheet, he was as concerned as me.

"Alice, what if it wasn't a coincidence the cupcakes you baked from scratch were used to poison Delphine?" I said.

"Holly, let's not get ahead of ourselves," Campbell said.

"You're thinking it, too."

His silent scowl told me everything.

Alice dropped onto the bed, her face pale. "Who would want to frame me for Delphine's murder?"

"All of your so-called friends spring to mind," I said. "Maybe one of them saw this as an opportunity too good to miss. They must have witnessed Delphine bullying you over the years, so figured you were the perfect fall guy. It finally got too much for you to bear, so you engineered a way to deal with Delphine once and for all. You lured her to the castle and then poisoned her."

"She wasn't that awful to me, just a terrible bully," Alice said.

We were quiet for a moment. Meatball hopped onto the bed and rested his head in Alice's lap.

"Who knew you baked those cupcakes?" Campbell said.

"You, Holly, Chef Heston, Rupert, the kitchen staff, and all my friends. After I'd finished icing them, I took a picture and sent it to them, to show them what they had to look forward to."

Campbell pinched the bridge of his nose. "That's not helpful."

"I'm trying to help. I just don't know how!"

"It must have been one of your friends," I said. "It wouldn't be anyone who works here, and it wasn't me, Rupert, or Campbell. It has to be someone who wanted to frame you." I paced the room. "Could it have been Delphine?"

"You think she poisoned herself?" Alice said.

"Delphine planted the poison, but her plan backfired after someone saw her do it. They drugged her with her own pills, then forced the cake into her mouth as punishment."

"You're stretching," Campbell said.

"I'm determined to save Alice. I'll stretch as much as I need to until we get to the truth."

He pressed his lips together, but nodded.

"How suspicious did the police sound when you spoke to them?" I said to Campbell.

"I didn't speak directly to them, but Saracen sounded worried. He said they asked a lot of questions about the cupcakes and how stable Alice seemed."

"I'm stable! What are they talking about?"

I continued pacing. "Why did Delphine have an overdose of sedatives in her system, and also the poisoned cupcake smeared all over her?"

"To ensure she didn't survive," Campbell said. "And to implicate Alice and take the heat off the actual killer."

"The evidence keeps pointing back to me." Alice's bottom lip jutted out. "If I didn't know I was innocent, I'd wonder if I'd done it, too! Campbell, promise me I won't get charged."

He hesitated. "We're working on it."

"We'll do whatever we have to, to prove you're innocent." I raised my eyebrows at Campbell. He must be so frustrated being stuck in bed while his girlfriend was under suspicion, but that was no reason for him to give up. "You keep trying to get through to the police. Find out everything they know, and how seriously they're looking at Alice for this crime."

Campbell nodded. "What will you do?"

"Keep questioning suspects. We need a clear timeline to find everyone who went into the kitchen, and also a timeline for everyone who saw Delphine after she went to her room. Until we have that information, we can't rule anybody out, and we'll keep going in circles."

"And I'll go to prison for the rest of my life. Worst Christmas ever."

"That'll never happen." I caught Campbell's gaze, and he discreetly shook his head.

I was as puzzled as he was. And as I hugged my best friend and considered this tricky problem, I had no idea how to get Alice out of this mess.

It had taken time and lots of questions, but I was back in Campbell's bedroom with Alice later that same day. And we had a timeline for everyone's movements on the night of Delphine's murder.

I'd also checked who'd gone into the kitchen and upstairs, so I knew who had an opportunity to get to Delphine and force cupcakes into her mouth.

I stood at the end of Campbell's bed. Meatball sat beside me. He'd brought his new girlfriend, Dottie, who we'd met in the corridor. Alice was snuggled next to Campbell on the bed.

"Delphine left the party with Emma at eleven o'clock that night," I said.

"And then Emma came back to the party at eleven twenty, after helping Delphine get ready for bed and giving her the usual dose of pills," Alice said.

"What about the fiancé, Clay?" Campbell said. "When did he arrive?"

"I was outside walking Meatball when Clay face-planted into the snow around ten-thirty. I can't get any closer than that, but he arrived before Delphine went upstairs. She came out with her friends to meet him."

Meatball's ears lifted at the sound of his name, and Dottie barked.

"Then my friends cooed over Clay for ages," Alice said.

"And Delphine was dead a couple of hours after Clay arrived. A coincidence?"

"I agree it seems suspicious," I said.

"Clay joined the party with the rest of you?" Campbell said. "He didn't want any alone time with Delphine?"

"He joined us as soon as he'd dried off," Alice said. "He kept telling everyone about his brave adventures through the snow. So many times."

"The guy walked less than three miles. It was hardly a hero's journey," Campbell said.

Meatball gave a single bark of agreement, and Dottie joined in.

"You can't judge. You can barely walk three feet, the state you're in." I crouched to pet the dogs to keep them calm. "Getting back to the timeline, Emma stayed at the party for about twenty minutes and then went to bed, too."

"Giving her time to drug and poison her employer," Campbell said.

"Agreed. But she has no motive." I strode around the room, Meatball beside me and his new fluffy friend trotting close behind. "At around the same time, Tabitha went upstairs and spoke to Delphine through the door. That was at eleven-thirty. She tried to get in, but Delphine had locked the door from the inside and wouldn't let her in. They argued."

"What did Tabitha do after that?" Campbell said.

"She got upset and left. She went to the bathroom, then re-joined the party."

"Could she have lied about the locked door? Perhaps she only said that to make us think someone else is involved."

"All the doors can be locked," Alice said. "We leave the key on the inside for guests. Some people can't sleep soundly if they know someone could come in."

"I checked with Paris. The door was unlocked when she discovered Delphine's body. She said it was closed, but when she didn't get an answer, she tried the handle, and it opened," I said.

"Was the key still in the door?" Campbell said.

"I remember taking it out and locking it so no one could disturb the scene." I drew in a breath. "Which means someone did this to Delphine. They locked the door while they killed her so they wouldn't be disturbed, then crept out, leaving the key behind."

"Verity and Paris went upstairs at around eleven-forty five," Alice said. "They saw Delphine in the corridor, so she was still alive then."

"They spoke to her?" Campbell said.

"No, they just saw her walking around," I said.

"They also saw me," Alice said. "Do you remember, I came up and checked on you at almost midnight?"

Campbell nodded. "So Delphine was still alive at midnight. Did anyone else see her? What about her fiancé?"

"Clay said he knocked on her door. He couldn't remember the exact time, but it was after midnight. He heard quiet talking and wondered if Delphine was on her phone. He called her name a few times, but then it went quiet. He tried the door, but it was locked."

"Was she on her phone? They were barely working that night," Campbell said.

"She could have been talking to her killer." I eased one of Campbell's smart black shoes from Dottie's mouth and hid it out of sight. He didn't need any more reasons to be grumpy.

"What an awful thought. There were so many opportunities to stop this murder from happening," Alice said.

"And we would have stopped it if we'd known someone planned to commit a murder," I said. "After that, everyone stayed downstairs. I don't recall anyone else leaving the party."

"We were in the same room for over an hour. It was only when the party broke up and we went to bed that Paris discovered Delphine," Alice said.

"So, between about twelve-fifteen and one-thirty in the morning, Delphine was killed," I said.

"She must have left her room more than once before she was murdered," Campbell said. "Delphine was in the upstairs corridor when your friends saw her, and then she went downstairs to get the cupcakes."

"Or perhaps the killer brought the cake and champagne with them," I said.

"That makes sense if they planned on using the cakes to frame Alice." Campbell squeezed her closer to his side.

"And whoever it was, Delphine let them into her bedroom, so she knew and trusted them."

"She hadn't wanted Tabitha in her bedroom, or Clay. So that leaves me, Paris, or Verity as the killer," Alice said.

"Not necessarily. What if her killer was in the room with her earlier in the evening? They locked the door to ensure Delphine couldn't get out and to make sure the pills had the desired effect. The killer could even have been there when Clay or Tabitha tried to get in."

"Emma knows all about Delphine's medication. And she was one of the first to leave the party. Perhaps we should focus on Emma," Alice said.

"What's her motive?" I said. "Delphine was Emma's lifeline. Now she's dead, her friends will ignore her again, and she'll become a social pariah. She'll lose everything she's gotten back."

Alice wrinkled her nose. "Paris? Those two have been so unpleasant to each other, ever since Delphine wrote a scathing review about Paris's catwalk exploits. She tripped on a gown in front of everyone, and Delphine published a picture and made less than subtle hints Paris had been drunk."

"This is getting us nowhere," Campbell said. "Everyone was coming and going from the party all night, so they all had an opportunity to kill Delphine. If I could, I'd arrest them all."

"I hope you're not including me or Holly in that sweeping statement," Alice said.

"Sorry. Of course I'm not." Campbell had the decency to look embarrassed. Only Alice could get that expression out of him.

I understood his frustration. I wanted this mystery solved, too, and to make sure Alice didn't stay on the suspect list. "The police will consider all opportunities and motives. And they'll be looking hard at the poisoned cakes."

"So, I'm still in the frame?" Alice flopped across the bed.

Meatball yipped and leaped up, covering Alice's face in doggy kisses until she laughed.

Campbell tried to look surly, but even he smiled when Dottie joined in.

"That's enough, you two. Leave Alice alone." I scooped the dogs off the bed. "For now, everyone is still in the frame."

Alice's smile faded. "And we still have no idea how to find the killer before the police make a big mistake and charge me with murder."

Since I had no way to give her definite hope that wouldn't happen, I unleashed Meatball again. Doggy distraction would have to suffice, until I discovered a clue to get Alice in the clear.

Chapter 14

"I can only think it's a problem with the supply line." Chef Heston appeared in the open kitchen doorway, stamping snow off his boots. "I can't see a problem with the tanks. And there's plenty of oil in them. But we can't go on like this. We've had no heat for over twenty-four hours."

After my less than satisfying conversation with Campbell and Alice the previous day as we'd tried to solve the murder, I'd found myself in the middle of another issue to untangle. After some investigation around the castle, and a chilly night in my cottage with Rupert and Meatball, I'd discovered no-one had heat.

And after a staggering amount of complaining, Chef Heston had ventured out to check the tanks and supply lines first thing the next morning.

I'd offered to do it myself, but that had only made him complain more. He secretly loved helping. He just sometimes forgot that truth.

"Even if we could reach a heating engineer, I doubt they'll come out in these conditions." I glanced over my shoulder at the banks of snow sitting against the castle walls. "And being so close to Christmas, no-one will want to come out, anyway."

"I'm sure you're right. But I have a bigger problem to focus on." Chef Heston kept his coat on but pulled off his gloves.

"What's that?"

He pointed at the range cooker. "No oil, no Christmas dinner."

"Um... yes, that's almost as important as not freezing to death."

"It is! This Christmas will be a disaster. No turkey, no figgy pudding, and no glazed ham."

"And let's not forget there's a dead body in a guest room."

He snorted. "If there's no heat, the body won't get unpleasantly smelly."

"True. Eau de Christmas Corpse is the last thing we need mingling with the cranberry pot-pourri."

Chef Heston's eyes widened, then he laughed. "Christmas is always unique when you're around."

"You make it sound like I'm a magnet for trouble." I poured him a mug of steaming coffee. Fortunately, we still had electric, so the kettle worked.

"Remind me again, how many murders you've been in the middle of?"

"One or two. I don't keep count."

He accepted the coffee. "I do. Mainly because when you'd sneak off to nose about, I was left in the lurch handling a busy lunchtime."

"I always got my tasks done before I went snooping."

He didn't look impressed.

I arched my eyebrows. "I'm a good employee."

"I can hardly say you aren't, since you married Lord Rupert."

"Don't use that as an excuse. Speak your mind."

After muttering under his breath, he sighed. "You always do a decent job."

It was as good a compliment as I'd get from Chef Heston. "How are the firewood supplies?"

"There's not great news there. If we bank up the fireplaces and run them throughout the day to keep the chill out, we'll run out of wood on Christmas Day."

"Hmmm.... Frostbite for Christmas. No thanks."

"That won't happen." Alice pushed open the kitchen door. She wore a white ski suit with pink and silver snowflakes all over it. "Trees surround the castle. And I've decided we're in charge of collecting firewood."

"We?" I said.

"Not me," Chef Heston said. "I have a nightmare Christmas dinner situation to puzzle through."

"No, not you. Food first. I asked my friends if they'd help, and all I got were excuses. Paris said she thought she was coming down with a cold. Clay simply disappeared, and Verity and Tabitha said they hadn't brought clothes for venturing outside. I offered them some of mine, but they weren't keen. And I can't find my annoying brother anywhere. So, it's up to us to save the day." She smiled at me.

"I'll keep working on the food crisis," Chef Heston said. "I'm not made for manual labor. I got a headache just looking at all those pipes."

I glanced outside. There'd been a few more inches of snow overnight, but it had stopped, and a weak sun peeked at us. "A walk in the woods will do us good."

"That's what I thought. It'll clear the cobwebs so we can figure out this murder and make sure I'm no longer in the frame."

"Chef, perhaps you could keep working on the oil tanks as well as the food," I said. "There's a kit in the storeroom that's used to flush through the pipes when there's a blockage. Or try to reach the filter and clean it."

"I trained at the finest culinary school in Paris. I'm not meant to grub around in oil tanks."

"You also don't want to work in a freezing castle while you cook a feast for everyone," I said. "And you need your range to make the delicious treats for the family."

"Do it for me, Chef Heston." Alice planted a kiss on his cheek. "You'll be a hero if you get the heating working. And it'll stop my friends from complaining."

He grumbled under his breath again, his cheeks flushed pink. "I'll see what I can do. But no promises."

"You're an angel. And maybe make some icing dusted mini chocolate yule logs for when we get back?"

"Alice! No heating means no freshly baked anything," I said.

Chef Heston glowered at the microwave. "I could improvise."

Alice clapped her hands together. "Go change into your ski suit, Holly."

"Um... I don't own a ski suit."

"No! One of mine. I've got five. They all have matching hats and gloves too. I put the lemon yellow one out for you."

"You won't lose me in the snow if I'm dressed like an overripe banana."

"Hurry! We have fires to stack."

Ten minutes later, I was shoving my feet into my boots, attaching Meatball's leash to his collar, and heading out with Alice, looking just as bad as I feared I would in the ski suit. But at least I was warm.

"I'm glad to be out of the castle." Alice pushed a wheelbarrow, which we planned to fill with wood. "My friends are being so grumpy. I told them it wasn't my fault Delphine got herself killed. Of course, Tabitha burst into tears when I said that, Clay and Emma looked miserable, and Verity and Paris started day drinking. Although, I think they were just looking for an excuse to crack open the breakfast bubbly."

I nodded as she complained about her friends. Why would any of them want to frame Alice for murder? She had eccentric ideas, and occasionally had a morbid obsession with dungeons, but she was a loyal friend. She'd survived her boarding school years, and the elite snobbery that came with it, relatively unscathed. Was that why she was a target? Someone was jealous of her happiness?

My phone buzzed in my pocket. "I've got a signal!" I pulled it out and discovered a message from Lady Philippa Audley.

NO SNOW! All in capital letters.

More messages pinged in, pushing down Lady Philippa's odd comment. Before looking at them, I called the police station.

It rang and rang before someone picked up. "Audley St. Mary station."

"This is Holly from Audley Castle. I need to know if there's been progress in the investigation into Delphine Augustus's death. We sent someone over to you with evidence. Saracen. Is he still there?"

"One moment, please. You'll need to speak to Detective Inspector Gerald. He's in charge of the case."

I grimaced. "Is that necessary? I just need to know what's going on. I don't want to trouble the detective."

"I'll put you through."

"Make sure you tell Detective Inspector Trying to Frame me for Murder that I didn't do it." Alice was looking at her own phone and pouting. "You're so lucky. I'm still not working."

My phone rang and rang, the line growing increasingly crackly. Then the connection died, and silence filled my ear.

"No! Why couldn't she have just told me what was going on? Maybe they've gotten more tests back, or found out something about a castle guest." I tilted my head. "Is that someone calling my name?"

Alice sighed. "I don't hear anything." She shook her phone.

I looked around and spotted Lady Philippa hanging out the window of her turret and waving at us. I lifted a hand. She was shouting, but I was too far away to hear her.

I slid my phone into my pocket and cupped my hands around my mouth. "I got your message. What did you mean by no snow?"

She kept waving and shouting, but I still couldn't hear her. "Maybe we should go back and see if your gran needs something."

"Ignore Granny. She's probably having one of her turns. You know what she's like."

I looked at the message again. It wouldn't be the first time Lady Philippa had sent me an odd message. She'd never gotten the hang of using her phone.

"We're going to collect firewood," I yelled. "I'll see you later."

Alice gave her a hearty wave. "We need to hurry and get the place warm before Granny freezes in that turret. I expect she won't close the window once she's finished hanging out of it."

"We should bring her downstairs while we fix the heating and find the killer," I said. "She may feel nervous about being on her own."

"Granny loves living in that turret. Despite what she tells everyone, it's her favorite place, even with all the ghosts."

When I'd arrived at Audley Castle, Lady Philippa revealed to me her family kept her a prisoner in the turret. It wasn't true, but they sometimes kept their distance when she was in one of her more eccentric moods.

I adored Lady Philippa, even when she had visions and predicted the future. Which often involved people dying!

Alice turned to me, dropped on one knee, and grabbed my hand. "Campbell Milligan, will you marry me?" She giggled.

"Um... yes? Is that how you're planning on doing it?"

"I'm keeping things traditional. Did I sound sincere?"

"The giggle gave the wrong impression."

"I'm nervous! Everyone giggles when they make a proposal that's so serious."

I pulled Alice to her feet. "However you ask, Campbell will say yes after a few seconds of being shocked to the core. You will give him time to freak out, won't you?"

"What if he doesn't say yes? He's seen how odd my family is. He could be waiting for an excuse to finish things with me. He's probably waiting until Christmas is over." Her bottom lip wobbled.

"Campbell adores you. He's seen you at your best and your worst, and he's still here."

"He's got no choice, since his foot is broken and he's confined to bed."

"That's true. He's probably counting down the days he can grab his expensive gifts, then escape in the dead of night with the family silver."

Alice thumped my arm. "He'd never do that."

"You're the only one doubting him." I nudged her with my elbow. "Even though you're so different, you're perfect for each other. You make him less grumpy, and he makes you..."

"Less ditzy?"

"You have the perfect level of ditziness. Maybe slightly more level-headed."

She frowned. "That sounds dull."

"Not dull, just the perfect balance."

Alice kicked her feet through the snow, throwing up clouds of white that made Meatball bark and leap in the air. "Perhaps I shouldn't do it. It's inappropriate to propose marriage when there's a dead body in the castle."

"I doubt there's any protocol for that. But you both deserve to be happy. And Delphine will be moved soon."

Alice huffed out a plume of air and kicked more snow. "I am happy, but I'm also not."

"You're sad about Delphine?"

"No! And I'm not sorry that I'm not sad. She wasn't a nice person. I should feel guilty about saying that, but the world won't be any worse off now she's not here to spread her poison. She made me feel terrible when she published those articles about my love life."

"Did she publish articles about the friends you've got staying here too?"

"Of course. Although I'm sure she had some even darker secrets on them. They were in Delphine's inner circle, though, so she promised them she'd keep their truly awful secrets forever."

"What secrets were they?"

"I have no idea, since I'm not a part of the hallowed inner circle. Clay used to be a bit of a playboy, so there could be a scandal there. And since Paris models, there could have been a secret affair or exploitation going on. We already know Tabitha's secret."

"And Verity?"

"Not a clue. She's a vegan. Maybe she got caught eating a steak at a pro-hunting rally."

"That's hardly the scandal of the century."

"Verity has a huge following online. They all listen to her green goddess advice. If she got snapped gnawing a hunk of dead cow while holding a banner saying: *wear fur, kill fluffies*, that would cause her problems."

"What about Emma? She had her fall from grace, although everyone already knows about it."

"It wasn't exactly her fall, but when her family lost their fortune, she lost her status. Emma would have been kicked out of every influential social group and event if it weren't for Delphine."

We'd almost arrived at the treeline. Snow blanketed the skeletal trees and crunched under our boots.

"I'm still wondering about Clay," I said.

Alice made a snowball and threw it for Meatball. "They all look guilty to me. I have no clue how to solve this."

I felt the same, but I wasn't giving up. I unclipped Meatball's leash, and after a few seconds of sniffing around, he bounded through the snow, heading to the trees.

"Meatball has the perfect idea. Forget our worries and simply run." Alice tipped her head back, laughed, and raced after him.

I swung my arms to keep warm, grabbed the wheelbarrow Alice had abandoned, and picked up the pace.

There had to be something I was missing in this puzzle. Delphine must have known something about one of her friends to make them do this. And it was someone calculating enough to bring poison with them in the hopes they could frame Alice.

Since their tactics were so underhanded, I needed to do some covert snooping. When we got back to the castle, I'd look through everyone's luggage and purses. It would be nothing less than the police would do if they were here.

I looked for Alice's blonde hair, but she'd disappeared from sight, her ski suit blending with the surroundings.

Meatball barked, and my heart sped up. His barking was frantic, and he only made that noise when he was stressed.

I broke into a clumsy jog, shoving the wheelbarrow through the snow. "Alice! If you've fallen and broken something, I'm not carrying you back to the castle."

Meatball kept barking. He sounded so agitated.

I reached the edge of the trees and headed along the well-worn path we often took during our daily walks. "Meatball. Where are you? Alice!" It was getting harder to remain calm when no response came back.

I followed Meatball's bark, which took me off the path, but the snow wasn't as deep under the trees, so it was easier to push the wheelbarrow.

I shoved past some bushes and froze, my eyes widening and my heart racing as I saw a trail of blood in the snow.

Chapter 15

"Alice! Where are you? Are you hurt? Meatball?" Who was bleeding? The blood looked fresh, and the few drops I'd seen were getting more frequent as I followed the trail.

Meatball burst through a bush, making me jump. He ran around me, barking, then raced off.

"Take me to Alice. Good boy!" I chased after him, my chest heaving as branches whipped against my face, leaving behind stinging cuts.

There was more blood in the snow. Lots of it. Had Alice fallen and injured herself? She could have tripped and hit her head on a rock hidden beneath the snow.

"Alice, if you can hear me, make a sound. Anything. I need to know you're okay."

Other than Meatball's panting and my rasping breath, there were no other sounds. Even the birds were silent, as if watching to see what would happen next.

A sick, tight feeling filled my stomach. There was more blood. It was a stark contrast to the pristine snow.

I pulled out my phone and stared at it, willing it to work. The no signal sign remained resolutely in place. I tried calling the castle anyway, but it wouldn't connect. I even tried Alice's number.

Meatball bounded ahead of me, but the snow slowed him down. He stopped and shook out his fur, before looking back and giving me a serious sounding bark.

"Keep going. Show me where Alice is." I caught up with him, and we stopped at another pathway.

There was more blood, but also footprints, and what looked like drag marks cutting through the snow. Someone else was out here with us. Had they attacked Alice?

I heard a weak scream, and my head shot up. I craned my neck as I figured out which direction the sound had come from. "Meatball. Follow that noise."

He launched himself through the snow, his ears back and his tail out behind him. He loved Alice as much as me.

"Keep going. She can't be much farther." My thighs ached as I fought to get through the snow. I wasn't giving up. Alice was injured and in danger. I had to get to her.

There was another feeble scream, a thump, and then footsteps hurrying away.

I peered through the trees, trying to see who it was, but I couldn't see anyone. I was panicked, anxious about Alice, and freezing.

Despite being cold, a chilly line of sweat coated the back of my neck. I shoved past more tree branches and gasped. Alice lay in a bloody heap on the ground.

Meatball raced over to her and licked her hand.

I dashed over and sank to my knees beside her, but kept looking around. Whoever had done this could return to finish the job. I grabbed the nearest large stick and waved it in the air. It wasn't much of a weapon, but it might be enough to deter them.

Alice groaned and her eyes flickered open. "Holly?"

"Yes, I'm here. So is Meatball. Who did this to you?"

"I don't know. I don't feel good. My head hurts. Feel sick." She tried to touch the injury on the side of her head, but I caught hold of her hand.

"You may have a concussion. We need to get you to the castle."

Her eyes fluttered closed. "I want to sleep."

"No! I have to keep you awake. Are you hurt anywhere else, or just your head?" I looked over her ski suit, which was dotted with blood from her head wound.

"Don't think so. Terrible headache, though."

"Do you remember what happened? I felt in the pockets of my borrowed ski suit, but there was nothing to help me patch up her head wound, which continued to bleed at a worryingly rapid rate.

"There was someone here. They surprised me. They were fast. Came from behind." Her words slurred.

I chewed on my bottom lip. "Meatball, go to the castle. Bark for as long as you have to until someone comes out. Then run back here. Make them follow you."

His ears pricked, and he licked Alice's hand again.

I blinked tears out of my eyes. My little dog was wonderful. I had to hope he was up to this challenge. "Meatball. Castle. Bark. Go."

He turned a couple of times, wagged his tail, and then set off through the snow toward the castle.

"He's such a good dog. He'll get help," Alice mumbled.

"Meatball's never let me down yet," I said. "But in case he gets distracted, I need you on your feet. You can't fall asleep with a head injury."

"Why not? The snow is soft."

"And cold and wet. It's what they always say on the TV shows. You must stay awake."

"That's fiction. I bet people with head injuries go to sleep all the time."

I bit my tongue. If they did, they most likely didn't wake up. I caught hold of her hands. "On three. Let's get you up."

"No! Leave me. I'll be fine."

"Here we go." I kept a firm grip on her hands and heaved her up.

Alice groaned and sank to her knees. "You're supposed to be my best friend. Stop moving me. It makes me feel sick."

I cast a look at the sky through the tree branches. It was getting gloomy and more snow was falling. We had little time before it got dark and even colder. "Put your arm around my shoulders, and let's move."

"Don't want to."

I scooped a handful of snow and pressed it against her face.

She squeaked and jerked away.

"Alice, this is serious. Since someone did this to you, they could still be out here. We're in danger. And I have to get you to the castle to treat your injury."

"What? Oh, I can't think straight. Hit me with more snow. It helped."

I picked up two handfuls of snow and smooshed them into her cheeks.

Alice's blue eyes snapped into focus, and she shuddered.

"You can do this. One step at a time. I'll be right by your side."

After much grunting, groaning, and more complaining, I got Alice on her feet. I wrapped one arm securely around her waist and made sure she had a hold on me.

Then we moved. Well, I moved, while Alice staggered, stumbled, and bled all over my ski suit. I'd heard head wounds bled a lot, but this seemed like a worrying amount of blood for her to lose.

"Is Meatball back with the limo yet?" she whispered.

"Not yet. And he doesn't have his full license to drive us anywhere. He'll find help and bring them to us."

"It won't be any of my friends." Alice sagged against me, and an icy plume of breath whooshed out of her mouth. "They're not really my friends, are they?"

"Don't think about that now. Focus on walking and keeping your eyes open."

She staggered a few more steps. "One of them killed Delphine. We both know that."

I blew out a breath. "We do."

"And they want me to look guilty, don't they?"

I hesitated. "Maybe."

"They planted my cupcakes at the scene. The poison. I'm such a trusting fool."

"Alice, trusting people is a great quality." I adjusted my grip on her waist. It was getting harder to hold her up as she leaned her weight on me.

"It's a stupid quality. And this isn't the first time I've been framed for murder, is it? I'm an easy target because I'm gullible." She shivered. "I'm so cold."

"Keep moving. The faster you move, the warmer you'll get." I was also freezing. My ski suit was wet through to my knees and my hands felt icy cold.

"Need a rest. Please, just for a minute."

I stopped walking. "Hold on to me. I'm going to try my mobile and see if I've got a signal." I pulled the phone out, but it was gloomily unhelpful.

Alice staggered forward and sank to her knees. She groaned and dropped face first into the snow.

I grabbed her shoulder and rolled her onto her back. She was unconscious. I tucked away my phone, slid my hands under her armpits, and dragged her.

The snow was falling again, and gloom crept in around us, but I kept going. The castle was behind me, and I had maybe a mile before we were there. I could do this. I wasn't letting Alice down.

I made it a few steps before falling and jarring my hip and knee. After rolling onto my feet, I jogged to the trees, found the wheelbarrow, and shoved it through the snow, back to Alice.

She was still out cold, so it took effort, but I got her in the wheelbarrow. "Perfect. Let's go."

The wheelbarrow didn't move.

I shoved, grunted, and strained and made it five feet before the snow ground us to a halt.

Alice jerked awake. "There was a knife!"

"What?"

"The person who hit me had a knife. And they wore white."

I stood in front of the wheelbarrow as I got my breath back, leaning forward with my hands clasping my waist. "Did you see their face?"

"No, but they were small, like a ninja. An evil Christmas ninja." Alice's head slumped back.

I kept shoving the wheelbarrow, inching us closer to home. There were no ninjas at Audley Castle, but there were plenty of underfed socialites. Paris was the smallest. All I'd seen her eat was a few salads and fruit.

Was it her? Why attack Alice? If she'd brought a knife with her, she meant business. I hadn't seen a weapon, but it would have been easy to hide in the snow. And I'd been so panicked about Alice, I hadn't paid attention to our surroundings.

My lungs burned and tears pricked my eyes as I stumbled. My arms were throbbing as I tried to push the wheelbarrow through another mountain of snow.

We weren't going to make it. I stopped pushing and hugged Alice. The snow was falling so hard, I could barely see my hand in front of my face.

Frantic barking reached my ears, and a sob slid out of me as Meatball raced into view. And he wasn't alone.

Dottie was beside him, looking excited. And she dragged a huge ham hock behind her.

Meatball reached me, and ran around in circles, Dottie following him after she'd dropped the ham hock.

"Good boy. You did your best. You brought Dottie and food." It wasn't the help we so desperately needed, though. Tears clogged my throat, and I grasped Alice's frozen hand.

"Holly! What are you doing out here?" Chef Heston's voice was the most welcome noise I'd ever heard.

I waved wildly at him. "Over here! It's Alice. She's hurt."

He broke into a jog, his eyes widening as he saw the blood dripping on the snow. "What happened?"

"I'll explain everything, but we must get Alice to the castle. She has a head injury, and I can't keep her awake."

Chef Heston stared at the wound on her head for a second before looping his arms under her knees and lifting her. "What were you thinking, bringing Princess Alice out in weather like this?"

I hurried along beside him. "You were there when she insisted we collect firewood. When Alice wants to do something, she does it."

"You let her go off alone?"

"Of course not! Alice ran ahead of me. That was when she was attacked." I checked behind me, glad to see Meatball and Dottie were following us. Dottie carried the ham hock, her head up so it didn't drag in the snow.

"Someone did this to her?" Chef Heston glanced at me as he waded through the snow.

"I think so. Alice said someone jumped her. She didn't see who it was."

"When your annoying dog came racing into the kitchen with Dottie, I knew something was wrong. He had the audacity to jump on a counter and kick the ham on the floor. He'd never behaved like that before. I shooed him out, but he grabbed my sleeve and tugged me to the door." Chef Heston shook his head. "Then Dottie snatched the ham hock, and they ran off."

"I'm so glad they misbehaved," I said. "I told Meatball to find someone to help."

Chef Heston snorted his surprise. "He certainly got my attention. Meatball is a credit to you, Holly, even though that's one less dish I'll serve at Christmas."

"Meatball is amazing. Best dog in the world."

"No doubt. I'll make him something special as a reward."

Chef Heston's surprising praise had my eyes flooding with tears again, while Meatball happily barked as if he understood he'd be getting a chef special for being such a good boy.

"I'm worried about Alice," I said. "She was awake for a short time, but keeps losing consciousness."

"It's no surprise, with a head injury like this."

"Is the landline working? I haven't been able to get a signal to call for an ambulance."

His expression tightened. "No, the last time I checked, it wasn't working."

My heart sank, but I grasped Alice's hand. We'd figure something out, but I didn't know what.

Chef Heston looked at me and nodded. "Hopefully, she isn't too badly hurt."

I gulped back tears as panic whacked into me like a ball of ice and chilled me to the core. What if she was? What would happen if I couldn't save my best friend?

Chapter 16

Alice was still unconscious, and I was failing to keep my emotions under control as we reached the entrance to the castle and trailed snow over the antique rugs.

"I know little first aid. Only the basics." Chef Heston wheezed as he walked. "There's a medical kit in the kitchen. Go get that."

"Campbell will know how to help. Get Alice to his room. I'll grab the kit." I squeezed Alice's unresponsive hand, then dashed into the kitchen, Meatball and Dottie by my side. My frozen fingers slid off the cupboard latch and I bent my fingernails back.

I closed my eyes for several seconds and took long, deep breaths. My panic wasn't helping. Alice was vulnerable and needed everyone to keep a level head. But how could I do that when someone just tried to kill her? Someone who had to be inside this castle, pretending as if nothing had happened.

Meatball pressed his front paws against my thigh and licked my hand. I opened my eyes and looked down at him. Trust and confidence radiated from his gaze. If Meatball believed in me, then I had to believe in myself, too.

Dottie ruffed gently, as if sensing the importance of this moment.

"We've got this. We can fall apart later. And we're finding out who tried to kill our beautiful Alice." I yanked open the door, grabbed a large green medical supplies kit, and dashed up the stairs two at a time with Meatball and Dottie on my heels.

Meatball knew this wasn't a game, but Dottie was enjoying herself, giving the occasional bark, her tail wagging. She must think Meatball led such an exciting life, dashing through the snow, barking at Chef Heston, stealing ham hocks, and finding a person covered in blood! No wonder she was so interested in him.

"What do you mean, someone did this to her?" Campbell's voice rattled with anger as I strode into the bedroom.

Chef Heston had placed Alice on the bed and wisely backed away. Blood stained his chef's whites. I deliberately didn't look at the marks for more than half a second to avoid triggering my panic.

"Explanations later. Can you treat her head injury?" I dropped the medical kit onto the bed. "Tell me what you need, and I'll get it."

Campbell had one arm protectively around Alice while his free hand examined the wound. "I need to know what happened to her."

I opened the medical supplies. "Does she need stitches?"

He drew in a breath. "The wound must be cleaned so I can see how bad things are. She may need stitches."

I passed him a clean, white cloth, then hurried to the bathroom and brought back a glass of cool water.

Campbell dipped the cloth into the water and carefully cleaned the blood off Alice's face.

"Is there anything I can do?" Chef Heston's voice quavered.

"Yes! Tell me what's going on."

"I... I... Holly?" It was a rare event for Chef Heston to be lost for words.

"I'll need a stiff drink if I don't get an explanation," Campbell growled out.

"Not with the pain medication you're on," I said.

"Holly, you must be frozen." Chef Heston touched my arm. "Your ski suit is soaked. I'll get towels and warm drinks, shall I?"

I nodded. Of course, Chef Heston needed to feel useful. There was nothing worse than wanting to help and not feeling able to. "Perfect. Get dried off, too. Bring everything up here when you're ready."

He cast a worried look at Alice, then hurried out of the bedroom.

Campbell placed Alice flat on her back as he cleaned her head wound. He muttered to himself, many of the words too rude to store to memory. "How's she looking?"

"Not as bad as I first thought." He pressed a clean, wadded piece of gauze to Alice's forehead.

"Do you think she has a concussion? I tried my phone on the way back, but there's still no signal, so I couldn't call for an ambulance." I choked on my words. "I don't know how badly she's hurt."

"It's hard to tell, but possibly. There's a huge lump under the wound." Campbell looked at me, and the pain in his eyes hit me in the gut.

I reached over and squeezed his shoulder, trying my hardest not to break down. "Alice will be okay. She was conscious for a short time and talking."

"This should never have happened. I'm supposed to protect her. What good am I like this?" He gestured to his broken foot.

"You would have been there for her if you hadn't been injured in that car accident. Campbell, this isn't your fault."

His nostrils flared. "No, it's yours. What were you thinking, taking her outside to mess about in the snow?"

I reined in my anger. Campbell was shouting because he was fearful of losing Alice. "We needed firewood. And Alice suggested we go outside. Neither of us knew what would happen."

"What exactly did happen? I'm still waiting for the full story." Campbell dabbed the injury and held more gauze against it.

I sat beside Alice and clasped her hand between both of mine. "I'm not certain. We went to gather firewood. Alice ran ahead with Meatball, and a few minutes later, he started barking. I could tell something was wrong, so I followed the noise and discovered blood in the snow. I followed the trail, and... it led me to Alice."

Campbell squeezed his eyes shut for a second. "Are you certain she didn't fall? Did you see who attacked her?"

"No, but I heard a couple of screams and then running feet. Alice said her attacker was small and dressed in white."

"Small male or small female?"

"We only have a few guys staying in the castle at the moment. None of them are small. I'm thinking it was a woman."

"One of her friends?" He checked the bleeding again, then nodded, replaced the wadded up gauze with a clean, white square, and wrapped a bandage around her head.

"Who else could it be? The snow is keeping everybody else away."

Muscles in his jaw ticked along with his grinding teeth. "Why try to kill Alice?"

"I don't know, but I'll find out. As soon as I know she's out of danger. Is she?"

Campbell finished wrapping the bandage and secured it in place. Then he wiped the dried blood off Alice's cheek and chin. It had splattered all over her white snowsuit and looked like macabre berries in the snow.

He spent several minutes not saying anything, simply holding Alice and making her comfortable.

As much as I wanted to interfere, Campbell was like a possessive lion guarding his favorite lioness. He'd only bite my head off if I got in the way. Besides, he had more medical knowledge than me and was doing everything he could to keep her safe.

Chef Heston knocked on the door and walked in. He had several towels tucked under his arm and a tray of steaming mugs. "It's coffee. I put sugar in all of them. I know how much Princess Alice likes sweet things."

"Thanks." I was shivering in my damp snowsuit but didn't want to leave Alice.

Chef Heston set down the tray. "Holly, Lady Philippa is in the corridor. She'd like to speak to you."

"Did you tell her about Alice?" It was rare Lady Philippa left her turret for anything less than an emergency, or a fancy party involving pink champagne and feather boas.

"She already knew. I don't know how. Perhaps she saw us coming back to the castle."

"Go. Get out of those soaking things and reassure Lady Philippa that Alice will be fine," Campbell said.

I hesitated. "I won't be long. And, Campbell, she will be fine."

His determined gaze met mine. "I have no doubt about that. But Holly, I want you to promise me something."

I raised my eyebrows, waiting for him to continue.

"You'll find out who did this to Alice and make them pay."

I gripped his shoulder. "I guarantee, whoever did this, they won't get away with it. I love Alice as much as you."

Campbell nodded and looked away, but I didn't miss the sheen of tears in his eyes.

I hurried into the corridor with Chef Heston, who nodded at Lady Philippa, and then dashed away along the corridor.

Lady Philippa wasn't alone. Horatio, her elderly, overweight corgi, had also made a rare appearance. Although he growled softly at Meatball, who'd accompanied me into the corridor, he was behaving himself.

"How is she?" Lady Philippa wore a jade green velvet onesie and had a huge white fur hat perched on her head with several large feathers adorning the top.

"Campbell thinks Alice will be fine. How did you know what happened to her?"

"My message! Why didn't you pay attention to it?"

"You sent me the words 'no snow.' Was that supposed to mean something?"

"Yes! Exactly. I was warning you not to take Alice out in the snow. I sensed she was in danger." Lady Philippa gripped my hand. "I don't sense any approaching death, though. She wasn't too badly injured."

I tried not to be unnerved by Lady Philippa's bizarre ability to predict the future. "Campbell's cleaned her head wound, and the cut isn't too deep. She's still unconscious, though."

"If only you'd turned back and not gone into the woods. I knew trouble was waiting for you. I yelled as loudly as I could from my window, but you didn't listen to me. No one listens to me."

"Sorry. We have to get you better at texting. If you'd sent: 'killer in the trees. Run!' we'd have paid attention."

She pursed her lips. "I was panicking. And my phone hasn't been behaving, so I needed to keep the message short."

"It's the snow. I don't suppose your prediction hinted at who attacked Alice?"

Lady Philippa shook her head, making the feathers dance. "I know for certain they wanted her dead, though."

"Why? This wasn't a random attack, was it?"

"I can't answer that, but I'm worried they'll try again. And I have a feeling the attack was because Alice has something they want, and they won't stop until they've gotten it from her."

"Money? Jewels? The castle antiques? What does Alice have that's worth killing her for?"

"I couldn't tell you, but I feel a deep sense of dread in my bones about this terrible situation."

I tilted my head. "You're sure that's not because the castle's heating is broken and you're cold?"

She tutted at me. "I know everyone thinks I'm kooky, but I know what I'm sensing. My dearest Alice is in deadly trouble, and with Campbell out of action, she only has you and Rupert to rely on. And as much as I adore Rupert, he's a gentle soul. Made to read poetry and think, not tackle deranged, knife-wielding killers."

"We'll all look out for Alice. Chef Heston stepped up to the mark. He carried Alice to the castle and brought her upstairs. He didn't complain once."

"For all his surliness, he's an excellent man. But he doesn't have Campbell's skills, or your ability to sleuth out a problem and put a stop to this madness." Her fingers wrapped around my arm and she leaned in close. "Because that's what this is. Someone unstable is hunting Alice."

"You're sure?" I chewed on my bottom lip. "Does the attack on Alice have anything to do with Delphine's murder?"

Lady Philippa blinked. "If it does, I couldn't tell you the connection. Although, I knew Delphine. She was an unpleasant sycophant. Every time we'd meet, she'd simper around me and attempt to wheedle out an exclusive story. She got nothing. That young lady would have misused the information and twisted it into an unpleasant scandal. And she was so spiteful to Alice when they were younger."

"Some things never change," I said. "I only got to see Delphine in action for a few hours, but she was unkind to everyone."

"And if you're unkind, look what happens," Lady Philippa said. "Still, there's nothing we can do for Delphine. You must focus on protecting Alice."

"What if there is a connection, though? Alice was worried someone put poison in her cupcakes because they wanted her guests to die. What if the killer is still intent on achieving that goal, but picking people off one by one instead?"

Lady Philippa tilted her head as she considered the option. "I heard about the bungled use of Alice's cakes as a murder weapon. It can't be that. I've had no visions about mass murder."

My gut told me the attempt on Alice's life had to be connected to Delphine, but I didn't know what that connection could be.

"You need backup." Lady Philippa gave my arm a decisive pat. "The police are useless, though. I heard they've been making excuses about bad roads to avoid doing their job."

"They're doing their best, but the snow is preventing anyone from getting in or out. Did you hear what happened to Saracen?"

"I did. Poor chap."

I nodded. "The terrible conditions are good in a way. The snow has trapped Delphine's killer in the castle."

"We should lock them up until the police get here. Maybe a few nights in the haunted turret will get them talking."

"It's not a terrible idea, but I can imagine Verity and Paris will complain about being imprisoned."

Lady Philippa tapped a finger against her lips. "Take Horatio to help. I'll command him to guard this room. He won't let anybody in, so Alice will be safe."

I repressed a groan. "Are you sure? He's old. I wouldn't want to stress him out."

Horatio growled at me and then Meatball, revealing a few yellow teeth. Surly old hound.

"When Horatio needs to, he can perform any task excellently. And he's excessively fond of Alice. He'll stay here and watch over the situation."

"I could leave Meatball, too. They can guard Alice together. And Dottie is inside. She's a passionate little dog."

Meatball lowered his head, and Horatio's growl grew more menacing.

"No, you need Meatball with you. If you're off to talk to potential killers, he'll need to step in and bite someone if they get feisty. Keep him by your side. And Dottie is too flighty to be relied upon."

"I use Meatball more for emotional support than as an attack dog." I leaned down and scratched Meatball between the ears. He'd attack if he had to, but who wanted to see their beloved pup go up against a bad guy?

"That's sensible. So, shall we get started?" Lady Philippa rubbed her hands together.

"What are we starting?"

"Questioning everyone in the castle. Someone tried to kill Alice, and I need to know who, so I can give them a thump."

"Oh, Lady Philippa, you don't need to do that."

"I absolutely do. And I insist on it. Alice is my dearest relative, and this is my castle. Well, not mine, but you know what I mean. If there's a killer within these walls, I'm helping you find them. Their deadly games come to an end."

I looked at Meatball and gave a small shrug while he flopped onto his belly and sighed. I could hardly tell Lady Philippa no, and even if I did, she'd follow me around, anyway. "We'd appreciate your help. And I know exactly who to speak to first."

Chapter 17

After a change out of the soggy ski suit, and borrowing one of Alice's less fluffy pink gowns from her walk-in closet, I was headed down the stairs with Lady Philippa and Meatball to begin our questioning.

And we were on a mission to find Paris.

"What makes you so suspicious of young Paris?" Lady Philippa said. "I met her at one of Alice's finishing school balls. She struck me as highly strung, but not deadly."

"Alice was only conscious for a short time when I found her, but she said her attacker was small. Paris is the smallest in the group. She models on the catwalks for big-name designers, so needs to stay tiny to fit into their miniscule dresses."

"All of Alice's friends are small. They have to keep up appearances for all the Insta apps and Whatbook thingy posts."

"True, but Paris is the skinniest."

"She must be tall to grace the catwalks."

I hesitated as we reached the bottom of the stairs. "Yes, I suppose she is. But we must start somewhere. Let's see if Alice has something Paris desperately wants and is willing to kill for it."

We'd already tried Paris's bedroom, and she hadn't been in there, so planned to search the downstairs rooms.

The library was empty, and so was the dining room.

"Meatball, can you sniff out Paris?" I said.

"She probably smells of hunger and self-righteousness." Lady Philippa chuckled to herself. "I've never met a happy catwalk model."

I shoved open the door to the ladies' parlor and discovered Paris on the couch. She jerked upright and shoved her hand under the cushion next to her before wiping her mouth. "Are you looking for me? I was just... about to take a nap."

I strode in with Lady Philippa and Meatball. "I need to know where you were an hour ago. Did you go outside?"

Her eyes narrowed. "I haven't been anywhere. I wouldn't mind getting out of here, but the roads still aren't cleared. Any news on when that'll happen?"

"You won't be going anywhere if you did something nasty to Alice." Lady Philippa did some excellent looming, despite her tiny frame and her feathers bobbing around.

"Oh, I know you." Paris stood and curtsied. "Sorry for my rudeness, Lady Philippa. It's a pleasure to see you again. What's wrong with Alice?"

"I think you already know what's wrong with her," I said. "Why did you attack her?"

Paris's mouth dropped open. "Me? Attack Alice?"

"Give me your hand, child." Lady Philippa grabbed Paris's hand, and she stared into her eyes.

"Um... What are you doing?" Paris glanced at me.

"Sensing your guilt," Lady Philippa said.

She glanced at the couch. "What am I supposed to feel guilty about?"

"Paris, this is serious," I said. "Alice could have died out there."

"Out where? I've been here. I got up late, had breakfast, and have been wandering about entertaining myself. Verity has a hangover from yesterday, so I've barely seen her. Tabitha's not talking to me, and Clay keeps moping around and trying to get a signal on his phone."

"Which means you've been on your own. You could have followed me and Alice into the woods." I was allowing my anger to get the better of me, but I was done sidling around the suspects. No one hurt my best friend and got away with it.

Paris attempted to tug her hand away from Lady Philippa, but she refused to let go and kept scrutinizing Paris like she was a stain that needed removing. "Why would I follow you?"

"She is hiding something," Lady Philippa said. "But I don't think it's a desire to murder anyone."

"Of course not! Alice is my friend. I'd never do anything to hurt her."

Meatball, who'd been snuffling around the couch, grabbed the cushion next to Paris and pulled it onto the floor. He revealed a half-eaten mint frosted cupcake and several empty food wrappers.

"I told you. All models smell like hunger. Poor thing is half-starved." Lady Philippa poked Paris in the ribs, then stepped back with a satisfied nod.

"Give me that!" Paris snatched the cushion from Meatball and slung it over the wrappers.

"My dear, have some decorum." Lady Philippa fluffed the cushion. "This was imported from an order of silk-weaving nuns who live in the Kalograion Monastery."

"Oh! Sorry. It was expensive?"

Lady Philippa arched an eyebrow. "Nuns are never cheap."

I walked over and lifted the cushion. "Why are you hiding food?"

Paris rolled her eyes. "I'm a catwalk model. I'm supposed to live on celery and thin air. If anyone sees me eating cake, they judge."

"You can eat as much cake as you like around here," I said. "As a baker, I love seeing people enjoy my food."

"Not you. You don't count." Paris glanced at the wrappers, and her cheeks flushed. "I mean, my friends. The girls always judge me. Delphine was the worst."

"What did she do when she saw you eating something you shouldn't?"

Paris looked away. "Nothing. It doesn't matter anymore."

"There are no secrets here, child," Lady Philippa said. "You're under my roof, and you'll tell us the truth. And you need to be honest, since we're looking at you as the brute who hurt Alice."

"I didn't. Alice is sweet. Stupid, but sweet." Paris's mouth twisted to the side.

I rolled my shoulders. It was important to get control of my emotions, so I missed nothing important. "You had a problem with Delphine? Did she have something on you?"

"Maybe. I mean, it's no big deal in my line of work." Paris looked at the slightly squashed cake and lowered her gaze. "I've been diagnosed with an eating disorder. I was getting on top of it, but Delphine spied on me one day and saw me coming out of the clinic after a therapy session. I'm not certain, but I think she paid my therapist to get her hands on my file. She knew everything about my problem."

"She threatened to expose your secret on her blog?"

"That's some friend," Lady Philippa said. "It's no wonder someone finished her off. Was that someone you?"

Lady Philippa was thinking the same as me.

"No! I begged Delphine not to publish the article. I've got several food sponsors, and I'm always promoting healthy living. I'd lose those deals if they learned about my eating disorder. It might even ruin my modeling career. And an agency who promotes body positivity to teenagers has just signed me. Imagine what they'll think when they learn about this?" She jabbed a finger at the cake.

"I thought Delphine looked after her inner circle? Wasn't that a perk of supporting her, no matter what she said about other people?" I said.

"She was supposed to, but Delphine had been losing followers to rival bloggers and was desperate. She had to do some huge exposés to get her numbers back, or risked losing major deals, too."

"Delphine picked business over her friendship with you?"

Paris wrapped her arms around her tiny waist. "She was going to."

I nodded slowly. Paris had just given herself an excellent motive for killing Delphine, but I couldn't work out how it tied into the attack on Alice.

"Did Alice know about your eating disorder, too?" I said.

"No. At least, I don't think so. Although she often said I should eat more." Paris grabbed the wrappers and scrunched them in her fist. "I promise, I didn't try to kill Alice. And I remember now, I have a witness. I was in the kitchen with your amazing chef when your dog ran in. I was sampling the food, and the chef was making something chocolatey in the microwave and complaining about it not being good enough for Alice. He tried to shoo your dog out, but then another dog came in and stole a ham."

I let out a breath, and my anger faded. That story tallied with what Chef Heston had told me.

"Your dog kept barking and running outside. It was odd. The chef started muttering, then went off to look for you. I took some goodies and came in here to stuff my face. I couldn't have hurt Alice. And why would I?"

I'd have to check with Chef Heston to make sure Paris wasn't lying, but their stories were almost identical. And, although my focus was on finding Alice's attacker, I'd just uncovered an excellent motive for Paris to kill Delphine.

"You need to sleep," Campbell said to Alice.

"You tell me sleep is for the weak. And I feel better. I've been resting all afternoon. You barely even let me get up to use the bathroom," Alice said.

I smiled as they gently bickered with each other. It was such a relief Alice was awake and none the worse for her head injury. I was back in Campbell's bedroom and had updated them after talking to Paris and her friends. Lady Philippa had gone to speak to Chef Heston to check Paris was with him at the time Alice was attacked, and then she was taking a nap. She said she'd find me if there were any discrepancies in Paris's story.

"Holly, make Alice see sense. She won't listen to me," Campbell said.

"I can speak for myself," Alice said. "Other than a sore head, I'm back to normal. I need to help Holly question the rest of the suspects about who tried to kill me. I'm sure, if I'm asking the questions, they won't be able to hide their guilt. They might even think I'm dead, and seeing me walking around will shock the truth out of them."

"I agree with Campbell. You stay in bed and sleep. And I've had help from Lady Philippa. Even Horatio has been guarding this bedroom to make sure no one comes in without his approval. The situation is under control."

It didn't feel under control. After speaking to Paris, I'd spoken to the rest of Alice's party about where they were at the time she was attacked, and they all had alibis. Emma had been speaking with Clay about Delphine's funeral, and Tabitha had been with Verity, and they were painting each other's toenails.

"Did you know about Paris's eating disorder?" I said to Alice.

She wrinkled her nose. "I had an idea something was wrong with her. Paris would often overindulge when we went to dinner, and then disappear a few minutes after she'd cleared her plate. When she returned to the table, she'd always look gray and would chew gum. I asked her about it once, but she said it was nothing, just a habit she'd picked up through her work."

"It's common in the fashion world. There's too much pressure on women to stay thin," Campbell said.

"You know much about that world?" I arched an eyebrow.

"Don't you dare tell me you've dated a supermodel," Alice said.

He smiled. "I've run security detail at a few high class fashion events. Those models had nothing on you."

Alice swooned while I inspected the wallpaper.

"Where's Saracen? He should be back by now? I need a professional here in case this killer strikes again," Campbell said.

Alice clutched his arm. "You don't think they will, do you?"

He gritted his teeth and glanced at me. "It's just a precaution."

From his stern expression, I could tell he didn't think it was a precaution. I had the same concern. If Lady

Philippa's prediction was right, and they usually were, the killer would try again. Alice wasn't out of danger.

Campbell picked up his phone, scowled at it, and threw it down. "Why does nothing work around here?"

"Saracen would get back if he could," I said. "Have you seen the snow? It's getting worse."

"He's a former special forces operative. Snow is irrelevant."

"Do special forces operatives eat snow for breakfast?"

"And rocks. Annoying bakers, too, if they get too irritating."

I chuckled. "I doubt Saracen thinks this terrible weather is irrelevant. I'm sure he's feeling guilty. He'll arrive when the police get the road clear enough to travel."

Campbell harrumphed out his dissatisfaction. "Maybe they'll arrive by the end of January, when we're all frozen and starved."

I plumped Alice's pillow and tried to do the same to Campbell's but got growled at, so gave up. "A positive attitude goes a long way to solving everything."

"Don't throw your positive nonsense at me. Saracen needs to get back here. I can't have an aged, flatulent corgi as Alice's only guard," Campbell said.

"We've also got Granny, Rupert, and Holly," Alice said.

"Forgive me for criticizing your family, but Lady Philippa has been warned by her doctor not to overexert herself. And Lord Rupert—"

I stiffened. "Yes? What about my excellent husband?"

Campbell shrugged. "I wouldn't pick him to go into battle with."

"Then you're losing an asset. Rupert is loyal and dependable," I said.

"Perhaps if he whacked someone with one of those hardback books he's always carrying, he could cause damage."

Alice thumped Campbell's chest. "Rupert would help, if I insisted. And we also have Chef Heston. He was such a hero, bringing me back through the snow. I'll have to get him a special Christmas gift."

"You focus on getting better," I said.

She sighed. "I am better. You two are fussing over nothing."

The landline at the bottom of the stairs rang.

I was already racing out the door as Campbell yelled at me to answer it. I sprinted down the stairs and grabbed it. "Hello? Audley Castle."

"Who is that?"

I recognized Detective Inspector Gerald's unfriendly, nasal tone. "It's Holly Holmes. Well, Holly Audley. Holly Audley-Holmes if you want to get into the nitty gritty. I tried to reach you earlier today. We've had a development. What progress have you made?"

There was a second of silence. "Is Lord Rupert there?"

"Yes, but I don't have time to get him. The line isn't stable. Tell me everything, and I'll pass on the information. When will you be able to get here?"

A huff came down the line. "The investigation is still ongoing. We have a snow plow. We'll be at the castle soon."

"Tonight? It's already pitch black. Are you sure it's safe?"

"Will... Let you... Later."

"Say that again. The line is breaking up. Did you say you'd get here later tonight?"

"You... Have... Situation..."

"Listen! This is important. You don't know about Alice. Someone attacked her today. She may have a concussion. You need to bring an ambulance with you. I think the killer is still active. And they want something from Alice. Something they're prepared to kill for."

There was a static hiss, and the line died.

I groaned and set the phone in its cradle. I had no idea when Detective Inspector Gerald would get here, or if he'd heard me when I'd told him about Alice. Would he risk life and limb to travel over the ice and snow when it was already dark? He didn't have an adventurous spirit, and he was no friend to me or the Audleys.

I had no choice but to keep poking around. It was time to do things the old-fashioned way. There had to be a clue somewhere to reveal who killed Delphine and attacked Alice. And that clue was hidden somewhere in the castle.

After climbing the stairs, I walked back into Campbell's bedroom.

"Who was it? Was it Saracen? Is he coming back?" he asked.

"It was Detective Inspector Gerald. I only got half the message, but he said they've got a snow plow, and they'll be here soon."

"In an hour? Two?"

"I don't know. The line broke up. He said something about a situation, though. I wonder if he meant Alice, or if he has information about Delphine's killer. I told him Alice had been attacked, but I don't think he heard me."

"The man is hopeless." Campbell thumped a hand on the bed. "I wouldn't put him in charge of a snowball fight, let alone solving a murder and a vicious attack on Alice."

"Which is why we have to solve this," I said. "I'm going to search everyone's things for evidence."

Campbell's snort was derisive. "People don't hide poison bottles and evil written plans to whack someone on the head in their sock drawer."

"I won't be looking for a bottle labeled aconite poison." There was a tart crispness to my tone. "But there are always clues if you look hard enough. Something is always left behind."

"You don't know what you're looking for, or even where to look," Campbell said. "It's a waste of time."

Alice whacked him on the arm. "Holly is doing her best. My head hurts, so I'm no good to her, and I know your foot is troubling you, even though you won't admit it. We have to trust Holly can do this."

"You can't rummage around randomly, hoping to find something useful," Campbell said.

"Have you got any better ideas?" I crossed my arms over my chest and summoned my sternest glower, even though I looked ridiculously unscary in Alice's pale pink gown.

He grumbled a few times but came up with no clever plan to flush out the killer.

"Didn't think so. Everyone has been questioned about where they were when Delphine was killed. I've also questioned everyone about where they were when Alice was attacked. That gave me nothing. All we have so far is evidence of the pills and the poisoned cupcakes, which link to Alice."

"And we know those cakes were planted at the crime scene," Campbell said.

"We do. And I'll admit, I don't know what I'm looking for, but I must do something. I'm not waiting for them to try again."

"What if they succeed the next time?" Alice clung to Campbell but gave me a sly wink. She knew just how to press his buttons and make sure he agreed to me snooping.

He was quiet for several seconds, his gaze on Alice. "You think there's a connection between Delphine's murder and what happened to Alice?"

"Most likely. And I know you don't think much of Lady Philippa's predictions, but she's certain Alice has something the killer wants."

Campbell sighed. "Don't listen to the ramblings of an eccentric old woman."

"Hey! That eccentric old woman is wonderful. Even if she can be a little strange," Alice said.

"I believe Lady Philippa," I said. "And one murder and another attempted murder within a few days of each other isn't a coincidence. I have to look into what connects them."

"I have no way of stopping you." Campbell gestured to his foot. "And I'm not leaving Alice."

"You're not. Although, I won't need your assistance in the bathroom again. That was humiliating. There are some things that must remain private between a couple." Alice reached over and took my hand. "You do what you have to do. But stay safe. If the killer knows you're onto them, you could be their next victim."

I put on a brave face, even though I didn't feel brave. "I'll take Meatball with me. He'll alert me if I'm in any danger."

Campbell opened his mouth as if to protest, but Alice pressed a finger against his lips. "No more criticism. Holly will solve this, and you'll thank her when she does. That thank you will include a huge Christmas present. Whatever she likes."

His eyes narrowed, but he nodded. "Don't get yourself killed, Holmes. Alice doesn't need another terrible early Christmas gift."

"Neither do I. I'll report back when I have news." I slid out of the bedroom with Meatball and eased the door shut. Horatio was outside. He was asleep and snoring.

I gently nudged him with my toe. "Hey, guard dog. Get up."

He grunted and rolled onto his side.

I shook my head. Some protector he was. I crept along the corridor to Paris's bedroom and pressed my ear against it. I heard footsteps as she walked around and the faint rustling of something plastic, suggesting she'd gotten her hands on more sweet treats.

Next, I went to Clay's room. The door was shut, and light filtered under the gap, suggesting he was in there.

I had better luck with Verity's room. There was no light on, and I waited for several seconds, listening for signs of life, but there were none.

I knocked. "Verity, are you there? I wanted to see if you needed anything." Why not play up to my obedient servant role if it got me what I wanted?

There was no response.

I tried the handle and found the door unlocked. I poked my head around it. "Verity. It's Holly. I just wondered if you needed tea or a snack." It took a moment for my eyes to adjust, but there was a bright moon already in the sky, which splayed light across the bedroom. The room was empty.

I sat Meatball by the door to alert me if anyone came near, then hurried in and turned on a bedside light. I started with Verity's luggage, flipping open the large case she'd brought with her and rifling through the pockets. There was nothing useful in there, unless you liked tiny slips of silk underwear. How does she keep her important bits warm in something so small?

There was an open laptop on the bed, but the screen was blank. I brought it to life, but it was password protected. I checked through the notepad left beside it.

Boarding school threesome.

Possible bribe by an unethical company?

Lied about family lineage.

Slept with a politician. An old one!

Horrible person who deserved everything she got.

I turned the page. Delphine's name was written several times and then scrubbed through with such viciousness there was a hole in the paper. Underneath the scribbled out name was a list of magazines and newspapers. Several were crossed through, but there were ticks beside a few.

I read through it all again. Had Verity been planning a hate campaign against Delphine? Everything on that list could relate to her dead friend. But why do that?

Footsteps approaching the door had me turning. I grabbed the notepad and looked for somewhere to hide. There was space under the bed. I dropped to my hands and knees and crawled underneath. "Meatball, follow me."

He wagged his tail and shimmied under the bed, getting in prime face licking position before I could stop him.

We made it just in time, because a second later, the door creaked open.

"Verity, are you in here?"

My eyes widened. It was Clay.

"Darling, where are you? No one else is about, so I thought we could have some fun before lights out."

I sucked in a breath and clapped a hand over my mouth. Verity and Clay were having an affair?

Dottie dashed into the room just as the door swung shut. She lifted her nose and sniffed, then headed for our hiding place.

I shook my head and gestured for her to go away.

Meatball gently whined, torn between his loyalty to me and his love for his new fluffy girlfriend.

Dottie bounced by the end of the bed, then barked and dropped into a play position, with her butt in the air and front legs pressed on the carpet.

"Hey! What are you doing in here?" Clay said.

Dottie continued barking, despite my efforts to shoo her away.

"Have you got something under there? It better not be Verity hiding from me." A second later, Clay's face appeared.

I could do nothing to conceal my location, so I smiled and waved. How would I explain this?

Chapter 18

"What are you doing under Verity's bed?" Clay blinked several times, suggesting he couldn't believe he'd seen me.

Dottie bounced around and then wriggled under the bed to join Meatball and engage in nose snuffling.

"I... I was looking for my dog. And here he is." I rolled out, clutching the notebook I'd taken with me to my chest.

"Oh! Of course. I suppose the little terror didn't want to come out." Clay glanced at the door, tugging on the tailored cuffs of his suit jacket. "I was looking for Verity. I see she's not here, though. I'll go."

"To have fun with her?" I said.

Clay had already turned and was walking to the door. He stopped and looked back at me. "Well, yes. I thought we could... play cards or something. There's not much to do around here."

The door opened and Verity appeared. Her eyebrows shot up as she looked at Clay and then at me. "What's going on here?"

"Nothing!" Clay hurried over and caught hold of her elbow. "Holly was looking for her dog."

Verity frowned and her gaze went to the notepad. Her expression tightened, and she marched over. "That's mine. What are you doing with it?"

I had no time to pull any punches. "You two are having an affair, aren't you?"

Verity leaned back as if my words stung her. "That's impossible. I'm single and Clay's fiancée is dead. Who would we be cheating on?"

"No!" Clay said rapidly. "I was engaged to Delphine. We were happy. I'd never cheat."

Verity's glare was tainted with rage. "Ignore Holly. She's stirring trouble. Alice told me you liked to poke around in things that are none of your business. Got a bit of a name for yourself."

"For being an excellent baker, you mean?"

Verity jabbed a finger in my face. "For being a nosy, irritating busybody who interferes in matters above her station."

"Steady on, V. Holly isn't here to cause problems." Clay looked at me. "Are you? We can keep this between us. No one's getting hurt."

"If you're not seeing each other, why call Verity darling?" I was undeterred by Verity's rudeness. It showed she had something to hide. "The fun you wanted had nothing to do with cards. You were seeing each other behind Delphine's back. Did she find out?"

Verity shot a vicious look at Clay. "Idiot! I told you somebody would figure it out if you showed up here. You should have stuck to the plan."

Clay gestured at me. "Holly knows nothing. I'm sure we can find something to convince her to forget ever being in this room and misunderstanding what she heard. Isn't that right?"

Verity stepped back and closed the bedroom door. "If she's half as saintly as Alice makes out, this one isn't open to being bribed."

I nodded. "Money doesn't interest me."

"Maybe the truth will. The truth about Delphine."

"Verity, maybe you shouldn't," Clay said.

She raised a hand, and Clay stopped talking. "What if we were seeing each other? Clay and Delphine were unhappy. Doesn't everyone deserve to be happy?"

"I never said I was unhappy with Delphine," he spluttered.

Verity stuck her hands onto her hips. "You hated her almost as much as I did."

"From my encounters with Delphine, I understand she was difficult to get along with. What did she do to you to make you dislike her so much?" I said.

"She was a spiteful cow who delighted in making other people miserable. There was something wrong with her. She was only happy if someone was crying."

"So you did something about it?"

"I didn't kill her, if that's what you're thinking," Verity said. "Although the thought crossed my mind more than once. I knew what Delphine was like when she targeted someone. She wouldn't let go until they were ruined. She even had a hit list of people she wanted to bring down. The people who'd stood up against her, or said something nasty about her. Delphine knew how to hold a grudge."

"Yet you remained friends. Did you fake the friendship to avoid her spite?" I said.

"Of course. Why else? Delphine was a horrible person, but she had power, money, and influence. It was a case of better the devil you know. I knew it wouldn't be long before someone snapped and dealt with her. Now, she's got a taste of her own medicine."

"Delphine never killed anyone, though."

"She killed reputations. And one girl took her own life not long after an article was posted about her. Delphine picked on a vulnerable person to bully," Verity said.

"We don't know that for certain," Clay said. "Delphine had a sharp side, but she was as troubled as everybody else."

"Because she found out you were cheating on her?" I said.

"Delphine would only have cared about that if there was a risk of it becoming public knowledge," Verity said. "She wasn't marrying Clay because she loved him."

"She cared for me," Clay said.

"She cared about your social standing and what your family name brought to the arrangement."

Clay frowned but didn't disagree. "I just wanted to keep the peace. You know what my parents are like."

"I don't," I said. "But I've heard they were keen on you and Delphine marrying."

He lifted one shoulder. "They're traditional."

Verity smirked. "Try Victorian. If they had their way, there'd still be balls to pick suitable partners. Clay has to marry within a certain class, or it's not seen as respectable. Unlike the Audleys, who let their children marry whoever they want."

"You're fortunate," Clay said. "As are Rupert and Alice. When I was growing up, my parents nudged me toward Delphine. I was never interested, and I thought they were joking. But on my eighteenth birthday, my father pulled me aside and said it was a serious match and I should get to know her better. I was stunned. I didn't want my future wife to be decided by my parents."

"But you dated her, anyway?" I said.

"He has his ginormous trust fund to consider," Verity said.

"I make no apologies for that. I wasn't academic and didn't excel in sport, so had no focus when I finished school. The older I got, the more the suggestion of marriage became an order. I had no choice but to give it a go."

"That sounds awful," I said.

"Fortunately for me, Delphine was always busy. She went out every night to get gossip for her blog, and when

192

she wasn't doing that, she acted like the perfect daughter and attended family events. I saw little her." Clay scuffed a foot across the carpet. "She didn't love me. Yes, she liked my family name and the fact we looked great together in pictures, but I was a commodity she could use."

"Just as you did to her," Verity said. "You've told me about the bonus your parents were giving you when you married."

"Thanks for sharing that." He glared at Verity. "That was meant to stay between us."

"If you were so unhappy with Delphine, why did you show up here?" I said.

"He got an ultimatum," Verity said. "His father told him if he didn't set a date for the wedding by New Year's Eve, his trust fund would be taken away."

"I told you that in secret," Clay said.

"Holly likes to know our secrets." Verity was staring at the notebook I still held.

"I'm not hunting for your secrets because I want to use them like Delphine, but someone is framing Alice for Delphine's murder. I know Alice didn't do it, so I need to find out who did."

"Why couldn't Alice have killed her?" Verity said. "Delphine was horrible to her when we were younger. She once locked her in a closet and wouldn't let her out for three hours. She picked on Alice because she was so sweet. She used to say no one could be that nice."

"Alice hinted about bad times at boarding school," I said. "But she's my closest friend, and I know she didn't do this."

"Don't let the guise of friendship fool you," Verity said. "It's easy to fake. I'd been doing it for years with Delphine. She never knew how much I loathed her."

"Looking through this notepad, you'd decided things had to change," I said. "You were planning on ruining Delphine, just as she'd done to other people."

Clay stared at Verity. "Was that your plan?"

Verity shrugged. "As I said, she needed a taste of her own medicine. She wasn't as perfect as she made out. She lied and cheated her way to fame. And your fake relationship would have been easy to expose."

"And take me down, too! Verity, say it isn't so. I thought we had something."

"We had fun. And it felt great to get one over on Little Miss Perfect by stealing you away from her. But that's all this was. I know you're not exclusive with me. You're seeing someone else."

Clay spent several seconds tugging at his cuffs again. "You said you cared about me."

"Oh, angel, I do in my own way. I cared very much about showing the world what a fake Delphine was." Verity patted his cheek. "No hard feelings."

He spluttered out a few words before drawing in a breath. "This is over."

"Fine by me. You're no use to me now, anyway. With Delphine dead, any scandal that comes out will be wiped away because of her tragic death." Verity focused on me. "That's why I didn't kill her. Delphine's no good to me dead. I can't see her breakdown when she's in the grave. My plan was to discredit everything she'd done, so she'd be left with nothing. She'd be worse off than Emma."

Clay shook his head. "Verity, that's spiteful."

"I earned my A-Grade in Spite from the best, angel. Besides, Delphine will be forgotten in a few months when the next Queen Bitch takes the top spot and exposes everyone's vulnerabilities."

"Is that what you were planning on becoming?" I said. "You wanted to step into her shoes?"

"I have no desire to become the next Delphine," Verity said. "Perhaps I intended to plant a few stories and get people asking questions about her to expose her as a fraud. I don't have to bother, anymore. Someone's done me a favor by getting rid of her. And if that someone was Alice, then I'll hug her."

"It wasn't Alice," I said. "But you've just given me excellent motives for wanting Delphine dead."

Clay gulped and glanced at Verity. "It wasn't either of us. I didn't like Delphine, but I'd never kill her."

"And as I've revealed, I wanted to look her in the eyes when I brought her to her knees," Verity said. "Besides, we were together the evening she died."

"That's right," Clay said. "I suggested to Verity we escape the party. I went to Delphine's room and checked if she was awake on my way to see Verity. I wanted to ensure she didn't catch us."

"Delphine trusted no one," Verity said. "She worried we were out to stab her in the back."

With these friends, she'd hit that assumption on the nose.

"I went to her room and heard Delphine talking," Clay said. "I wondered if she was talking to another guy on her phone. She never admitted she cheated, but we hadn't been romantic with each other for some time."

"It's convenient you now alibi for each other," I said. "All that suggests is you were in on this together."

"I have proof! Pictures. They're time stamped." Verity pulled out her phone, scrolled for a few seconds, and handed it to me.

My cheeks flushed at the lewd images of Verity and Clay together in various stages of undress.

"Those are for our private use," Clay said. "You're not supposed to share."

"Idiot! I'll share them with whoever I like if it stops me from being a murder suspect. You see. We weren't killing

Delphine, we were having fun. The kind of fun lacking in Delphine and Clay's fake relationship."

After a skim through the images, I handed the phone back. I was no tech expert, but maybe picture timestamps could be faked. As far as I was concerned, they stayed on my suspect list.

"I'll have that notepad back, too," Verity said.

I held onto it. "It's evidence in the murder investigation."

"It's evidence you're snooping into something that doesn't concern you." Verity tried to yank the notepad out of my hand. "Give it to me. It's mine."

Meatball stopped flirting with Dottie and growled at Verity.

"Keep that flea-bitten thing away from me." She got hold of the notepad.

I let her have it. Although it was a useful source of evidence, I could remember the names of the newspapers and journalists Verity contacted to smear Delphine's reputation. The police could contact them and verify what Verity had been attempting.

"Holly, don't think badly of us." Clay's tone was placating. "We were in a difficult situation. Delphine had control over us. If we'd tried to change things, she'd have destroyed us. All I want is a quiet life."

"And your trust fund money." A smirk distorted Verity's pretty face.

"Money is important. Anyone who tells you otherwise is lying," he said.

"If you hadn't been with me that night, I'd have thought you'd done it," Verity said.

Clay's forehead furrowed. "Likewise. All you did when we were together was complain about Delphine. It got boring." He looked at me and clasped his hands together. "Are you sure there's nothing you need that'll help you forget this unfortunate mess?"

"Any information I find that'll clear Alice's name will go to the police. They have to know about your relationship and what you were planning, Verity."

"I'll show them the pictures," she said. "I have nothing to hide. If giving the police a thrill by seeing me straddling Clay is what it takes, I'll do it. Now, it's late and I'm tired. Tired of being accused of something I didn't do."

Clay looked almost apologetic as Verity hustled me to the door. "I'm sure this'll be cleared up once the police have poked around."

"Get rid of those mutts, Clay. Do something useful for once," Verity snapped.

Clay needn't have worried about the dogs. Where I went, Meatball followed. And it seemed so did Dottie, but she was much more interested in Meatball than me.

I'd gotten plenty of information out of Clay and Verity thanks to this surprise encounter. Perhaps it was enough to ensure the police would focus on them and not Alice when they finally arrived.

Verity opened the bedroom door. "Good night and good riddance."

I walked out with Clay, Meatball, and Dottie, and the door slammed behind us.

He looked at me and shrugged. "I'm not a bad person. I'm just not great at making good decisions. As you can see, my decisions about women are never sensible. Good night, Holly."

I nodded a good night as I pondered this new information. Tomorrow would be Christmas Eve, and I had to figure this mystery out by then, or we'd be remembering the season for all the wrong reasons.

Chapter 19

"Hey! Wake up."

I surfaced from sleep to feel my nose being pinched. I cracked open an eye. "Alice! What are you doing in our bedroom?" I glanced over to see Rupert on his side, fortunately still fast asleep.

"I had to talk to you, and my silly phone's not working, so I couldn't send you a message."

I pressed a finger to my lips. I'd gotten back late from my snooping around the castle, and then stayed up talking to Rupert about what my next step should be. When I'd finally gotten to sleep, all I'd dreamed about was who the killer was.

Alice raised her eyebrows and sniffed, and as I blinked the sleep out of my eyes, I saw her cheeks were blotchy and her eyes puffy. I pointed at the bedroom door, then slid out of bed, grabbed my thickest robe, and ushered her out, easing the door shut behind me.

Meatball lifted his head and watched us for a second from a warm spot by the hearth, before shutting his eyes again. It was too early for him, too.

"What's the matter?" I whispered.

Alice heaved out a sigh. "I've made an awful discovery."

"It's not the police, is it? They're not here to arrest you?"

"No, this has nothing to do with the police. Look at this." She thrust a photograph at me.

I headed into the kitchen and switched on the light so I could get a better look. I also turned on the kettle and grabbed a blanket off the back of the couch and threw it over my shoulders.

"Do you see?" Alice followed me around the kitchen like a sad, sniffy shadow.

"It's a picture of Campbell."

"Yes! With another woman. Holly, he's cheating on me."

I brought the picture closer to my tired eyes. "How can you tell?"

"He has his arm around her shoulders and he looks happy. He rarely looks that happy when he's with me."

I handed her back the picture and massaged my forehead with my fingertips. "Before we go any further, I need caffeine. Do you want anything?"

"A huge hot chocolate and to bury my face in a cake. A big one with extra frosting and caramel drizzle. I can't believe this. Campbell told me he loved me. He said he wanted to be with me for the rest of our lives. Now, I find this!" She waved the picture in the air.

I couldn't muster the energy to make hot chocolate, so brewed strong coffee and lifted mint frosted cupcakes, the unpoisoned kind, out of the fridge and set them in front of Alice. I grabbed squirty cream and topped her coffee with it. "This will have to do."

Alice grabbed a cupcake and bit into it. "Should I leave him? Confront him and demand answers? What about the other woman? What sort of person cheats? I've been such an idiot to think I found my happily ever after. Everyone knows I'm a disaster with relationships. But... but I thought this time was different."

I took several sips of my coffee, while Meatball moseyed over and comforted Alice by licking her hand.

She lifted him onto her lap and hugged him. "I'll become one of those crazy spinsters who has hundreds of animals and lives in a crumbling old castle alone. I'm done with men. At least you can rely on Meatball not to run off with another woman."

"Not so much these days since he's got Dottie," I said. "But you're right. Dogs are loyal."

"Unlike men. Unlike Campbell. I don't know what to do. There was I, about to propose to him, and he's seeing someone else."

Now the coffee pleasantly roamed through my system, I could get my thoughts in order. "Let me look at the picture again."

She thumped it on the kitchen worktop. "Keep it. I never want to look at it again. Although the hideous image is burned into my eyes for eternity."

I slid the picture closer and inspected it. "Alice, this is old. And who prints photographs, anymore? Everyone stores them on their cameras or in the cloud."

"Campbell must have had this one printed because she's so important to him." Alice ate another cupcake, while Meatball licked her chin to get the frosting that had missed her mouth.

I took a good look at the photograph. "This must be at least five years old. Campbell looks less wrinkled and has more hair."

"He's got plenty of hair! He just keeps it short. Not that I care what he does with his hair. He can grow it to his waist. See how many women want him then. Cheating swine!"

"Take off your jealousy goggles and have another look. This wasn't taken recently."

Her red-rimmed eyes narrowed. "Do I have to?"

"Yes, unless you want a reason to break up with Campbell."

"Of course not. I love him. Well, I loved him until I found out what he's been up to behind my back. When does he even have the time to cheat on me?"

"That's another reason to take a pause. Campbell is always busy. He's either working or he's with you. And he rarely goes out on his own."

"He did three weeks ago. I begged to go with him because I was bored, but he said he needed to get something special for my Christmas gift and didn't want to spoil the surprise."

"You think he went to see this mystery woman in the old photograph?"

"Why not? It's possible."

"The better question to ask is why would he do that when he's got you?"

Alice huffed out a breath and fed Meatball a dollop of frosting.

"I don't think he's cheating. Take a deep breath and have another look." I'd had my disagreements with Campbell over the years, but I couldn't deny he was perfect for Alice. They made each other blissfully happy.

Alice ate her third cupcake before she was fortified enough to grab the photograph. She stared at it for several minutes.

I said nothing, simply drank coffee and petted Meatball.

Her mouth twisted to the side. "Maybe you're right. He does look a little younger. Still so handsome, don't you think?"

"Divine. Alice, you've both had relationships with other people. I expect you have a few old pictures of former boyfriends tucked away somewhere."

"Unfortunately. I had to do a ghastly photoshoot with that awful man I got engaged to," Alice said. "There were dozens of pictures of us in awkward poses pretending to be happy. The Duke even wanted to put one in the portrait gallery."

"And I expect Campbell has seen them. He didn't jump to conclusions and assume you were cheating, did he?"

She let out a slow breath. "No. And... you're right. He wouldn't cheat. I just found the picture and panicked. It's the stress of this murder, the poison found in my cupcakes, and figuring out the perfect proposal. I'm not thinking straight."

"You've also had rotten luck with men, so I get why you're cautious. But that's in the past. Focus on your present with Campbell."

"And our future? When we're married?"

"Exactly! Let's celebrate with more coffee and squirty cream, shall we?" I topped up our mugs. "Where did you find that picture, anyway?"

"Campbell insisted I stay in bed and rest, but I got bored. When he fell asleep, I had a look around. I found a box in the back of his closet and opened it."

I grimaced. "Never do that. When someone puts a box in the back of anywhere, it means they don't want anyone to look inside it."

"And I know that now, but I needed something to do. There were lots of letters and pictures of Campbell with friends. Even pictures of him in his military uniform, and some medals. He looked so handsome. But my heart almost stopped when I found this picture of him with another woman."

I pulled the picture back to me. I couldn't place her, but the woman looked familiar. I'd only known Campbell since moving to Audley St. Mary, and I didn't think she lived around here.

"What's going on?" Rupert stumbled out of the bedroom. "It's only just gone six in the morning. Alice, what are you doing here?"

"Nothing. Go back to bed," she said.

"I can't. I woke to find Holly gone, and then I heard voices." He rubbed his eyes. "It's not news from the police, is it?"

I grinned at Alice. "Just a small misunderstanding. Everything is sorted."

"Holly fixed it. You know what I'm like, always jumping to the wrong conclusions," Alice said. "Stop standing there and making the place look messy."

Rupert's expression turned exasperated. "This is my home. If I want to stand here and make it look messy, I will."

"Or you could sit with us and have a coffee," I gently suggested.

"Or Alice could go home and let us sleep peacefully in our bed."

As they bickered, I kept looking at the picture. The more I stared at the woman's face, the more I was certain I knew her. I lifted it close to my face and then moved it away.

"Holly, tell Rupert he's an idiot," Alice said.

"I'm Switzerland in your arguments," I said. "I'm not taking sides with either my husband or my sister-in-law. It would be reckless."

"He's being annoying, as usual."

"And you're being ditzy. Why aren't you resting, anyway?"

Alice groaned. "You sound like Campbell."

"Only posher." I slid the photo into my robe pocket. "Rupert, could I have a word in private?"

"Don't keep secrets from me." Alice's bottom lip jutted out. "I knew this would happen once you got married."

"It's about your Christmas gift. You don't want to spoil the surprise, do you?"

Her pouting lessened. "I suppose not."

"Please, take me away. It's too early in the day to be Aliced," Rupert said.

I grabbed his hand and tugged him back into the bedroom before he continued the argument. "I need to visit the castle. And I need you to keep Alice distracted while I'm gone."

"Why? What's going on?"

"I have to check on something. I could be wrong, but I must be sure."

Rupert grimaced. "It's not something dangerous, is it?"

"It's a hunch. Go talk to Alice about her planned proposal to Campbell. That'll get her attention, and she won't notice me leave. I won't be long."

"I should come with you."

"No, I'll be fine. And Alice has already had a stressful start to the day. I don't want to give her anything else to worry about until I'm certain."

"Certain about..."

I kissed him, and Rupert sighed, knowing he wouldn't win this battle.

"Be safe. Don't do anything too heroic," he said.

"I'll only be the hero if I absolutely have to."

While Rupert returned to bicker with his sister, I dressed and slipped back into the living room. I tiptoed past the kitchen, stopping when I discovered Meatball waiting expectantly at the door.

I pressed a finger to my lips and slid the front door open. I eased it shut, and we hurried away through the snow. I walked briskly to the castle, while Meatball dived about, did his business, and had a marvelous time eating snow.

There was a worn path straight to the front door, since no new snow had fallen overnight, so it didn't take me long to get there.

I slipped off my boots and tiptoed up the stairs. I went to Emma's room and tapped on the door.

When there was no answer, I pushed it open. The bed was made, and the curtains pulled back, despite it still being gloomy outside.

I took out the photograph and looked at it. I couldn't be certain, but this young woman might be Emma. Different hairstyle and color. She'd possibly had work done on her nose, and I hadn't ever seen her without her glasses, but they could be sisters. Or maybe the same person.

After easing the door shut, I left Meatball standing beside it. I hurried to the closet and opened the door. There were a few items of clothing hung up, and underneath them was a small suitcase. I pulled it out, opened it, and looked through the contents. It wasn't until I got to the last pocket that I found travel documents for two people. Emma Colby and Campbell Milligan.

For a second, I was thrown back to Alice's discovery. Was Campbell having an affair?

That made no sense. Campbell was a man of honor. The whole time I'd worked in the Audley Castle kitchen, he'd been in love with Alice. He'd kept it well hidden, but I'd seen by the way he looked at her, protected her, and made sure no one spoke badly about her. His love was deep and enduring. Campbell would never cheat.

So why did Emma have travel documents for both of them?

I found nothing else useful, but I kept the documents out and placed them on the bed.

I searched the desk in the room, and then moved to Emma's laptop that sat on the bed. She had papers beside it, and I sorted through them. There was a travel itinerary and a list of wedding chapels.

Her phone pinged, making me jump. I grabbed it off the bedside cabinet. I could only read a small amount of the message, but that wasn't what caught my eye. The image on Emma's lock screen was of Campbell. And it had been taken recently.

I laid everything out and studied it. There were no coincidences. Emma hadn't gotten her job with Delphine by accident. She had pictures of Campbell, old and new. And even though his name was on the travel documents, I was certain he had no knowledge of this planned trip.

And then there was Campbell's car accident. Had it been an accident? Or a way to stop him from recognizing Emma while she put her plan into action?

Meatball yipped and backed away from the door.

I grabbed the paperwork and looked around, but before I could hide, the bedroom door opened, and Emma stood outside. "Holly! Do you need something?"

I sucked in a breath as her gaze skittered over the evidence I had clasped in my hands. "Yes. I need a confession that you murdered Delphine and attempted to frame Alice for it."

Her eyes widened, then she gave a forced laugh. "I heard about Alice being attacked. You must be so stressed." She walked into the room. "Although that doesn't give you the right to poke around in my things."

"You left me no choice. After the attack on Alice, I realized the killer was stepping things up. I had to stop her."

Emma licked her lips. "Is that so? What are they planning on doing next, since you're so knowledgeable about the killer?"

"They were leaving, after Alice was charged with murdering Delphine."

Emma strode to the bed and grabbed the photograph of Campbell I'd missed. Her breathing grew shallow as she stared at it. "Where did you get this?"

"It's you, isn't it? You're older now, with different hair, and you've had work done on your nose and maybe cheek filler, too. But I recognize you. That's you with Campbell."

She brushed a thumb across the photo. "This was such a happy day. Campbell took me deep sea fishing. I didn't like to tell him, but I'm terrified of the sea. You never know what's lurking beneath the waves. But he was so calm and confident, and he showed me exactly what to do. He even talked about getting a boat and sailing off into the sunset."

"You planned to be with him when that happened?" I said.

"Campbell kept this picture, didn't he? That's how you found it." A smile lit her face. "I knew he still loved me."

"I didn't find it. Alice did. Emma, this was all you, wasn't it? You set this up so you could get to Campbell and get rid of Alice at the same time. But then things went wrong."

She narrowed her eyes as her icy gaze settled on me. "Prove it. And even if you can, you need to get out of this room alive."

Chapter 20

I took a step back. Anger blotted red marks across Emma's face and chest as she continued stroking the picture.

My heart beat out an erratic rhythm. I'd been so determined to reveal who tried to kill Alice, I hadn't stopped to think she'd want to silence me, too.

A movement in the corridor caught my eye, and although I remained focused on Emma, I spotted Verity with her phone held up. Was she calling for help, or taking a selfie?

"The proof of your involvement is right here." I lifted the papers. "And you've given yourself away by admitting you know Campbell. You said he still loves you. You do look happy in that picture."

"We were. And he does love me. He was terrible at showing his feelings, though. I once said he reminded me of an iceberg. All that silent, invisible power, with so much more beneath the surface." Despite Emma's threat to kill me, she was fixated on the photograph.

"How long were you together?"

"Long enough to know he was perfect for me."

"Six weeks, six months, six years?"

"It's not important. It's what we felt for each other that mattered." She pressed the picture against her heart. "I knew Campbell wouldn't be able to hold out once

I came back into his life. He'd realize how deep his feelings for me were. He'd declare his love, and we'd leave together."

"And if he didn't?"

"That was never an option. Even if he'd resisted, he'd have come with me in the end. Nothing will stop us from being together."

"Campbell is a man of principles. He'd never up and leave everyone here."

Her top lip curled. "I know. He'd never abandon his position to follow his heart. He pledged to protect the Audley family, so that's what he's doing, even though his soul tells him true happiness is with me."

"His heart and soul tell him he's in love with Princess Alice Audley. That gives him even more reason to stay."

Emma smirked. "I've known Alice a long time, and despite her being sweet, she can't offer Campbell half of what I can."

"A life on the run from the police? Or an unstable, obsessional love that he doesn't feel for you?"

She scowled at me. "You've clearly never been in love."

"You know I'm happily married to Rupert."

"You got lucky there. You wouldn't have been interested if it weren't for the money and castle that comes with him."

I glowered at her. "I'd have married Rupert wherever he lived or whatever he did for a living."

She shrugged. "Then you know a little about matters of the heart. Campbell has been denying his feelings and putting his duty before his desires. I decided to make him see sense."

There was more movement in the corridor, although I couldn't see who it was.

I moved closer to the bed to keep Emma's attention. If she realized we had an audience, she'd stop talking.

"You've been planning this for a while. That picture of Campbell on your phone shows you've been watching him. You must have thought you landed on your feet when you got a job with Delphine, because you knew she'd be spending Christmas at Audley Castle, giving you access to Campbell."

"I made a few suggestions to Delphine about Christmas, and how she needed me by her side. She didn't protest. Especially since I kept groveling about how grateful I was for the job as her lowly assistant. She got a kick out of seeing me put in my place. She paid me the minimum wage and said I should be grateful."

"And you were, but not because of the money. It was an opportunity to get into the castle without question. Then what were you planning? Campbell is a big, tough guy. You can't have expected him to take your hand and walk off into the sunset."

"As I'm sure you're aware, Campbell has a stubborn streak. It would have taken me time and work, but I'd have gotten him to see sense."

"You're deluded if you think he'd have left with you."

A smile trembled across her mouth. "He wouldn't have had a choice. Not in his current situation. And I had other resources if he proved difficult."

"Delphine's pills. You had access to her medication. She wouldn't have noticed if a few pills went missing. You stole from her supply so you could drug Campbell?"

"Delphine always got so chatty when drugged. I figured the pills would do the same to Campbell. Lower his resistance until he confessed his feelings." Emma went to turn to the door, but I grabbed her arm.

"Campbell's car accident was no accident. You caused that, didn't you? You damaged the brakes."

"Again, that's something you'll never prove. And everyone keeps saying the roads around here are treacherous. What would seem more logical to the police: an accident because of bad weather, or a girlfriend tampering with her errant lover's brakes?"

"It was you. And you needed to make sure Campbell stayed in bed, because if he saw you, he'd recognize you. You've never been in the same room together since you got here. Delphine and her friends were obsessed with meeting Campbell, but you knew if he saw you, he'd reveal who you were."

"What if he did? I just needed time. And he'd be easier to deal with while injured."

"He wouldn't have been able to run away from you, you mean?"

Emma made a tsking sound several times. "After Campbell's anger fades, he'll be grateful to me. I'm getting him out of a dreadful situation. He can't seriously want to be with Alice. She's nice but hasn't had a sensible thought in her head for over a decade."

I heard a tiny squeak in the corridor, but kept a tight hold on Emma's arm so she only paid attention to me. "What went wrong? I don't think you planned to murder Alice, did you? Your plan was to have her blamed for Delphine's murder. With Alice out of the way, you had a clear path to Campbell. Of course, he'd have been heartbroken at losing her, but you'd have been there to comfort him."

She dug her fingernails into my hand. "That's enough guessing. I've got work to do, and you're stopping me."

"I can't let you leave with Campbell." I dashed to her closet and pulled out her luggage. I threw it on the floor and flipped the lid open.

"What are you doing?" Emma rushed over and tried to stop me.

"Looking for more evidence."

She caught hold of my hand. "There's nothing in there."

Meatball barked from the other side of the room. He was nosing at a carrier bag tucked beside the bed.

Emma lunged at him. "No! Get away from that."

I chased after Emma as she ran at Meatball. He grabbed the bag and dodged away with it in his mouth.

"Here, boy. Give me the bag." I jumped across the bed as Meatball did a circuit of the room, pursued by Emma.

Emma shrieked. "Stop him!"

"I plan to. Then I plan to see what you're hiding."

Meatball leaped onto the bed, and I gently tugged the bag out of his mouth. "What's in here? More evidence of your guilt?"

"It's nothing." Emma glared at Meatball. "I'm warning you, Holly, you don't want to mess with me."

Since there was definitely more than one person listening in the corridor, I took a chance. I opened the bag.

Emma screamed and tried to slap my face, but I dodged the blow and kept a firm hold on the bag while I wrestled her for it. Meatball barked and bounced up and down on the bed.

"You're crazy," Emma yelled. "Go away and leave me alone."

"Not as crazy as you. How could you think this would work?" I shoved her away, but she came back at me. "Campbell is happy in his job, and he loves Alice. She loves him. You're ancient history."

Emma slammed a hand against my shoulder so hard the bone jarred. "I'm his future. I'm all he wants."

I threw myself at Emma, sending her tumbling back. I landed on top of her and finally got the bag open and tipped it up. A long, silky dark wig fell out.

I rolled off Emma, held it up, and shook it out. "This looks like Delphine's hair."

Emma scrambled to her feet. "What if it does? It could be hers."

I drew in a breath. "It's yours. The timeline for Delphine's murder is wrong. Delphine died not long after she went to bed, didn't she? And when people saw her in the corridor, it was you impersonating her by using this wig." My gaze ran over her. "You're a similar build and height, so you could pull it off."

"It's only a wig! It proves nothing."

"You went up with Delphine the night you arrived. You gave her the usual amount of pills, but then what, you added more to the champagne? Did you bring that champagne up to her room and convince her to have a glass?"

Emma scowled at the wig. She paced the room, her fingers tapping against her arms. She was so engrossed in her thoughts, she didn't notice we had an audience.

"You made a mistake, didn't you?" I had to press for a confession. "That night, you planned to kill Delphine, but she had to be pliable before you fed her bitter tasting poisoned cupcakes to implicate Alice. Did you mess up the dosage of her sedative?"

"My plan was perfect." Emma turned and stalked toward me. "It was stupid Delphine. She must have been taking other medication without me knowing. She was always looking for some miracle pill to blot out her vacuous lifestyle."

"Delphine took those pills earlier in the evening. You gave her the usual dose of sedatives when she went to bed, and then added extra to her champagne. But because she already had drugs in her system, it was too much and she overdosed," I said. "Which meant you couldn't feed her the cupcakes you put poison in. The cakes that would have framed Alice."

Emma made a noise of disgust. "Delphine was the most poisonous thing here. She deserved everything she got."

"She wasn't nice, but no one deserves that. When you realized Delphine was dying, you had to force feed her cake. But you were too late. The cake never reached her stomach." A shiver of fear zigzagged down my spine, but I kept my chin up. "It must get easier to commit murder once you've done it before. That's why you went after Alice."

The smile Emma gave me sent another shiver through me. "You could be right. Delphine was a thorn in my side, and I hated her for treating me like a dogsbody. But I knew her connections would bring me to Campbell. The Christmas parties are always planned well in advance, and I followed Delphine on social media, so I knew everyone would be here. Although she didn't name the place, she dropped enough hints for me to know this was my chance."

"And you've been keeping tabs on Campbell, as those creepy photos you've taken with your phone show. You knew he worked here."

"Don't tell me you don't cyber-stalk old boyfriends. Everyone does it. That's what they created the internet for."

"No, I don't. It's creepy and inappropriate."

Emma rasped out her anger. "I always knew I'd be with Campbell forever. I just needed to find the right time. And it needed to be the right time for him, too. When we parted, he said he wasn't ready for commitment."

"That must have angered you." I needed to keep her talking, but I also needed an escape route in case things turned nasty and Emma blocked the only way out.

"Most men are slow on the uptake with commitment. I was willing to wait for him, though. And everything lined up when I got the job with Delphine and had less than a year to wait until I was right where I needed to be."

"Giving yourself time to plan what you'd do once you had access to Campbell."

"I went through dozens of scenarios, but the best one involved getting rid of Delphine, removing Alice by framing her for murder, and taking Campbell for myself." Emma pointed a finger at me and nodded. "Don't get me wrong, I like Alice. She was the least awful one in that group of skinny, snippy, nightmares."

"But Alice was in the way of your happily ever after. She was with Campbell, so you had to get rid of her." I glanced around the room. "And when the poisoned cupcakes didn't get her arrested, you needed to get her out of Campbell's life for good."

Emma's fingers flexed as her attention turned to Meatball. "If it weren't for your annoying dog chasing me away after I'd whacked Alice, I'd have succeeded."

Meatball bared his teeth at Emma.

"I expect you've gone as far as planting evidence in Alice's room to ensure the police have no doubt she's the killer."

Emma narrowed her eyes, then shrugged. "I should have recruited you as my sidekick, since you know it all."

"I'm Alice's sidekick, and she's mine. We look out for each other. That's what true friends do. We don't stab each other in the back, poison cakes we've made for friends, and then frame each other for murder because we have an unhealthy obsession with our past."

She sneered at me. "I didn't like you the second I saw you. Some people are too clever for their own good. But you're not that smart. It's just the two of us, and the evidence you have of my guilt is also here. And, as I've already made clear, you're not leaving this room alive."

The bedroom door slammed against the wall.

Emma jumped and spun around. Verity stood with her phone raised, recording everything. Alice, Clay, Paris, and Tabitha were also there. And behind them, balanced on his crutches, was Campbell. A very shocked, angry looking Campbell.

A breath whooshed out of Emma, and she reached for him. "You shouldn't be out of bed. I still have things to do before we leave."

He moved forward slowly on his crutches, assisted by Alice. "I wouldn't have believed any of this if I hadn't heard it come out of your mouth."

"Neither would we, but I got it recorded." Verity waved her phone in the air. "This'll create the biggest scandal. And what a shame, Delphine's not here to see it."

Clay glanced at her. "Now's not the time to gloat."

Verity shrugged. "It's no less than Delphine would have done."

"Not now!" Alice clutched Campbell's elbow as they moved closer. "Emma, how could you? We're friends."

Emma's focus was on Campbell, desperation in her eyes.

"We only dated for a couple of months," Campbell said. "I quickly realized Emma needed help. She was obsessional and clingy, and after our second date, she started talking about marriage and kids."

Emma sucked in a breath. "You told me you wanted six children."

"I was joking, and I thought you were, too. Then I found the wedding magazines and the fertility drugs. I knew then I had to call things off."

She giggled. "Campbell, you feel obligated to the Audley family and you don't want to hurt Alice, but we're perfect for each other. We're meant to be together. Leave Alice and come to me."

"He's not a dog. He doesn't obey commands." Alice's color was up, but her tone was even.

"I want nothing to do with you," Campbell said, not so calmly. "You messed with my life back then. You almost got me killed in a car crash. You murdered Delphine, and tried to frame the woman I intend to spend the rest of my life with."

"You mean me, right?" Alice whispered.

Campbell nodded.

"Emma, the game is up," I said. "Everyone heard you. There's nothing you can do to change what happens next."

She looked around the group, her eyes wide. "My friends won't believe you. Everyone, this is a joke. Don't believe this common piece of nothing over me!"

"We wouldn't have believed it if we hadn't heard you confess," Paris said.

"How did you know we were here?" I said.

Tabitha shook her head, as if not believing what she was seeing. "Alice told us."

I raised my eyebrows. "You were supposed to stay with Rupert while I checked out my suspicions about Emma."

Alice pursed her lips. "I knew my silly brother was up to something when he talked about rings and wed—" She froze. "I mean, dresses for you, Holly. After I twisted his arm, he told me you'd come here. So, I followed you. I overheard what was going on, so went and grabbed everyone else for backup, even though I wanted to charge in and smack you, Emma."

"We'd never have thought you capable of this," Paris said. "You were always so... bland."

"I'd say more beige," Verity said. "Maybe taupe on a good day."

Tabitha shrugged. "I always thought you were okay. Kind of forgettable, though."

Clay made no comment.

"The police will be here soon," I said after a few seconds of tense silence. "Let's all wait downstairs."

Emma raced to the window and pulled it open. "You're not spoiling my dream. It won't end like this."

Alice made a move to grab her, but Campbell held her back. "Emma, what you've done is terrible, but you're unwell. We can get you help."

"I want Campbell. He was never yours. You were a holding place while he got himself together and realized what he'd been missing." Emma leaned out of the window.

"I didn't miss you for a second," Campbell said.

"You'll be sorry you said that." Emma forced the window higher.

I inched toward her as she swung one leg over the ledge. "There are other options. I know you think you love Campbell, but there's so much more to life than chasing an impossible dream. Campbell's grumpy and he never talks about his feelings. You said yourself, he's like an iceberg. Who wants to hug an iceberg?"

Her gaze flickered to Campbell. "For all his faults, I still love him. And he loves me, too."

"Then explore that possibility together." I rubbed my hands up and down my arms as an icy wind blew through the room. "You and Campbell can talk and find a solution that works for both of you."

Emma hesitated, then shook her head. "You're tricking me. Everyone does that. It happened when my family lost their money. Then Delphine told me this job would lead to better things, but all I did was run around picking up her dry-cleaning and drugs. Even Campbell tricked me. He said the time wasn't right for us when we broke up. I thought he'd come back, but he never did. I waited for so long. Then I got tired of waiting. And I got tired of being lied to and deceived by everyone who should have looked after me."

I edged closer to the window. "I understand your anger, but there's a much better world waiting for you. And people can be nice. Not everyone wants to use you and then walk away."

Alice drew in a breath as she clutched Campbell's arm. "I'm not angry with you for trying to kill me and steal Campbell."

"I am," Campbell said.

I shot him a glare. That wasn't helpful. "Everyone has different feelings to work through, but we can do it together. You're not alone anymore, Emma. We're here to help you."

Emma's gaze went to Campbell and then Alice. "Liars! All of you." She pitched off the window ledge.

I raced forward and grabbed her shoulders. For a second, I had her, but Emma was being dragged down by gravity, and I was off balance.

Then, we were falling.

Chapter 21

The icy air froze my lungs as I plummeted, still clinging to Emma's shoulders.

I couldn't see her face, but she was screaming, and so was I. The rapid tumble through the air ended as we hit snow and it sprayed around us in a frosty cloud. My forehead whacked into the back of Emma's head, sending a ramrod of pain down my nose and jarring my teeth.

Then silence surrounded me.

And so did snow. We'd landed in an enormous bank of snow piled against the castle wall. Snow wasn't soft to land on, but it was more forgiving than concrete, and it had just saved my life. I'd also been clinging to Emma's back, so she hit the ground first and cushioned my fall.

My brain took a few seconds to catch up with the fact we'd stopped falling. I wriggled my fingers and toes. Everything worked.

I drew in a breath and nothing hurt other than my head. But I was alive, and all thanks to the snow that had caused so many problems.

Emma shifted beneath me and groaned.

I released my grip on her shoulders, slowly rolled away, and lay flat on my back, staring at the yellow and gray sky. There was a hint of weak winter sun poking through and looking down at me.

Verity, Tabitha, and Clay were peering out of the window I'd fallen from.

I tried to raise a hand to let them know I was alive, but nothing happened. It must be the shock. But I was breathing, nothing was broken, and I'd just uncovered who murdered Delphine and why.

If I hadn't been stunned, freezing, and processing the events of the last few minutes, I'd be smiling.

I looked at Emma. She was moving, her eyes open, but she must be in a world of hurt after that fall.

"Are you..." I coughed and tasted blood in my mouth. "Are you injured?"

Emma blinked once.

"Holly! Don't move." Alice skidded around the side of the castle. Chef Heston followed her, and not far behind him was Campbell on his crutches.

A small, sturdy ball of tan and white fur caught my attention as it blurred toward me. Meatball dashed through the snow on jet propelled paws, overtaking everyone.

He jumped and landed on my stomach. His nose dabbed mine, his tongue swiped my face, and he whined.

"I'm good. Although winded, thanks to those chunky paws." I hugged him and let him lick every inch of my face until he was reassured I was okay.

There was a second, higher-pitched bark, and Dottie trotted through the snow, shaking it off her dainty paws every few steps, not looking amused at being dragged outside to follow her new guy.

"Sorry, Dottie, but if you're sticking with Meatball, you'll have to get used to roughing it occasionally," I said.

She barked again, tilted her head from side to side, then wagged her tail.

"How badly are you broken?" Alice had slipped over and was being assisted by Chef Heston to get back on her feet.

I mustered my energy and gave her a weak wave.

Alice almost fell on me as she arrived. She caught hold of my hand, tears on her cheeks. "My heart leaped out of my chest when you went out of the window."

"I meant to stop Emma, not go down with her." I coughed again, and my ribs twinged. Maybe something had gotten bruised or cracked, after all.

"He's mine," Emma whispered. "Stay away from him."

Alice gasped, her eyes narrowing. "How are you alive?"

"We have the snow to thank for that." I looked at Emma. "Focus on your broken bones, not Campbell."

"You have the luck of the devil," Alice said to her. "I can usually find something nice to say about everyone, but there's nothing good about you. You tried to steal my boyfriend, frame me for murder, then kill me. And if that wasn't enough, you wanted to take my best friend with you when you swan dived out the window. You're a terrible, terrible person."

"I love him." Emma's gaze shifted as Campbell arrived with Chef Heston.

Meatball hopped off my stomach and danced around me, alternating between licking my face and barking.

I quietened him with several pets. "Help me up," I said to Alice. "It's freezing down here."

"You shouldn't move." Campbell's face was almost as white as the snow.

"Neither should you, but I don't see you following that instruction. I'm okay. I landed on Emma. I hit my head and bit my tongue, but everything is intact. Maybe some bruised ribs." I held up a hand and wriggled my fingers at Alice.

"It's a Christmas miracle." Chef Heston assisted me up. "When I heard everyone running down the stairs and yelling, I couldn't believe what they were saying."

"Stay away from him." Emma was also moving. She shuffled onto her side and closed her eyes for a second. "Campbell wants to be with me."

"What's she talking about?" Chef Heston said.

Rapid, crunching footsteps through the snow had me looking up. Rupert was running toward me. "I saw the fall. I was outside the cottage. I didn't know it was you! Are you hurt?"

I was happy to be engulfed in his warm hug. "No, just shocked. I'm not so sure about Emma, though."

"She's still talking, unfortunately," Campbell muttered.

Rupert peered into my face, one hand cupping my frozen cheek. "This was what you went to investigate? I've missed a lot."

I nodded. Overcome with exhaustion, I needed tea and cake to get my energy back before I could explain everything.

"You always miss the important things," Alice said. "Holly figured out who murdered Delphine and who tried to kill me."

"It was Emma?" Rupert said. "Why?"

"Because we love each other." There was a dribble of fresh blood at the corner of Emma's mouth.

I looked up at the window we'd fallen from. We should be dead. I shivered and leaned against Rupert for comfort, which he happily supplied.

Despite everything Emma had done, I felt a trickle of sympathy for her. She looked pitiful lying in the snow, her longing gaze on Campbell.

I crouched in the snow beside her. "I'm not sure how badly you're injured, so now is the right time to lay to rest your demons. Everything you've done shows your love was a fantasy. Campbell's happy with Alice."

"I'll get him back." Emma amazed me by struggling into a seated position. She wrapped an arm around her ribs as the color drained from her face, but she remained conscious. "Campbell is living a lie. I know him better than anybody else."

"You don't." Campbell's tone was as cold as the snow. "We weren't right for each other. My life is exactly how I want it to be. You've made a mistake."

"A big one," Alice said. "And it's caught up with you."

"I'm confused," Chef Heston said.

"So am I," Rupert said.

"Astonishing! You're both alive." Clay appeared with Verity, Paris, and Tabitha. Unlike the others, who were missing coats and hats, they'd taken their time to bundle up in warm clothing. Verity had her phone out and was taking pictures.

"We should go inside," Rupert said. "You need to get warm, and I should check your injuries."

"We will. But if Emma won't reveal the reason we're out here, I'll do it for her."

"No one will believe you," Emma said.

"After what I overheard, I'm willing to believe anything," Clay said.

"I'll make this quick. Despite Delphine giving you excellent motives for wanting her dead, you're all innocent," I said.

"I could have told you that," Verity said.

I arched an eyebrow but lowered it when it made my head throb. "Verity, you were running a hate campaign against Delphine and having an affair with Clay."

Verity's cheeks flushed, and she glanced at Clay.

"And Clay, you didn't even like the woman you were engaged to, which was why you couldn't keep your hands off other women. Not just Verity. You were seeing Emma, too. That was why you gave her an alibi for the time of Alice's attack."

224

He ducked his head and stuffed his hands into the pockets of his coat. "I never thought timid little Emma would do that. When she insisted we'd been together, I went along with it. I didn't realize I was covering up her sneaky attack."

Emma bared her teeth at him. "You're pathetic. Nothing like my Campbell."

Clay took a step back. "I'm just glad I found out before you came for me, too."

"You're not worth the effort."

"And Paris, you had an excellent reason for wanting Delphine gone." I wouldn't mention her eating disorder in front of everyone. It was a demon she needed to conquer, and with the friends she had, it was unlikely she'd get support from them.

Paris nodded and hugged herself.

"And Tabitha, you loved Delphine. She exploited that. She betrayed your friendship and your affection."

Tabitha's bottom lip jutted out. "I think she loved me a little."

"Despite these motives, none of you did it. Emma killed Delphine to frame Alice, so she could get Campbell to herself."

"Emma loves the bodyguard, too?" Paris's mouth dropped open.

"Emma and Campbell briefly dated years ago," I said. "Emma never accepted they'd split, so she devised a plan to get Campbell back."

"What's so special about this bodyguard that you're all falling in love with him?" Verity said. "I mean, he's easy on the eye, but am I missing something?"

I smiled as Campbell blushed. "He has a certain appeal. But Emma's love turned into an unhealthy obsession, and she decided to take Campbell. What tipped me off was an old photograph Alice found in Campbell's room. It showed him with Emma."

"It's proof he still loves me," Emma said.

"It's proof I forgot to throw it out," Campbell growled.

"There were also travel documents in Emma's room with their names on," I said. "And a wig she wore to impersonate Delphine after she'd killed her to muddle the timeline."

"Delphine hired someone who was crazy!" Verity said. "This has to go on her blog."

"No! This isn't some sordid tale to gossip about. These are people's lives. Everyone's been affected by this. Give me your phone so I can delete the pictures you've taken."

Verity shook her head. "They're mine."

Meatball jumped, knocking Verity into the snow and sending her phone flying.

"Good boy," I said as he leaped on Verity, happily assisted by Dottie.

Verity squealed and protested until Clay yanked her out of the snow.

"Delphine wasn't kind in the way she treated you all, gossiped about others, and used their misfortune to bring her fame, but be better people," I said.

After a moment of quiet, they mumbled their agreement. I wasn't convinced, but it was the best I could do.

A low rumbling reached my ears. As I looked around, a sigh of relief came out of me. A snow plow trundled along the drive, and behind it was a police car, an ambulance, and a tractor with Saracen at the wheel.

"Just when you figure everything out, the police swoop in and take the glory." Alice frowned and crossed her arms over her chest.

"I'm happy for them to swoop." I took a step toward the vehicles, but my knees wobbled.

Rupert kept a firm hold on me. "Stay where you are. Chef Heston, please greet our guests. Ask them to arrest

Emma and take her away as soon as she's fit to be moved. Let them know where Delphine's body is and that we're available for interviews, after my wife has received medical treatment."

I leaned against my marvelous husband, happy to let him take control. Falling out of a window had knocked the wind out of my sails, and from the pain in my forehead, I'd be sporting colorful bruises on Christmas morning. Goodness, that was tomorrow! What a lead up to the special day.

Chef Heston pulled his shoulders back. "Holly, will you fill in the gaps if I miss anything?"

"Of course, boss. That's what I'm here for."

Alice dived toward me and hugged me. "You did it. You've cleared my name, found the killer, and made sure our Christmas will be wonderful. Have I ever told you you're the best sister-in-law in the world?"

I grinned. "Once or twice. I feel the same about you."

"I want to hear everything. How you figured out it was Emma. Was it the picture? Yes, of course it was. What did she say when you confronted her? What about that wig Meatball found? Where did that come from? And—"

"Alice, later." Rupert gently nudged his sister back.

"I promise, we'll talk soon," I said. "What I need now, though, is to collapse on a couch with a cupcake and some pain pills."

Chapter 22

"Have a lovely Christmas." Alice waved wildly as she stood beside Campbell outside Audley Castle. I was with her, standing with Rupert to see off her friends, who were squashed into a police car, along with their luggage.

After such an eventful evening yesterday, they'd decided not to stay in the 'murder castle' and booked rooms in a nearby town.

"It's a shame they can't stay longer," Alice said.

"You don't mean that," Campbell said. "And Detective Inspector Gerald was prepared to drive them wherever they needed to go."

Alice huffed a little snort through her nose. "I should think so, too. After the mess he made of this investigation, he owes us."

"I'm glad you made him chauffeur them away," I said to Campbell, who I'd spotted talking intently to Detective Inspector Gerald when he'd arrived this morning.

He shrugged. "Like Alice said, he owed us. And this Christmas is about family, not who'll win the biggest, fakest, socialite contest."

"They're not that bad." Alice wrapped an arm around Campbell's waist.

"Whatever you say, Princess." He shared an amused look over the top of her head with me and Rupert.

I couldn't deny that any of us were sad to see them go. And I was exhausted. I wasn't sure my social skills could have handled anymore fake nice entertaining.

After giving her friends a last wave, Alice carefully escorted Campbell inside the castle. He was still on his crutches and complaining with almost every step, but he'd insisted on getting out of bed on Christmas morning and joining us.

Chef Heston met us inside the door. "The Christmas Day breakfast buffet is waiting. It'll be different from other years, since I've had to improvise."

We still had no heat, but the fires were roaring, and most of the rooms were pleasantly warm.

"Whatever you've made, it'll be amazing." Alice danced over and hugged him. "Happy Christmas, Chef Heston. I insist you join us. I consider you family."

"That's good of you, but I'm fine in the kitchen."

"You're coming with us," I said. "Alice is right, you are family."

A flush spread up his neck, and he smiled. "I'd like that. Thank you."

The Duke and Duchess descended the stairs. Lady Philippa was with them, resplendent in a crimson onesie with a white feather boa draped around her neck. There was a round of Christmas greetings and kisses.

Meatball almost knocked Lady Philippa over in his haste to get to Dottie. They jigged around each other, barked and tussled, while the rest of the Duchess's corgis looked on with disgust on their furry faces.

It was their loss if they chose not to join in. Meatball was an excellent friend to have.

"Will you look at that? We have another love match in the castle." Duchess Isabella looked on with amusement as the dogs bounced around us.

"They can't stay away from each other," I said. "It's true love."

"Perhaps a litter of puppies in the castle is just what we need."

My eyes widened. "Dottie hasn't been spayed?"

"I was considering breeding from her. And who better than the handsome Meatball? Wouldn't you agree?"

I didn't have the heart to tell her Meatball had gotten the snip when he was a youngster. "Whatever the outcome of their relationship, I'm sure they'll be happy."

"Let's eat. I'm famished." The Duke marched into the dining room.

Duchess Isabella let out a gentle sigh. "He's like an excited child on Christmas Day. He even insists on getting a stocking from Father Christmas. Shall we?"

I glanced along the corridor and spotted Saracen lurking in the shadows. "You go ahead. I'll be right in." I headed over to him. "Won't you join us?"

Saracen shrugged. "Campbell's still not talking to me. Well, I'm getting one-word answers. I told him I was sorry about crashing the tractor, but he's still angry."

"Ignore Campbell. You must come for the Christmas breakfast." I tugged on his arm.

"I doubt I'll be able to eat anything."

"There'll be something for you. And if there isn't, I'll make you something special. No one's getting left out today. Come on."

He shuffled from foot to foot and smiled. "Thanks, Holly."

Christmas Day was unusual in the castle, because everyone served themselves from a huge buffet table set on one side of the dining room.

As I surveyed the table, festooned with a glittering tinsel surround, I was amazed how well Chef Heston had done with just a microwave and an electric cooker.

I caught his eye and nodded my approval.

He accepted my silent praise with good grace and a head bow.

I handed Saracen a plate, and we hunted out breakfast treats for him.

"What's he doing here?" Campbell loomed over us.

I piled my plate with cranberry muffins, sweet breakfast rolls, and gingerbread french toast, and nudged Saracen along to get a coffee. "Celebrating this special day with friends."

"If he hadn't crashed the tractor, we wouldn't have had a body left in a bedroom for days. Alice wouldn't have been injured, and you wouldn't have—"

I thumped down my plate. "Campbell, bury the hatchet. Saracen got the evidence to the police, and he came back as soon as he could, despite being injured."

Campbell grunted.

"We're not having the Grinch at the table. You know he did his best. He always does."

Saracen set down his plate. "I messed up. I'm really sorry. I was pushing the tractor too hard."

Campbell placed several slices of maple bacon on his plate.

"Campbell! Don't make me get Alice to order you to wear the Christmas Grinch costume. You know she has one. And if I plant the idea in her head, she won't stop asking you to put it on."

"You wouldn't dare."

"I would, if you don't make up with your oldest friend."

Campbell glowered at me, then stuck out his hand to Saracen. "I suppose, since it's Christmas. I was frustrated because I couldn't help Alice, and I took it out on you. Sorry you got injured."

Saracen grinned, relief on his face as he shook Campbell's hand. "It was nothing. Just glad I could help."

"Excellent," I said. "Now you've made up, let's join everyone and start these celebrations."

"Just a minute, Holly." Campbell waited until Saracen had left before speaking. "With everything that went on yesterday, I didn't have time to thank you."

I arched an eyebrow. "I expect those words feel strange coming out of your mouth."

He pursed his lips. "Now's not the time to get cute. I was out of action and panicking about Alice. I couldn't do anything trapped in bed with this stupid broken foot and no solution. If it hadn't been for you..."

"You can say it. I'm brilliant."

"And don't get cocky, either."

"Oh, no. I leave the cockiness to you." I hugged him. "Happy Christmas, Campbell."

He hugged me back. "You're annoying, nosy, and stubborn, but I wouldn't have you any other way. Let's eat."

Once everyone was settled around the table, we tucked into our delicious Christmas breakfast.

"I trust everything is getting back to normal." Duchess Isabella's voice was soft as she leaned close while buttering a sweet roll. "I must admit, I was out of the loop with this situation, but Alice's predicament was alarming."

"It was nothing to worry about."

Her eyebrows rose. "A friend murdered, accusations of poisoning, motives galore to sort through, and this dreadful weather. I'd say that's more than nothing."

"Well, it wasn't the Christmas I had planned." I looked around the table. "But everything seems much as it always has been." The Duke studied an oil painting while munching on a candied pear. Alice and Rupert were bickering. Campbell looked surly, but at least he was talking to Saracen. Lady Philippa had Horatio on her lap and was feeding him sausage while chatting to an invisible companion, and Chef Heston worried over the food.

Duchess Isabella chuckled as she took in the scene of family normalcy. "Yes, everything is as it should be. And you? You're content? We're a unique family and have strange ways of doing things, but you've brought so much joy into our lives. I hope that never changes. You've brought Audley Castle back to life."

"That's kind of you to say. And yes, I'm content. More than content."

She took a small bite from a cranberry muffin. "I'm also aware we don't participate as much as we should in everyday life, but that doesn't mean I don't pay attention. You help keep us safe and solve mysteries others don't seem able to. For that, you have my eternal gratitude and friendship."

"You're too kind. Since I've moved here, I've never been happier. Audley St. Mary and this castle have a special place in my heart. For all the stresses it sometimes brings me, I wouldn't change a thing."

"Could you pass the fruit pudding, my dear?" the Duke said.

Duchess Isabella squeezed my hand, gave me a wink, and then turned to tend to her husband.

Alice kicked me under the table. "Have the police been in touch yet?"

"They said they would after my interview yesterday, but I've heard nothing."

"I spoke to Detective Inspector Gerald this morning," Campbell said.

"You kept that quiet. Go on, what did he tell you?" Alice said.

Campbell shifted in his seat, not comfortable being the center of attention as all eyes fixed on him. I could understand why. After all, a woman who was literally madly in love with him had gone on a killing spree to win him back.

"There's no doubt of Emma's guilt. After the police searched her room and took the evidence, they also checked Alice's room. You were right, Holly. Emma had planted a bottle of aconite poison for them to find."

Alice's mouth dropped open. "Why am I only just learning this? Does this mean I'm still a suspect?"

"I didn't want to worry you." He kissed her cheek. "And no, you're not a suspect, not after the police gathered everyone's statements. Emma is sticking to her story, though. She believes I'd have followed her anywhere once she revealed who she was."

"And send Alice down for a murder she didn't commit by planting evidence." I shook my head. "She really didn't know you."

He adjusted his shirt collar. "We weren't together that long. In truth, I'd forgotten about Emma."

"You still kept that picture of her," Alice said tartly.

Campbell winced. "I forgot it was in the box. I'd have thrown it out if I'd remembered."

"I'm glad you didn't," I said. "That picture was the missing puzzle piece I needed to figure everything out."

"As soon as I saw her, I knew who she was," Campbell said.

"That was why Emma kept away from you. She was never around when you were. She always had an excuse for being somewhere else."

"Emma sounds like an unwell woman." Duchess Isabella turned away from her husband. "I hope she'll be properly looked after."

"She will," Campbell said. "The police are holding her for now, but they're arranging a psychiatric evaluation once she's well enough."

"There really must be something wrong with her." Rupert munched on a piece of spiced french toast. "Campbell's a decent chap but not worth killing over."

There was a stunned silence, then the Duke roared with laughter.

Rupert's cheeks flushed red. "Oh! Campbell! No offence. I mean, I'm sure someone would kill for you. You're... err... quite wonderful."

"I appreciate that, Lord Rupert," Campbell said.

"Isn't it time you stopped calling him Lord Rupert?" Alice said. "We've been dating for ages."

"It wouldn't be appropriate to call him anything else." Campbell slathered festive chutney over his bacon.

Alice shoved back her chair. "Then it's time things changed. All this near death business has gotten me thinking."

"That's never a safe thing to happen," Rupert muttered to me.

I nudged him with my elbow. I had a good idea what Alice was about to do, and I couldn't help but smile in anticipation.

Alice turned to Campbell, took his knife and fork away and placed them on his plate, before taking hold of one of his hands. "This is a traditional family, and you're an old-fashioned guy, but a woman can only wait so long before she moves things along."

It sounded like Alice was scolding Campbell. It wasn't the romantic proposal I was expecting her to launch into.

"So, it's time things changed around here," Alice said. "And it's the reason you need to stop calling my brother, Lord. He's plain old Rupert to you."

"I don't mind what you call me," Rupert said affably. He leaned over until his mouth was close to my ear. "Is she about to do what I think she is?"

I nodded. Alice always had a unique way of doing things.

Campbell looked uncomfortable. "Are you unhappy? I know I've been busy with work, and then getting the foot injury, I haven't been able to pay you as much attention as I'd like. That'll change."

She pressed a finger against his lips. "Shush. You're wonderful. But you are slow on the uptake with romance."

Rupert chuckled, and only another nudge from me stopped him.

Alice looked at everyone. "I love Campbell. He's not perfect, but neither am I, and I've never been happier than when I'm with him. He's never once called me ridiculous or laughed at me. We spend so much time laughing with each other."

I pressed my lips together. I could count on both hands the number of times I'd heard Campbell laugh in my company. Alice had definitely changed him.

Campbell shifted in his seat again. "Why are you telling me this now?"

Alice dropped to one knee, rifled in the bust of her red dress, and pulled out a small black ring box. "Campbell Milligan, will you marry me?"

Nobody moved as they watched to see what Campbell would do.

He stayed in his seat, his mouth slightly open as he stared at Alice.

She gulped and glanced at me.

I shook my head. I told her an unexpected proposal might shock him.

Alice gently tugged on his hand. "Did you hear me? I asked for your hand in marriage. I want to spend the rest of my life with you. Do you want that, too? To have me as your wife."

Campbell grabbed a crutch and slowly stood, lifting Alice so she was in front of him. "I didn't realize this was what you had planned."

"I wasn't planning it for today. I thought I'd do it on New Year's Eve, but with all the murder business,

I decided to seize the moment. Everyone I love and cherish is in this room, and I want them to witness this."

Campbell looked around. His gaze caught mine, and I gestured for him to say something. Anything. Because Alice was sweating, and soon, she'd panic, race out of the room, and never speak to Campbell again.

He cleared his throat, balanced on one leg, and reached into his pocket. He pulled out an identical black ring box.

Alice stared at the box. "Oh!"

"Alice Audley, from the moment I met you, my life has been full of surprises. From the time you learned to swim like a mermaid, to the time when you were almost charged with murder and I gave up everything to be with you. I knew I'd find no one else as unique."

"I've almost been charged with murder twice, now. How's that for something special?" Her giggle was panicky.

"A world with you in it makes everything brighter. You dazzle me. Not just your beauty, but your huge, open heart. You take everyone into your trust, and you're so kind. You're always looking for the best in people."

"Even Campbell," I whispered to Rupert.

He dabbed his eyes with a napkin. "I never knew Campbell was so poetic."

I squeezed his hand. I had a lump in my throat, too.

Campbell flipped open the ring box to reveal a stunning diamond solitaire. "I've wanted to propose ever since we got together, but I kept thinking you'd realize I wasn't good enough for you."

"Campbell! You know how much I love you," Alice said.

"Those two are as bad as each other for not getting to the point," Rupert whispered.

I chuckled softly. It had taken me and Rupert long enough to dance around our feelings before we finally got past our fears and found our happily ever after. Rupert glanced at me, grinned, and shrugged.

I smiled as Campbell wobbled his way onto one knee and held Alice's hand. "I accept your proposal. Will you accept mine?" He slid the engagement ring onto Alice's finger.

She stared at it, then kneeled and kissed him, before giving him his own ring. "Of course! Always."

Everyone broke into applause, while Meatball and the corgis raced around barking with excitement.

The Duke stood and clapped Campbell on the back, before helping himself to more breakfast from the buffet.

Alice dashed around the table, hugged Duchess Isabella, and then flung herself into my arms, laughing and crying at the same time. "Did you see? I proposed, and he proposed right back. It couldn't have been more perfect. And look at my ring. It's stunning. When did he get this?"

"It's a mystery I don't know the answer to."

Rupert was the next to hug Alice. "Congratulations."

"Campbell! Rupert should be your best man," Alice said.

Campbell looked a little shifty, then glanced at Saracen. "I've got someone else in mind for that job. But Lord... I mean, Rupert, as a happily married man, I'd appreciate all the advice you can give me. And I'll need someone to plan my bachelor party."

"I'd be honored," Rupert said.

As Christmas carols played softly in the air, the fire crackled, and there was another round of celebratory hugs and kisses, I settled back into my seat.

I looked at Meatball as he stopped bounding around to receive a brief pet and a breakfast sausage. "Best Christmas ever?"

He gave a single joyful bark, and as I petted him, I was happy to immerse myself in my wonderfully messy, unique family.

Audley Castle was safe again, my best friend had her true love by her side, and no one had mentioned the lack of figgy pudding. It was the most perfect Christmas gift ever.

About Author

K.E. O'Connor (Karen) is a cozy mystery author living in the beautiful British countryside. She loves all things mystery, animals, and cake.

When she's not writing, she volunteers at a local animal sanctuary, reads a ton of books, binge watches mystery series, and dreams about living somewhere warmer.

Stay in touch!
(and receive an exclusive **FREE** Holly Holmes novella)

Newsletter: https://BookHip.com/SQZPPHC
Website: www.keoconnor.com
Facebook: www.facebook.com/keoconnorauthor

Also By

Enjoy the complete Holly Holmes cozy culinary
mysteries in paperback or e-book.

READING ORDER

Cream Caramel and Murder
Chocolate Swirls and Murder
Vanilla Whip and Murder
Cherry Cream and Murder
Blueberry Blast and Murder
Mocha Cream and Murder
Lemon Drizzle and Murder
Maple Glaze and Murder
Mint Frosting and Murder

Recipe – Mint Frosted Cupcakes (poison free!)

Prep time: 20 minutes   **Cook time:** 20 minutes

MAKES 20

Recipe can be made dairy and egg-free. Substitute milk for a plant/nut alternative, use dairy-free spread, and mix 3 tbsp flaxseed with 1 tbsp water to create one flax egg as a binding agent (this recipe requires 6 tbsp flaxseed to substitute 2 eggs.) Substitute plant-based cream for the heavy (double) cream in the frosting.

INGREDIENTS

Cupcakes
2 tablespoons vegetable oil
6 tablespoons softened, unsalted butter
½ cup (100 grams) granulated sugar
½ cup (100 grams) light brown sugar
2 large eggs

2 teaspoons vanilla extract
1 cup (130 grams) all-purpose plain flour
6 tablespoons unsweetened cocoa powder
½ teaspoon baking soda
¼ teaspoon baking powder
¼ teaspoon salt
¾ cup (180 milliliters) milk

Frosting
1 cup (225 grams) unsalted soft butter
3 cups (360 grams) powdered or icing sugar
2 tablespoons heavy (double) cream
4 drops green food coloring
½ teaspoon mint extract

INSTRUCTIONS

1. Preheat the oven to 350°F (175c.) If using a muffin tray, line cups with paper cases or use a silicone tray.

2. Using a mixer fitted with a paddle attachment, beat the oil, butter, and sugars until fluffy, for about 3 minutes (or 6 if hand beating.)

3. Add the eggs one at a time mixing well. Beat in the vanilla.

4. In a separate bowl, combine the flour, cocoa powder, baking soda, baking powder, and salt. Stir.

5. Add half the flour mix to the butter mixture. Mix until almost combined.

6. Add the milk, followed by the remaining flour mix, and mix until blended.

7. Fill the muffin cups half full.

8. Bake for 20 minutes or until a wooden toothpick inserted comes out clean.

9. Remove cupcakes from the tin or leave to cool completely in the silicone tray.

10. For the frosting, combine butter, sugar, cream, and peppermint extract. Beat until smooth.

11. Add the food coloring. Beat until blended. Top the cupcakes with yummy frosting.

How about another treat?

Santa may be coming to town, but so is revenge. Add a dash of Christmas spite and a ghost, and this holiday season will be remembered for all the wrong reasons...

Lorna Shadow and her best friend Helen Holiday, take on a last-minute job hosting a Winter Wonderland Gala at Drew House in the beautiful Berkshire countryside.

What should have been an easy job to earn extra Christmas money, turns dark when they're warned of bad luck tainting the family. And when a recent death is discovered, the festive season doesn't seem so bright.

Forever the optimists, Lorna and Helen roll up their sleeves and don their Christmas hats. But when the ghost of Lord Albert Drew appears, insisting his death was no accident, they start the search for justice.

Throw in a troubled teenager, a secret Helen's determined to keep from Lorna, and a hint of adultery, and Christmas may be over before it has begun.

Enjoy this Christmas-packed cozy murder mystery. It's the perfect festive read to lose yourself in while curled on the couch with a mug of hot chocolate and a plate of cookies.

Ghostly Surprises is available in e-book on Amazon or in paperback at all good bookstores.

Want a peek at the mystery? Keep reading...

Chapter 1

Snow was banked on either side of Helen's little red car as we zoomed through the Berkshire countryside. The heating was on high, but I still wore my thick winter coat and gloves to keep out the chill.

"I can't believe we had this much snowfall overnight. It's so rare. I should invest in snow tires." Helen had to raise her voice so I could hear her over the Christmas tunes blasting from the stereo.

I gripped the door handle as the back wheels skidded on ice before the road straightened out in front of us. "Slow down! We're not late. Lady Drew isn't expecting us for another half hour. And I want to get there in one piece."

"I can't wait to arrive. Christmas is my favorite time of year, and we lucked out by getting this last-minute assignment to host an OMG sparkletastic Christmas party." She flipped her blonde hair back, revealing a pair of Christmas pudding earrings dangling from her lobes.

"I expect the personal assistant who broke her ankle doesn't think it was all that lucky. We got these jobs because of her accident." I opened the emails on my phone and re-read the message from the recruitment agency that arrived two days ago.

Emergency! I'm in desperate need of an excellent event planner and caterer to oversee the Winter Wonderland Christmas Gala at the Drew estate. Double your usual rate guaranteed, and Flipper is welcome, too. Please, Lorna, I'm desperate. This is a long-standing client, and I can't let her down!!! I know you're not taking many assignments anymore, but think of all the Christmas goodies you can buy with the extra cash.

When I'd seen how much Lady Kate Drew was offering for Helen and me to work for two weeks in the lead up to Christmas, I hadn't been able to turn down the job. Plus, I enjoyed Christmas. Although I didn't turn into a be-tinseled Christmas elf like my best friend, and terrible driver, Helen Holiday.

"Do you think we'll have any input into the finishing touches for the gala?" Helen said. "I've got so many ideas that I couldn't sleep last night."

"I doubt it." I reached back and scratched behind my dog's ears. Flipper was passed out in the back, as usual. He did it every time he went on a car journey. Next to him, snuggled up close, was Helen's feisty bald Chinese crested dog, Milly. "It's two weeks out, so everything has been planned. And when I spoke to the PA, Annie, she sounded organized. She kept apologizing for dropping us in it at the last minute."

"She's dropping us into tinsel heaven. And it was hardly her fault she fell off a ladder and broke her foot," Helen said. "Will Annie be around? I can run my ideas past her, see if she has any budget left for more sparkle."

"Annie's still working but only doing basic admin. It sounded like a bad break."

"With the extra money, we can treat everyone at Christmas and then take January off. Maybe we could try skiing again. Or..." She slid me a glance.

"Or what?" I gestured for Helen to watch the slippery road. The lane was getting narrower the deeper we went into the English countryside. "You want a vacation somewhere warm?"

"I wasn't thinking about a vacation. How about you spend January looking at venues for your wedding?"

"I'm not getting married yet." My hand tightened around the car door handle.

"Only because you won't fix a date with Zach. He keeps asking when he can make an honest woman of you, and you give him the brushoff. The guy will think you're not interested or you've changed your mind about marrying him."

"Zach knows I'm interested. I said yes to his proposal."

"Saying yes and setting a date are two different things. What's holding you back?" Helen barely eased off the gas as we zoomed around a blind bend.

I squeezed my eyes shut so I wouldn't see how close we were to the ditch. "I've been busy."

"We're all busy. You've got enough time to squeeze in venue hunting. Things get booked up years in advance. You don't want to miss out on your dream place."

I opened my eyes, relieved to see we were on a flat road, zooming past bare brown fields and hibernating trees overhanging the road. "We can have a ceremony in the backyard at home. Venue found."

Helen poked her tongue out. "No! Where's the fun in that?"

"It's less stressful."

"It's dull."

"I like dull."

"Impossible. You're best friends with me." Helen giggled. "It doesn't have to be a big wedding but at least hold it somewhere pretty."

"You're suggesting our yard is ugly?"

"I'm suggesting you're digging your heels in for no reason."

"I love Zach, and we have a great life together. Why change things?"

"Because he wants to marry you. What's the harm in that? And I desperately want to make your dress. I also want to make my own, so I can be the most stunning bridesmaid ever to walk up an aisle."

"I won't have an aisle if we marry in the backyard."

"There definitely won't be if you don't hurry and fix the date."

I settled back in my seat. Life had been busy. Although I wasn't working so much, I was part owner of a large house with Zach, Helen, and her husband, Gunner Booth, who was also Zach's brother. I kept myself busy around the house, took on freelance admin work now and again, and spent lots of time with Flipper. It was nice to take a break from my usual life.

Or should I say, my unusual life. I'd seen my fair share of ghosts over the years, mainly in the beautiful old houses I was sent to work in as an executive personal assistant. And although I helped them when they needed it, I didn't miss the freezing temperatures, icy fingers, nor the occasional blast of ectoplasm, or my fainting spells.

"Lorna, Zach's a patient man, but even his patience will run out. I know you don't like change, but this'll be a great change." Helen pursed her lips. "Although I don't see things changing much."

"Agreed. A ring on my finger changes nothing, so why bother?"

"Because it's romantic. Will you keep your last name like I did?"

"It would be strange to be called anything other than Lorna Shadow," I said. "Maybe Zach could become Mr. Zach Shadow."

"You could ask him. But neither of you will change your names if you don't get married soon."

Helen had a point. I didn't love change. It could be scary. And I was known for being stubborn and set in my ways. When I'd first met Zach, it almost broke us up several times. That and me always putting myself in danger when helping ghosts figure out how they died.

"We'll figure something out," I said. "Right now, we have our Winter Wonderland extravaganza to focus on."

"I'll be focused, but I won't forget your wedding." Helen drove on for another ten minutes as we both sang along to the festive tunes. "Oh, I see the house through the trees."

I peered through the ice-skimmed foliage and got a glimpse of the huge, detached pale cream mansion we'd be spending the next two weeks working and living in. A few minutes later, we discovered the gated entrance, and once through the gates, we headed along a winding gravel driveway.

"This is stunning," Helen said. "It'll look so beautiful when decorated. I'm surprised it's not sparkling and festive already."

"You always put up the Christmas decorations too soon."

"The first day in December is ideal. Then we get over a month to enjoy them."

"Gunner has tripped over that glowing reindeer by the fireplace three times."

"I keep telling him to be careful. His feet are too big, and Gunner never looks where he's going."

"That reindeer is huge."

"Hugely adorable."

"Just remember, we're not here to take over; we're here to oversee what's already been planned."

"Yes, mistress. Although I may make a few tweaks to the food if it's not festive enough," Helen said. "And

251

when the dressers come to stage the decorations, I've got some ideas to run past them."

"Don't take over. You don't want to upset Annie."

"I won't get in her way. I'll be the soul of discretion. Just a nosy soul. Hey, that's a stunning fir tree in front of the house. It'll look beautiful covered in lights."

I repressed a groan and shook my head. Helen was the best friend a woman could ever want, four-legged fur babies not included, but she always went crazy over the top at Christmas. And then there was Easter, Valentines, Thanksgiving, and Halloween. Okay, she just loved an excuse to over-indulge on treats and dress up. That's kind of why I loved her.

A person dashed out in front of the car.

Helen squeaked and yanked the steering wheel to the left to avoid hitting them, and the car slid sideways on a patch of ice.

"Brake! You're going to hit that tree!"

Helen stamped on the brake, but the car continued to slide. "It's not responding."

The back of the car slid to the right, and I braced for impact as we collided with a tree.

The airbags deployed, and it took a few seconds before I could see what was going on. "Helen! Are you okay?"

She shoved down her airbag. "I think so. Where did that boy come from?"

"I have no idea." I checked the back seat. Flipper and Milly were awake and looking around, but seemed unconcerned, considering the car just crashed.

Once we'd deflated the airbags, we hopped out and checked to make sure the fuel line wasn't leaking and there was no fire risk.

Helen sighed as she looked at the dent in the side of the car and the deflating tire. "This is bad. I'm going to need my car. Why did that guy rush out of the trees? And where's he gone? We could be injured and need help. He just ran off."

I looked around, but the teenager I'd glimpsed for a second was nowhere to be seen. "He looked startled. Maybe he was being chased."

"Unless he was being chased by the abominable snowman who wants him for the festive pot, I'm not happy." Helen patted her damaged car. "At least we don't have far to walk."

"Are you okay?" A thin woman with gray hair dashed toward us from the direction of the road. "I was passing when I heard the bang. You hit a tree?"

"We did. Thanks for checking on us, but we're fine," I said. "Just shaken up. The car didn't make it through so well, though."

The woman looked around, her thin lips pursed. "Are you going to the Drew House?"

"That's right."

"For a visit?"

"No, we're working here for a couple of weeks." I tilted my head, waiting for her to introduce herself and explain her interest.

The woman shook her head and tutted. "You should leave while you have the chance."

"Leave? We've only just gotten here," Helen said. "We're working for the family until Christmas, organizing their Winter Wonderland extravaganza."

"Are you now?" The woman's eyebrows arched. "My advice to you is this, call a cab and go. Bad luck follows this family, and you don't want it attached to you."

"Bad luck?" I shivered as an icy wind cut through my thick, green winter coat. "What kind of bad luck?"

The woman glanced around and adjusted her red woolen hat. "I used to work here. I'm the former cook, Emma Smedley. And I'm paying the price because of the dark shadow cast across this household. It's not a nice place."

"I don't like the sound of that," Helen muttered to me.

"What dark shadow?" I said.

Emma's eyes widened. "You must know about Lord Albert Drew."

"No. We've only ever dealt with Lady Kate Drew. She hired us."

"Lady Kate." Emma sniffed. "She's part of the problem. I lost my job because of her."

"She didn't like your cooking?" Helen said.

"She doesn't like anything that has to do with the old ways. I suppose she'll be selling up soon and running off with the money."

"Why? Isn't she happy living here?" I said.

"I can't imagine she is. Who'd want to stay anywhere associated with such a tragic death?"

"Who died?" Helen almost whispered the question.

"Lord Albert. Six weeks ago. He had an allergic reaction to some nuts. Of course, the finger got pointed at me because I made the meals. But I knew about his allergies. I worked for the family for over thirty years. I'd never make a mistake like that."

"I'm sorry to hear he died," I said. "That must have been a shock for the family."

"It was a shock for me. I lost my job, and everyone thinks I'm incompetent. And the bad luck is affecting other people. Don't get me started on what happened to Annie Saunderson. Do you know her?"

"In a way. That's why we're here," I said. "We were hired because Annie injured her foot."

"She was injured because she was asked to do too much by Lady Muck. Annie was halfway up a ladder when she fell. It's not her job to scurry up and down ladders like some Victorian chimney sweep. She's in so much pain." Emma tightened the scarf around her neck and eyed the dark clouds overhead. "This place is cursed. Everyone gets injured or their lives ruined if they stay too long. Escape while you can. This place was lovely before Lady Kate got her Prada-clad toes under the table."

I glanced at Helen, uncertain what to do, and she shrugged at me.

"We're going to stay. Check things out for ourselves," I said.

"Your lives will be changed forever if you spend time in this house. No amount of money could convince me to return."

"You make it sound like the place is toxic."

"It ruined my life, killed Lord Albert, and injured Annie. How much more proof do you need? And Annie is such a kind woman." Emma's gaze drifted over us. "You seem like nice women, too, so I'm only telling you what I tell everyone else. Stay away from Drew House. The beautiful outside hides a rotten heart."

"Any more slanderous talk like that, Emma Smedley, and I'll have you arrested."

Enjoyed the sample? Indulge in Ghostly Surprises today.

CPSIA information can be obtained
at www.ICGtesting.com
Printed in the USA
LVHW040528091222
734840LV00003B/399

9 781916 357389